Published in the United States of America
ISBN: 978-1-7371472-4-4

Cover Photographer: Britt & Bean Photography LLC

Cover Models: Alexa and Javin

Cover Designer: RBA Designs

Editing:

Marion Archer, Making Manuscripts

Jenny Sims, Editing4Indies

Proofreading: Kristen Johnson

Beta Reading: Andrea Johnston

ALSO BY S.L. SCOTT

To keep up to date with her writing and more, visit her website:
www.slscottauthor.com

To receive the Scott Scoop about all of her publishing adventures,
free books, giveaways, steals and more visit her website.

Join S.L.'s Facebook group: S.L. Scott Books

Read the Bestselling Book that's been called **"The Most Romantic
Book Ever"** by readers and have them raving. We Were Once is
now available and FREE in Kindle Unlimited.

We Were Once

Audiobooks available on Audible

Complementary to Crazy in Love

Never Got Over You

The One I Want

We Were Once

Everest

Missing Grace

Finding Solace

Until I Met You

Hard to Resist Series (Stand-Alones)

The Resistance

The Reckoning

The Redemption

Playboy in Paradise Box Set

Talk to Me Duet (Stand-Alones)

Sweet Talk

Dirty Talk

Stand-Alone Books

We Were Once

Never Got Over You

The One I Want

Missing Grace

Until I Met You

Drunk on Love

Naturally, Charlie

A Prior Engagement

Lost in Translation

Sleeping with Mr. Sexy

Morning Glory

From the Inside Out

CRAZY IN LOVE

S.L. SCOTT

PROLOGUE

Harrison Decker

CATALINA ISLAND - AVALON

I DON'T FALL for chicks.

Don't get me wrong. I'm not heartless. I'm just wise as to why they're trying to pin me down. If I've learned one thing while growing up in Los Angeles with my last name, it's that nothing comes without strings attached. Everyone wants something from me. *Besides my good looks.*

At this point in my life, I'm more interested in building my career in real estate and proving to my dad that I've earned a spot in the family business. Women are fun but a major distraction. I leave my dates sexually satisfied while keeping my emotions out of it. I get in, in every sense, and I get out.

So why am I staring at the woman sleeping naked beside me, trying to figure out how to make this last more than one night?

I'm not sure if it was being on a yacht in Catalina Harbor where her smile stole my attention away from the sunset, or how her laughter was the prettiest song I ever heard. She was a siren who called me to her restless sea. And I dived in headfirst, getting lost in her deep ocean.

On the yacht. On her balcony. Within her sheets.

Honestly, I'm surprised either of us is awake after the physical fun we've had. But just after midnight, she looked up at me. Bare before me as she lay on the bed, she was a study in art and composition with her tanned skin and dark hair poised on a background of crumpled white sheets.

"We should make a pact."

"Oh yeah?" I like that I don't know what to expect from her. She's been up for anything and has made me forget the stress I have back home. I grin stupidly while rubbing my hand down her back. "What kind?"

She's caught me at the right time. I would give her anything she wants to be able to spend more time together. Our connection is more than our physical attraction. We might be more than just a wild night in Catalina. I've never before felt chemistry with someone like what's sparking between us.

An unfamiliar feeling in my chest I can't quite describe.

A longing.

A desire that sex won't satisfy.

I can tell she's feeling it, too. It doesn't matter that we live across the country from each other. I make good money, so we have the freedom to travel and, more importantly, the desire to make something work. *Who cares if it's long-distance?*

There's so much I want to discover about her. I'd make the effort because we're more than a weekend.

It's a flight.

A three-day road trip.

At worst, a week apart.

Reaching up, she caresses my scruffy cheek. I slide down next to her and angle my body to look into her eyes. I'm what my little sister would call smitten.

Being with her has me feeling happier than I have in years. *That's because of Tate.* She makes me feel like more than just a one-track robot doing what my dad expects of me.

"I think we need to keep this simple," Tatum whispers.

"All right."

She curls to the side and strokes my cheek. "This is so good, the best night ever."

"Yeah, I think so, too."

"Good," she says, smiling softly. "Let's not blow it by pretending it can be more."

"What?" My heart sinks . . .

"Let's not be one of those ridiculous couples who think they're different, that they're special enough to survive a long-distance relationship. I know this is just another night for you, and I'm not the clingy type." Her eyes dip closed, her smile going with it. She's hard to read, but her expression doesn't seem to match her words. *Does she actually want more too, but isn't sure what I want?*

"You're not?" It's not what I want to ask.

Her eyes find mine in the moonlight. "I can't even keep a plant alive, much less a vacation fling." Her mood lightens. "I know how this goes, so let's just set the ground rules and continue the fun."

I'm still lost in where this went so horribly wrong when she slips her hand under the sheet and runs her fingertips across my abs. She kisses my shoulder, and then asks, "Are you in?" Right now, I'm not even sure I have a choice.

I rub my temple and then scrub my hand over my face, utterly confused. "What are we agreeing to?"

With a smile still residing on her face like she's just given me a million dollars with no strings attached, she laughs and then taps my nose. "One good night does not make us destined to be together." Rolling onto her back again, she stares up at the ceiling, but then her gaze slides over to mine. "We're having fun, am I right?"

Is there any other answer I can give her? I am having fun, so did I just break a cardinal rule—don't fall for a one-night stand? *Get in. Get out. Move on with my life.* "Yeah, sure."

My mind is reeling that I'm being dumped by the only woman I considered worthy of more time. Sure, I've had girlfriends, but I didn't feel like this . . . how I felt before she just rejected me, that is. *What the fuck is happening?*

As if her idea energizes her, she sits up and faces me. "You don't have to pretend this is the best sex you've ever had."

"It is."

Giggling, she says, "Me too. Well, you don't have to lie to me in the morning about an early flight or that you'll call me. I'm letting you off the hook, Harrison. It is what it is. A one-night stand. I'm so glad we're on the same page."

"What if—?"

A finger silences me. "No what-ifs. Those will only get us in trouble." As her hand takes hold of my dick under the sheet, her eyes close, and her mouth presses to mine.

She's just given me a free pass to move on without guilt if I don't call or text her. *Ever.*

Great tits. Firm ass. Fan-fucking-tastic mouth. Likes sex. *A lot.* All without commitment. She's a wet dream come true for most guys. But if it's such a good deal, why do I feel like I just got punched in the chest?

Holding out her hand, she asks, "Deal?"

Is it the early morning hour messing with my head? This is an offer I can't resist and one I shouldn't refuse. I should be celebrating, but all I can think about is that I'm going to be leaving this room in a few hours, and I'll have no way of ever contacting her again. *Fuck.*

I take her hand, and she begins to shake it.

Her brows pull together. "Are you okay?" *I am not okay.*

This not only surprises me but also hurts my ego. Yet I don't care because there's no way I'm going to become the clingy one. *Fuck that.* I cup her face and move in so close that my breath is hers, and hers becomes mine. The faintest hint of wine still lingers from the bottle we finished hours ago, her lips full from the impact of kissing most of the night. "I'm more than okay, baby."

Just as she grins, I kiss her. I kiss her so fucking hard that an inferno burns inside, a blaze that only an orgasm can tame. Fuck it.

If I only get one night with her, it's going to be the best night of our lives.

1

Tatum Devreux

"I CAME AS FAST as I could," I say, barreling forward as soon as the front door opens and hitting a wall of solid muscle dressed in a black button-down.

"That's not how I remember it." The voice—*deep and seductive*—causes my insides to tighten. The scent of the man I spent one night with years ago fills my nostrils, my entire being never forgetting. Slowly looking up, I'm greeted by a day's, *maybe two,* worth of growth covering the drift of a defined jaw and that Southern California tan I remember so well.

Only six words were spoken, but Catalina comes racing back to my thoughts like it was last night. It happens every time I see him. *Damn him.*

"If I remember correctly, and I remember every one of your orgasms, your body betrays your words, Tate," he says.

"It's Tatum to you." I hate that my cheeks heat. Only Harrison Decker can do that to me. And I think he knows it. I cross my arms because each time I see him, I swear he gets better looking, and he was sexy as hell to begin with. Hence the vacation fling hookup in Catalina.

I wanted Harrison from the moment I saw him, although he was a complete stranger, within ten minutes of our introduction I ran off with him.

If the sight of him before me wasn't already unnerving, the fact that I still have such a strong reaction to him is. It was one dang night. *And one broken promise.*

But I haven't been able to look him in the eyes since— not at my best friend's wedding or the few times he's flown to New York to visit Natalie's husband, Nick—his best friend.

I will never understand why he gets under my skin. *Why can't he be water under the bridge like any other one-night stand?* Like the others since him have been.

I'm usually better at hiding my emotions, but I should have been given a heads-up that he was here.

Daring to look into his Mediterranean blue eyes, I snap, "I didn't know you were visiting?" *Ugh.* Why'd I let my voice lilt at the end? The last thing I want is to show how he affects me.

Leaning against the doorframe, he crosses his arms, wholly amused by the interaction, like he always seems to be around me. I swear he gets off on making me mad or blush, which I do both too easily around him. His biceps tug the fabric tighter, and I can't help but notice that his muscles have gotten bigger. *Wonder what they'd feel like wrapped around my body?* "You mean you weren't warned?"

So smug. I roll my eyes. "Same difference."

"If it's different, then it's not the same. *Technically.*"

I rolled my eyes too soon. Now would have been the perfect spot to interject that reaction. Fortunately, the door swings wider, and Nick claps him on the shoulder. "Ready to go?" When the wall of a man moves out of my way, Nick sees me and smiles. Natalie definitely scored with that one. "Hey, Tatum. Natalie's on her way downstairs. Go on in."

"Thanks." Since they're blocking the entrance, though, I wait for them to exit first.

Harrison steps onto the stoop beside me, and we stand there awkwardly, too couple-y feeling for my liking. "What?"

"Just waiting for Nick."

"Let's not make this weird, okay?"

"Too late, I suspect," he says, nudging me gently in the arm with his elbow.

Nick holds the door open for me, and I'm quick to exchange places with him. If I don't get away from Harrison soon, I have a feeling my eyes will be on a constant rolling loop. Taking the door in hand, I wave with the other. "Don't have too much fun."

"Not without you," Harrison replies.

"Just like old times." Nick chuckles as he trots down the steps of his brownstone. "See you later."

Harrison looks back from the sidewalk. "Hey, Tate?"

So close to getting the door closed . . . I know he calls me that just to piss me off. I open the door just wide enough to peer out again. "What?"

"I like your hair." He winks and then gives me that smile that got me in bed the first time. "You look good as a blond." *Damn that delicious grin.*

I shut the door and lean against the back of it. Closing my eyes, I try to bleach my brain of that stupidly handsome face of his. He tried to apologize once . . . but was smart to back off after that. Too little. *Too late.*

"What are you doing?"

My eyes fly open to see my friend coming toward me. I push off the wood door and wave off the crazy emotions Harrison Decker stirs inside me. It honestly makes no sense why I care at all. I need to forget him like he forgot about me back then. "I ran—"

"In Jimmy Choos?" Curiosity angles Natalie's brows as she looks at my shoes. "Are those new?"

"Fresh off the display. Only one pair in Manhattan and I scored these babies."

"Babies," she says with a softened smile. She suddenly hugs me like she didn't just see me yesterday or the four days before that. My best friend since birth is the most happy-spirited and hug-loving person I know. "Miss me much, Nat?" I joke, wondering why she's so sentimental today. I hug her back just as tight. *Two peas in a pod.*

"I did, actually." She takes my hand and pulls me deeper into the newly renovated, four-story townhome. "Word on the avenue is that my next-door neighbors are putting their house on the market after they finish the renovation. I think you should look into it."

Her design and décor are a stunning testament to her impeccable taste, and I might add mine since I helped make a lot of the decisions. "I can't afford a townhome on the Upper East Side, especially the way the market is right now."

She nods toward the kitchen. "I'm starving. Hungry?"

"I just ate lunch—"

"How about something light?" There's an unusual nervous edge in her tone.

"Where are they moving?"

She pulls a fruit and cheese platter from the fridge and sets it on the island between us. Natalie is the only person I know, besides her mom, who would have a handy-dandy cheese platter ready to go just in case company stops by. She replies, "Connecticut. Dolores is pregnant with her third baby, and they want land. They bought an old farm they're redoing on some acreage."

"Sounds like a lot of work."

"Her current home is going to be gorgeous. I saw the designs this morning." She pops a grape in her mouth as she gazes off into the distance. Her fingers tap against the cold stone of the counter, and I notice her lips twisting to the side. Her nerves are palpable, the frenzied energy contagious. *What is going on with her today?*

"I think I'm hungry, after all." Taking a piece of brie, I pop it into my mouth and set my Birkin bag on the floor. She doesn't miss the bag, as I knew she wouldn't, and cocks an eyebrow at me before tugging open the door to the wine fridge set in the large island. "New bag?"

"New *guilt* bag."

"You have enough of those to fill a penthouse on Park Avenue." She smirks. "Or the townhome next door."

"Nice try, but I'm not selling my bags. Though I might be swayed, depending on the size of their closet." I laugh. "The bags need a closet of their own."

"Maybe an apartment at this point."

"I'm not complaining." Out loud, at least. I'd rather have my parents than an expensive bag any day. Glancing down at my newest pretty, I add, "My mom was invited to preview their private collection in Paris. Figured I'd carry it today since Hermés fits the Upper East Side." Pulling out a barstool, I slide onto it and watch as she moves around the kitchen like a ballerina on stage—lithe and gracefully, as if she was born for the role of Mrs. Christiansen.

She's so at ease in her own skin that sometimes it makes

me uneasy in mine. I'm not jealous of her, but she has a lot to envy—a husband who adores her and would pluck the stars from the sky if she asked him to. She owns a business she loves, and she has the most awesome best friend ever if I do say so myself. *Mine isn't too shabby either.* I laugh lightly to myself. But lately, there's been a niggle, a bothersome feeling in my gut as though I'm forgetting something or missing out perhaps.

Though it sounds like it, I know it's not jealousy. I'm fully aware we each find our destiny on our own timeline. Natalie St. James, now Christiansen, is fortunate to be smack dab in the middle of her love story. And one day, I hope to be that lucky.

"You make the Upper East Side sound like our parents— all fundraisers and no fun," she says.

"I didn't say you weren't any fun. We have fun all the time. It's just different. You're married, and I'm still single. *Painfully single.* Everyone around me is pairing off like lobsters and swans, and I'm over here still hoping to meet someone, get asked out, and fall in love before your anniversary party just so I have a date."

Her palm is pressed to the marble countertop, and I'm leveled with a look. "The party is Saturday night."

I shrug. As a professional gift giver and experience architect, I make people's dreams come true, from finding the perfect present to creating an unforgettable special event in their lives, or even elevating a simple date night to impress a significant other. I'm a tried-and-true people pleaser and I get paid for it. "That's two days. I've accomplished greater feats in less time."

Setting a bottle of wine on the island, she laughs. "As much as that's true, you don't have to bring a date. There's no pressure. It's not that kind of soiree. It's friends, who are your friends too, and family. Just a small-*ish* celebration. Wine or water?"

"Wine. Make it a double."

"Stop worrying. You're witty and smart."

"Pretty."

She grins. "Beautiful. A great catch."

"I'm so ready to be caught. Maybe just for the night."

Bursting out laughing, she adds, "I'm sure you have a phone full of the *right guy for tonight*. As for love, it will happen when it's supposed to for you. Don't force something because of someone else's timeline." Grabbing a glass from a cabinet, she sets it in front of me and starts to pour the wine. "You'll know when it's right." A gentle smile slides into place. "There will be no denying no matter how hard you try. And I know you love to deny some very good opportunities."

She takes a deep breath, peace softening her features. When she pushes the glass toward me, I ask, "You're not drinking?"

Tapping the counter, she perks up. "No. I have too much to get done. I still need to make sure Mr. Wriggler's surprise for his wife gets delivered."

"I thought that was handled?"

"Me too." She sighs and rolls her eyes. Yep, two peas. One pod. "But the jeweler can't deliver the necklace until tomorrow night at nine. The dessert cart is scheduled for nine fifteen. If there are any delays, the necklace won't be served when dessert is."

"There won't be. It will work out perfectly," I reassure.

I've worked with Natalie since she conceived the idea for her business back in college. I used to work for free, but since the company's grown into a multimillion-dollar business, my salary is more than enough to live off in one of the most expensive cities in the world. Of course, my current lifestyle wouldn't be possible without the monthly blank checks from my parents—money that eases the burden of their guilt for always traveling when I was growing up. I'm not going to deny them the pleasure even though I'm now twenty-six.

Without those checks, I wouldn't be able to live in the apartment I do. "You have your party to worry about. I can make sure the necklace arrives on time," I say.

"It will be fine. I'll be in constant communication with the jeweler but thanks. I appreciate it."

"Happy to help. You know me when it comes to diamonds. There can never be..." "Too many of the two main C's—clarity and carats," we say in unison, and break into a fit of giggles. Natalie has quite the collection of diamonds herself, so she understands my love of the sparkly gems.

"I have a surprise upstairs. Want to see?" she asks.

"Do you even need to ask?" This house is incredible and a great leg workout. The basement has a secondary living room and a home gym. The main floor is the kitchen, the living room, and the dining room. We're already climbing the stairs to the second floor, which has the main bedroom and two spares. I glance up just as I hit the landing. The top floor has one empty room and a guest bedroom. I've slept up there a few times over the years when I was too tired or too drunk to go home. We've also had a few sleepovers when Nick is out of town. Slipping on our panda onesies and snuggling in for movies or *Friends* reruns. I love those nights.

With my glass in hand, I ask, "What is it?"

"It's called a surprise for a reason, Tate." Her laughter permeates her words.

"Guess you have a point."

One of the rooms on the second floor is her home office. STJ, the company, which stands for St. James—her maiden name—is housed in a great space in SoHo. It's been slow, but she's been making headway in moving everything out of the house. Sometimes we bring our work home if it's going to be a late night, though, preferring to be here rather than in an office. It reminds us of old times when we were room-mates still building this dream, wrapping gifts on the floor of our apartment, and honestly, it brings me comfort. With so much constantly changing in our lives, it's nice to have something consistent.

She walks into the room, stops in the middle of it, and turns around. Staring at me with wide eyes and her hands clasped in front of her chest, she whispers, "Surprise."

Gripping tightly to the stem of the glass, I dart my eyes from the sketched wall mural to the two stuffed animals on the new chair in the corner, from the creamy color palette to the shelves with a small collection of children's books, and from the dresser to the crib.

"What happened to the office?" I ask, swallowing so hard that a lump gets stuck in my throat.

Her hands remain clasped, hope held inside by the look in her eyes. "I thought the one in SoHo was enough. And my furniture finally came in yesterday afternoon."

"You're really prepared." Still taking it in, I turn back to her just as tears glisten in her eyes. I set my glass down on the changing table and rush to my friend. "What's wrong?"

Worry wrangles her expression. "Tatum, look around."

"I am." I finally swallow down the lump, and ask, "You and Nick are trying to have a baby?"

"Nick and I *are* having a baby. I'm pregnant." Her words are whispered as she grips the side of the tall dresser.

Oh.

My.

God.

"Natalie," I say, the breath knocked from me. My gaze dips to her middle. "What do you mean?" I catch the question just after voicing it. "I know what it means, but I . . . I didn't realize you were trying."

"I know. It was a shock for me and . . ." She walks to the window and looks into the backyard. When she turns back, she says, "I didn't tell you because I didn't know if I could. It took longer than we thought, and I started to lose hope." Her smile returns. "When the test came back positive, Nick and I thought it was best to wait before telling anyone, just in case the worst happened. And then," she adds shyly, "it just felt like something Nick and I were sharing, something just for the two of us. But now, saying it out loud, I feel as if I've betrayed you."

"No," I say, shaking my head. "Don't think that. You didn't betray me. You're telling me now when it was right for you to share." I bring her into an embrace, my eyes filling with tears as I realize what this means for all of us. "You're having a baby," I whisper, resting my head on her shoulder. "That's amazing." Leaning back, I look into her eyes. "I'm so happy for you and Nick."

"You mean that?" We've been through crushes, heartbreak, drama, and life, but this is different. This is her bringing life into the world, *our world*.

"I do." Though my chest feels tight, happiness fills my heart. "I remember you talking about being a mom when you were twelve. Your dream is coming true. How can anyone not be happy for you?"

"You've always been there for me. Now you'll be here for my baby, too."

"For every moment." I smile so big my cheeks ache. "You're going to be a mom, Nat. Guess our crazy days are behind us."

Stepping back, she rubs her stomach. "I don't know. This might be the craziest thing I've ever done."

I laugh with her and then reach to cover her hand. "It just might be." I'm not sure why I suddenly feel insecure, but I raise my chin and hold tighter to the happiness I feel for my friend.

Taking my hand between both of hers, she releases a sigh of relief. "I wanted to tell you sooner, but I had this fear that something could go wrong, and I didn't know how I would handle that."

"You wouldn't. Not alone. We would. You, Nick, and I. I love you guys, and I'll always be here for you through good and bad."

"That's why I wanted you to be the first to know."

A soft gasp fills my chest. "You haven't told anyone else?"

"No," she admits, smiling. "We were debating if we should at the party, but as I said, it's early. Just two and a half months."

I squeeze her hand. "You should. This party will have all your closest friends and family. This baby should be celebrated and showered with love." Speaking of the party has me thinking of another. "Can I throw you a baby shower?"

Her laughter wipes any doubts or fears from her eyes. "I can't think of a better person to throw me a party." She rubs her stomach. "Or this baby." She goes into the closet, and I see she still has a few of our office supplies tucked away in there. Taking a gray binder from the shelf, she holds it up, and says, "I swear I've already lost some of my mind growing this baby."

"If that isn't writing on the wall for how the next seven months are going to be, I don't know what is."

"Let's go back downstairs. I'm hungry all the time now." I hear her laughing as she walks into the hallway.

I reach the door, but then say, "Oops. I forgot my wine." I dash back into the office—I mean nursery. That's going to take some getting used to. Just like my friend being pregnant. I'm quick to grab the glass but stop and look around once more.

Time is moving on, and our lives are forever changing. I smile, knowing not only will she always play a part in my life but now her child will also have the best *and most stylish* aunt ever. I can't wait to spoil this baby rotten.

In the meantime, I down my wine before I reach the kitchen, not sure what's come over me. Sitting down on the barstool again, I open the binder.

After she eats a cracker, she asks, "Did you know Harrison's staying with us?"

"You forgot to mention it, and I ran into him when I got here." Literally, but I leave that detail out of the story. I push the empty glass forward. "I'm going to need a refill."

She laughs as she pours, pushing it back to me and tilting her head. "It's not that bad."

"So says you." I take a big gulp, hoping to stop my head from spinning. He does that to me. Something I'll never admit. "How long is he staying?"

"Two months."

The liquid spews from my lips, covering the surface in front of me and Natalie's white pants.

Natalie hurries to my rescue, hooking her arm over my back and patting me with the other hand. "Are you all right?"

"Months?" I scratch out when I finally catch my breath.

She giggles and rolls her eyes, returning to the other side of the island, closer to the platter. "Is that what all the hacking was about? Harrison? Good grief, Tatum. Sometimes you make it hard to know if you like him or hate him."

"Hate him," I mumble, and then take a slow sip, letting that hit of reality sink in.

Natalie is wrong. Two months.

It is *that bad*.

Damn him.

I expected my world to change when my best friend told me she was pregnant. And even though those two words have significant implications for our lives, they have nothing on that arrogant and frustratingly sexy man and these two words—*Harrison Decker*.

2

_____

Harrison Decker

"The Manhattan office runs smoothly and is performing financially. If support is needed, headquarters is listening in LA. So, I'm here not only to represent the Decker brand in the city but also to establish myself individually now that I have my real estate license for New York."

I don't shift or fidget. I'm confident in my ability to sell property, so a rock star doesn't intimidate me. I've sold homes to Oscar winners, baseball hall of famers, Super Bowl quarterbacks, and rock 'n' roll legends. I've known Kaz Fabian—guitarist, descended from Russian royalty, pianist prodigy—for years back in LA. He's one of the most interesting people I know, and his band, The Resistance, stands in a league of their own. But at the end of a long day, everyone needs a place to lay their head.

They come to me to make their real estate dreams come true.

In the past six years, I've used my connections to go from

a floundering agent with a well-known last name to a top agent who has to turn away clients due to my busy schedule.

My dad made me work my way up to prove myself. He demands excellence at the expense of anything and everything else, including a personal life.

Kaz says, "Lara's design business has outgrown her LA office. She needs a space when she's here, a place to stay and work, and I don't want her in a hotel. Although she'll be splitting her time between LA and New York, I want twenty-four-hour security, a doorman, amenities."

"Many of my California clients have multiple homes and regularly travel between the two coasts. For a client of your discretion and need for privacy, I'll make sure you get all that and more."

"So I'm your first New York client?" Kaz says, chuckling. "You must have been losing a lot of money to make it worth the effort to get your license here."

He's right. I'm not doing this for fun, although I have a good time. "I was handing over millions to local co-listing agents."

"My brother, Andrew, was flipping the fuck out at the losses," Nick says.

Kaz nods. "You're working with him, too?"

"Nobody manages my money better than the Christiansens," I reply. Look, I could lie to get my friends more business, but fortunately, I don't have to. I grew up with Nick, so he's like a brother to me. I'm basically a third Christiansen son. They do manage my money, though, so no lies are being told today.

Christiansen Wealth Management already handles most of the band's money as well, so we're safe in our discussions.

Kaz stands and shakes my hand. "I have to run but send the paperwork over. You did us right in LA, so I trust you in

New York." While he shakes Nick's hand, he adds, "Ultimately, it's not me you have to please. Lara has a whole list of other things she needs to make it feel like a home. Take care of her."

"I will. You never mentioned a budget, though," I say.

"It's only a part-time home, so I'd like to stay under ten mil."

Got to love that celebrity money. "I can do that. Let her know I have some listings I can send. If any interest her, we'll take a look."

"Will do." He takes a few steps around to the other side of the table to the exit.

Balancing on the back legs of his chair, Nick says, "Break a leg."

"I'm not superstitious," Kaz says, laughing. "You guys coming to the show?"

I was in LA at the time, but I heard it was a nightmare to score any tickets to The Resistance's tour, so I say, "Sold out in under a minute."

"I can leave tickets if you want."

Nick's eyes land on mine. "I'm in, and I know Natalie would love it."

My beer glass is almost empty, tempting me to order another. With this meeting out of the way, we can just fuck off for the rest of the afternoon until the concert. "Count me in."

"Going solo?" Kaz asks. "I can help you with the extra ticket, Decker, but not the date."

They're laughing a little too hard. I can dish it, but I can also take it. Chuckling, I reply, "You guys are real assholes, you know that?" I can find a date just fine.

"We do," Nick replies through a chuckle.

Still laughing, Kaz finally starts walking away. "Tickets

will be at Will Call." He points at me. "I'm giving you two, Decker. Don't disappoint me."

"Thanks." I finish my beer, then look at my friend. "I don't have a date."

One tap on the screen of my phone lights it up. When I start scrolling my black book of contacts, Nick asks, "What about that flight attendant you were seeing a few months back? Wasn't she out of LaGuardia?"

"Talon got engaged to a pilot two weeks ago." I search New York but don't see any names that intrigue me.

"Damn, she was ready to settle down. Fitting name as well."

"Scarily fitting. I dodged those claws." Jenny Marie rings a bell. Good time. Summer. Bonfire. Decent in bed. "There's a girl out in Jersey I went on a few dates with when she came out to audition for a pilot. Broadway actress looking to make it big in Hollywood."

I get the receipt and my credit card back and sign.

"Why'd you only go on a few dates?" he asks.

Setting the pen down, I close the book and slide it to the middle of the table. "She liked the access to my client list more than she liked me."

"Man, you're dropping some honesty like you might have gotten your feelings hurt."

"Nah. You know what it's like out there. Everyone has stars in their eyes until they're burned and jaded and head back to their hometown."

"That's why I'm in New York."

Watching a leggy blonde cross the restaurant has me thinking this city isn't so bad. "I thought you moved here because Natalie wanted to live in the city?"

"That too." He leans forward, resting his arms on the

table. Lowering his voice, he says, "I know you might not want to hear this, but you could always ask Tatum."

"That ship has sailed, like four times over."

"What is it with you two? You're oil and water. Over what? A one-night stand that didn't pan out to be more?" He finishes his beer and sets the glass down to spin it between his fingers. "That's not how I saw things going after how you two spent the night in Catalina, but you fucked up. One text could have changed it from one night—"

"Evening, all night, and sunrise, but who's counting . . ."

"Apparently, you are."

"Natalie, actually, since she was the one locked out of her room all night while you two got it on."

"The operative part of that sentence is 'the one.' That's the same *one* you married. So, you're welcome." Considering three years have passed since the wedding, I doubt Tatum has thought much about me since Catalina, much less from the reception. *Even though I've thought of her more than once or twice over that time.* Nick's smile makes me chuckle. "Damn, dude, you still have it that bad for your wife?"

"I'll never get over how lucky I am." Standing, he adds, "Now that my brother's life is sorted, according to my mom, she's turning her attention on you, so be careful, or you just might find yourself in my shoes."

"Smiling like a loon in the middle of a restaurant? No, thank you. Cookie Christiansen may believe she's a match-maker, but fixing her sons' lives was easy compared to the mess I've made of my love life." I stand and walk around to his side of the table. "Anyway, just because you found your one and only doesn't mean I have to fall for the same shenanigans." *Although, after looking at my* black book*, I can't help wondering. Do I want more than one night as well?*

Leading us out of the restaurant, I look up at the

skyscrapers blocking the sunshine. "Do you ever get used to this? I've been here a day, and I miss the wide blue sky and the ocean."

Shoving his hands into his pockets, Nick gazes upward. When he looks back at me, he says, "The pros outweigh the cons. Andrew and I can take you to the shore sometime. There's surfing. Admittedly, the Atlantic isn't the same as the Pacific, but it works when you need to be with the sea."

He nods toward the car waiting at the curb. When we start walking, he adds, "I'll be honest, I felt out of place here for months. Maybe being with Natalie made it easier. She showed me how great this city can be. We can walk to so many places, restaurants, shops, the store. I don't miss sitting in my car for two to three hours a day." He stops and opens the door before clapping me on the shoulder. "So yeah, it's not LA, but New York's kind of won my heart over. Give it a chance, and you might find it's not so bad."

"I'm here. I'm giving it a chance." I duck into the back, and he follows. For someone who apparently walks so much, it must be nice to have a car on call day and night. "As for Tatum, that's a hard no. You saw how she reacted when she saw me. The woman hates me. With her, there are no second chances."

"Maybe give it the night, and you two can become friends. Natalie would like that."

His wife is cool enough for me to consider the option. "Look, I won't say no to Natalie, but that means me taking a risk. Tatum is more than bark. She bites."

"Keep your sexual escapades to yourself, dude."

It's a punch to the arm he can handle, especially since it doesn't seem to faze him from teasing me the rest of the way home. The thing is, I liked Tatum. I fucked up by not calling her despite our agreement. Maybe we could have worked out like Nick and Natalie, given how their relationship started the same night.

Fuck. I run a hand over my head. *What am I talking about?*

No way am I ready to be married and settled down at twenty-nine. Life's just getting interesting.

When the car arrives, we head up to the stoop. "I think I should have had another beer before doing this."

Patting me on the back, he says, "You got this."

Nick opens the door, and we're greeted with laughter echoing from deeper inside the house. We walk toward the sound, and when Nick sees Natalie, he opens his arms. "There's my beautiful wife." She rushes to him as if they've been apart for more than a few hours.

I hang back in the doorway, feeling like an intruder to their intimate moment. I can't help but glance toward Tatum, who's sipping a glass of wine while perched on a barstool.

She angles my way but is quick to turn toward the back-yard, blocking all of us from her view. While Nick and Natalie whisper to each other, I decide to throw my balls on the Tatum chopping block once more. I shove my hands in my pockets and join her at the large island. I make sure to keep space between us. Matters like Tatum have to be handled delicately.

"Hi," I say, keeping my voice quiet between us.

Glancing my way, she then turns toward the half-eaten platter of snacks and grabs a cracker. "Hi," she replies even quieter, eyes on the food before taking a bite.

When the room goes silent and tension fills the air, I find Nick and Natalie sneaking away. *Fuck.* No pressure or anything. "*Soooo yeah*, Nick and I scored some tickets tonight—"

"Oh my God, are you asking me out?" Panic rises in her voice, reaching her eyes as she stares wide-eyed at me.

My arms fly up in surrender. "Just as friends. I know you prefer keeping your distance from me, but I was hoping we could maybe move past, *well*, the past. Or maybe not as friends, but just not enemies." I need to shut the fuck up. It's incredible that I can date a Miss Universe, an Oscar-nominated actress, and the top real estate agent in LA—after me, of course—without so much as a second thought. But Tatum Devreux has me rambling like an insecure teen asking a girl out for the first time.

She angles my way, spinning her body to the side. The panic has disappeared, and I'm not sure how to read her. Is that calm settling the choppy waters of her deep brown eyes? A smile doesn't follow to calm mine, and the tension still felt like a tight lasso around my chest. She sighs in resolve, but then says, "I think you're right, Harrison."

"I am?" It's been so long since she's said my first name that I'd almost forgotten how sweet it sounds coming from her lips. "About?"

"Being enemies. It's not good for either of us or our friends. If you're going to be in the city for a while, which it sounds like you plan to be, we'll naturally be seeing more of each other." She holds her hand out. "So I agree with you. We should wipe the slate clean and leave the past in the past."

I take her hand, the memories of holding it that night in Catalina coming back like it was yesterday. "Deal." I pull back, not willing to let the heat of our connection trap me back in the night I can't seem to forget.

She stands, and a smile finally graces her full pink lips. "Great. Now about those tickets . . ."

3

Harrison

Tatum said yes to tonight before knowing if we had tickets to a movie, a concert, a baseball game, or even the subway. My point being, she said yes before knowing anything about the offer.

She said yes to me.

I could let that feed my ego, but that's not what she intended. I'll take the good, though, and hope we can actually reach a peaceful existence for our best friends. Or even better, become friends.

She makes it hard, *literally*, to think of her platonically when seeing her in a short skirt like she is now. I'm reminded I was once given full access to what's underneath it. There was a time I had to peel her off me, not because I wanted her to stop, but I didn't want us to get arrested for public indecency. She's got a wild side that she has me missing.

Bumping into me, she says, "Thank you."

"For what?"

She takes a sip of her drink and smiles. There's a shyness to it that doesn't quite fit the vibrant woman I know her to be. "For asking me to come with you guys. You could have brought anyone."

When I think about scrolling through my contacts earlier, I now know why I couldn't find anyone I wanted to call. I'm a fucking glutton for punishment. "I'm glad you came."

A smirk tilts her grin up on one side. A little nudge to my ribs with her elbow is enough for me to realize the double meaning of what I said. Tatum's still giggling when she replies, "Me too."

The lights go down. Natalie and Tatum loop their arms around each other's and raise their free arms into the air, screaming in excitement for the band. I catch Nick's eyes over their heads, and we fist bump. He nods toward Tatum and waggles his eyebrows. *Ass.* I give him a shrug because I'm the dumbass who keeps trying to get back on her good side.

When the lights flash on, the band members own their spots on the stage, Johnny Outlaw front and center, Dex on the drums, Derrick on the left, and Kaz in front of us. Twenty-thousand fans scream at the same time, and Dex kicks in on the drums.

Spending the next hour rocking out to the music, I'd finished my drink by the second song. Not wanting to miss any of the show, I stayed to watch.

We're only an hour in when Tatum turns to me and tilts her head to look at my hand. "Empty?"

"Yeah."

"Want to come with me? I'll buy your next."

Fuck yeah, I do. Screw the band. Tatum is much more

interesting. I follow her to the nearest door, and a bouncer swings it open for us.

The VIP section has its perks, and proximity to a private bar and facilities are two of them. She orders as I step around some guy trying to weasel in next to her and come between them. Tatum doesn't even notice how guys look at her, how they go out of their way to be near her, to hit on her, to touch her. *Fuckers.* All of them.

Blocking that guy, I lean on the counter and hold out a bill to the bartender.

"I'm supposed to be buying your drink." She tries to snatch the money but misses when I raise my hand. "Put it away, Decker. Your money's no good here."

The bartender sets the drinks in front of us and laughs. "The drinks are free," he says, "but I don't mind that as a tip."

Tatum catches me off guard when she snags the bill from my hand. She tucks it in the bartender's tip jar, and then tells him, "Thank you."

Leaving him with a huge smile and shock widening his eyes, he trips over his words. "Wow. Thanks."

I don't mind paying the guy the money, but she's sneaky. She tugs me by the sleeve away from the bar. We're quickly replaced when we walk away. "I thought my money wasn't any good?"

Laughing, she winks. "It wasn't good for the drinks, but you just made his day with that tip. So maybe your money's not so bad after all."

I chuckle. "Guess not."

Although the band is well into the set when we enter through the doors, Tatum doesn't seem to be in a hurry to get back. Standing off to the side out of the walkway, she sways to the music while sipping her drink. I stay behind her so I don't block anyone trying to get by. Watching the band from this angle isn't the best, but I'm okay with it. I'm near her and like the view of her dancing, even if it is from behind.

See? *Glutton.*

When she peeks back, she appears to be relaxed around me. Usually, her shoulders are tense and her mouth is tight-lipped. Not tonight. Maybe we really are moving forward with a fresh start. "I heard you got your real estate license for the state."

It's not a question, but I hear the lilt. I like that I'm on her mind. "I did."

"And you're staying with Nick and Natalie for the next two months."

Again, not a question, but I'll take the lead-in. "You sure are hearing a lot about me." I give her a wink. "I'm not sure how long I'll be here, actually. I have to fly back to LA every week. We'll see how the commute goes."

"I got the impression you were moving here." Her tongue dips out and swings the straw closer, and she peers up at me while drinking.

She's so hard to read. Her interest in where I live belies the cool casualness. "Don't worry. I won't be here forever. I didn't even plan to stay at Nick's place, but he offered when he heard I was planning to live in a hotel while here. Natalie insisted, and you know how hard it is to turn her down."

"I do. When she sets her mind to something, she usually gets what she wants." She glances back at the band and then at me again. "You don't have to worry about me ruining your visit. I'll respect your time with your friend."

"It's okay. You don't ruin anything."

Turning all the way around to face me, she lowers her gaze to her drink, and she fidgets with the straw. "Things are changing." Something behind grabs both of our attention. A guy is arguing with the bouncer, so I shift us away and closer to the audience. Her guard is down, her shoulders at ease, and with an arena behind her, she looks smaller to me, more vulnerable even. I angle to keep her safe from any scuffle that might break out, careful not to make her uncomfortable.

"I'm sure it will be good for you and Nick to hang out again," she says.

"LA's not the same without him, and it's been a couple of months since I've seen him. It's been good so far. I'm sure he'll get sick of me invading his house soon enough." I chuckle.

She takes another sip and then laughs lightly, momentarily appearing lost in her thoughts of her own. "I'm sure that won't happen. On the bright side, maybe you'll find that New York's not so bad." The smile on her face is genuine with no ill will attached.

"I'm sure it's not. Are you ready to go back?" I'm not in a hurry, but I don't want to circle around what happened in Catalina. It's been too good with her to ruin the night.

Nodding, she pushes off the wall and starts working her way back to Natalie's side, who's quick to wrap an arm over Tatum's shoulders. They dance and sing, competing with the lead vocals. Kaz points at us after a solo riff, giving me a nod of approval. I suppose it's because of my date. I'll take it from the guy who laughed that I couldn't find one.

Tatum's more than a stand-in to prove him wrong, but she's making me look good nonetheless. Nick disappears for drinks, bringing a bottle of water for Natalie and another round for the rest of us. It's probably best if one of us stays sober, and I'm glad it's Natalie and not me because I'm enjoying this glass of whiskey and Coke.

With a free weekend, I drink up since I have nothing to lose but the night ahead. Between the main set and the encore, a large security guy invites us to the bar where they're hosting the after-party. We're given the address and then continue enjoying the rest of the concert.

Nudging me, Tatum lifts high toward my ear. "They're probably going to bail. What do you think? Still want to go?"

For a brief second, I question if she's asking me out. "Me?" Guess I did that out loud. I might want to slow down on the alcohol.

She doesn't hold back her laughter as the band leaves the stage. Dex remains on the drums, closing out the show like the badass he is. I sold him a beach retreat with a killer setup for his drum kit last year. Tatum swings her long hair over her shoulder and bumps into me. "What do you think?" she yells so I can hear. I look around because I think the entire arena heard.

I lean down, not wanting to yell, and say, "I'll go with you."

She rolls her eyes. "It's not like you're doing me a favor, but thanks." Still laughing, she nudges me with her elbow.

The show ends, and the crowd is quick to stream from the arena. Sticking together, the four of us make it a few blocks before stopping to talk, though the girls have been talking a mile a minute the whole time.

"What are your plans?" Nick asks.

"Tatum wants to go to the after-party."

He smirks. "Oh, yeah?"

"I can't compete with rock stars, brother."

"They're all married, and you know as well as I do, they don't fuck around."

"True." I peek over at Tatum, smiling from seeing her

animated expression as she uses her arms to tell Nat a story. *God, she's gorgeous.*

"We're gonna head home," Nick says. "Make sure Tatum gets home safe, okay?" When I nod, he adds. "You know the code. Just let yourself in, but remember to set the alarm."

We shake hands and then bring it in for a shoulder bump. "Thanks for having me."

"I'm glad you're here." When he steps back, Natalie's and his hands clasp as if the universe pulled them together.

I don't know if this weird tightening in my chest is from witnessing what I don't have or what I'm starting to think I want. It's best to leave before I overanalyze the situation or emotion. I shove my hands in my pockets and turn to Tatum. "You ready?"

She turns to say goodbye to the others, then plucks the front of my shirt and says, "I'm all yours, Decker," as she raises her chin and marches past me. I grin and follow like a good friend, probably like her boyfriends do, trailing her like love-sick puppies.

Is that what I am?

Not on your life.

A great fuck, especially since it only happened one time, does not make me love-sick or her follower. Though I vaguely remember being smitten for a short time in our history. I quickly catch up to her, and we walk down the block together before we hop into the car I ordered.

Silence is another passenger hitching a ride between us. As a salesman, I'm trained to wait it out once the deal is on the table. But the deal isn't closed with Tatum. Just an awkwardness of wondering what's going to happen tonight.

Once we exit the car, she moves closer to my side as we walk down the alley toward the private entrance. It's not far, but I like her company. After we step inside, she stays close to me. Maybe it's because she appears to dislike the unwanted leers she's receiving. This is not the woman I've heard stories about from Nick. He said Tatum and Nat used to dance on bars and were the queens of the spotlight, owning the attention of every person in the place. Tonight, she doesn't seem to crave that life.

"I'm happy to be your wingman," I say.

She giggles. "I don't need help getting a date—"

"What? No, I meant bodyguard, not wingman." *What the fuck?* Helping her get a date with some other asshole is the last thing I plan to do.

Wrapping her arm around mine, she tugs me toward the velvet ropes. A bouncer gives us a nod and steps aside, allowing us entrance to the section. "Does my body need guarding, Decker?"

Abso-fucking-lutely. "I'm up for the job if you're offering."

"I know firsthand you're up for it."

I've been drinking.

She's been drinking.

"There's that trouble with a capital T that I remember so well," I say, giving her a once-over. I cared earlier, careful to watch her when she wasn't looking. That care is gone, and I'll give it right back to her. Her hair is lighter than it was in Catalina, but it's still long, if not longer. The loose waves are so fucking sexy. It's as if she just rolled out of bed after a night of sex. I know how the night's going to go down. Every guy is going to be eyeing her, talking to her, and one of those fuckers might win the lottery and get to take her home.

Fuck. What am I doing? Why am I setting myself up for this kind of torture?

That short skirt, a shirt that highlights her assets, and those long legs I remember being wrapped around me. She takes hold of my shirtsleeve like we're a couple walking into the VIP section.

Despite the band coming in behind us, you'd think Tatum was the rock star since all eyes are on her. We find a seat on a couch against the wall while the guys who came out tonight settle around a low table. I greet Kaz, then introduce Tatum. Most women are starstruck when they meet my famous friends. Hell, most men are as well. *Except Tatum.*

The band might be put on pedestals by everyone else, but Tatum's poised and confident not only in her own skin but also in the sky-high heels she's been wearing all night. I don't know near enough as I'd like about her, but maybe her world includes megastars and musicians.

The band's manager, Tommy, makes sure the table is loaded with bottles of options. Derrick and Kaz pour drinks like they didn't just sweat for over two hours on a stage.

Even they take notice of Tatum and that short, even shorter when she sits, skirt of hers. They're all married, but if they weren't, I might be worried they'd find her more interesting than she finds me.

I have no right to feel possessive or even jealous, but some feelings I've ignored up to this point have unexpectedly resurfaced, causing my gut to twist and my head to spin when it comes to her. I'm not one to get hung up on a woman. I wholeheartedly admit I only made one phone call that I don't even think she's aware of. I made decisions, and now I have to live with the consequences. I chose my family and work back then, and I'm regretting that now.

Not that I'm in love with the woman, but sitting next to her makes me realize there was a time we had a real chance at what Nick and Natalie have. My chest tightens, thinking of that time after Catalina and what happened. I can't change that, but maybe if Tatum knew . . .

She's been holding on to that grudge like a life preserver. Even when I tried to make it right at Nick and Natalie's wedding reception. No move I made or thing I said was going to change her mind. *Too little. Too late.*

I tried to tell her the truth. My timing might have sucked, but it wasn't because I hadn't been thinking of her. Sometimes life is shit and gets in the way. If I could change what happened, I would—for her, for me, but most of all, for my sister.

She's let me back in tonight, but what will tomorrow bring?

I have my reasons, but what are hers—the real ones. I'm fucking confused and ready to put this to bed, so I ask, "What happened between us?"

4

___

Tatum

I'M TWO COCKTAILS PAST THE POINT OF GETTING DEFENSIVE OR even bothering to protect my heart or other body parts that Harrison Decker has the innate ability to arouse.

After a few rapid blinks, I riddle through the alcohol fog that I was happily letting sink into my body when I was blindsided. "I thought we decided to move forward. Forget the past and all that jazz?" Enjoying the cocktail and the company of this after-party a little too much, I take another sip.

Harrison's knee is bouncing, and he looks down at the floor between his feet. "We did, but I have questions that I can't seem to answer." When he looks at me again, a tenderness tinges his eyes. No smile is found, which is odd, considering his demeanor is usually jovial. Or maybe that's just the impression I've gotten over the years.

Not sure where we're going with this, I settle in, resting back on a hand against the low leather couch. The motion has the toe of my shoes bumped against his, and I don't bother moving it. "What's the question again?"

"Why'd you make me promise not to contact you?"

"You were right there agreeing with me. At first, it was a joke, like this will be fun, meaningless sex, a romp on a yacht in the harbor, but . . ."

"But then?"

I look away. "You had my number, Harrison. I didn't have yours." I finish the ice-filled drink, wishing I had ordered one without so I'd still have some vodka left. I'm thinking I'll need it for this conversation. "We should leave the heavier topics for another day and get another drink instead."

He doesn't bother dancing around the topic and steps right into the fire. "Nick and Natalie have been together practically since the minute they met, which happens to be the same time we met." He looks up at a small scuffle beyond the velvet ropes. When our gazes meet again, he adds, "You could have gotten my number when they got together."

I rest my hand on his knee, trying to calm the anxiety revealing itself. "Harrison . . ." I find myself sighing as if I'm giving up; hopefully, the angrier side I've been holding so tightly to when it comes to him. *Is it so bad to give in?* "Natalie and I are a lot alike, but we're not the same person. Her heart is open, so exposed and ready to be hurt—"

"Nick won't hurt her."

Getting to know my best friend's husband over the years has shown me that true love exists. I've borne witness to it. Nick would do anything for Natalie, and she would do anything for him. They're committed in legal ways, but this baby cements them as forever tied to each other. "I know he won't. I meant before him. Natalie and I, God, we've done some crazy things, partied more than our fair share, and been the life of them. We never ran from being the center of attention. Worse, I ran into the arms of the baddest boy in the room. They were easy to find, usually with a cigarette or joint hanging out of the side of their mouths. We've both lived carelessly—her with her gentle heart, me with my willingness to prove to the world how I didn't need anyone."

"Didn't?"

"Don't. I *don't* need anyone, Harrison. That's your warning. If you proceed, do it cautiously because I always hurt the innocent. And I don't think I'll ever change."

"Do you want to?" he asks with no fear heard in his voice. I detect a little disappointment, though.

"And set myself up to be hurt again? Not really into that either."

He shakes his head in seeming disbelief. Then he drinks, his gaze sliding around the crowd in front of us. "You know, Tatum, I think you're right. I think we need another round of drinks." He stands and passes the table full of bottles, a free setup spread across the white lacquer top. Watching him, he weaves around the bouncer who lifts the red rope for him to pass.

Sitting forward on the backless couch, I set my glass down on the table and then stand to peer across the top of the crowded bar. The VIP area has a good vantage point, and as the sexiest man in the place, Harrison easily stands out. Then my heart sinks to the pit of my stomach as two women strike up a conversation with him. They're leaning in, flirting, and he's eating it right up with that stupid smirk on his face. Anger flares inside. *Anger or jealousy?* I'm not sure because the burn feels the same either way.

I knew he was a player. Standing up, I stalk toward the

exit, and my glare alone warns the bouncer to lift the ropes. I shouldn't bother giving Harrison another second of my time, but I'm too mad, insulted even, and irritated that I actually started to believe I'd made a mistake in Catalina. He's no less the playboy I met back then.

That wasn't tenderness in his eyes earlier. *I'm so dumb.*

Why do I always have to fall for the bad boys? Surely, there's one good man in this universe who's made just for me.

When I approach, he turns his attention to me, angling my way. I don't care if I make a scene or embarrass him when I say, "Why did I think we could be anything more than enemies?"

Confusion contorts his expression, furrowing his brow. "What are you talking about, Tatum?" He holds a drink forward. "I was getting us drinks."

The two women standing on either side of him have the gall to look away from me awkwardly as though I'm the one who should be ashamed. "I don't want another drink with you. I thought . . ." My twisted emotions get caught in my throat. Taking a breath, I look around to calm down. I refuse to fill the irrational female role. "I thought we could actually get a second chance at being friends, but you're no different than when you had the first chance and blew it." I take the drink, gulping some down, and then empty the rest on his chest.

The women squeal in horror as they jump back, both shaking their hands from the liquid that splattered on them.

"Fuck," he growls. That fire I felt earlier flickers to life in his eyes, and I recognize the feeling, finding comfort that it wasn't jealousy.

Why would I be jealous of anything having to do with

this man? "Go to hell, Harrison." I turn and squeeze my way through the crowd to get to the exit.

When I make it outside, the early June air hits. It's not quite cool anymore like last month but not insufferable like August. Yet somehow, a chill runs down my spine as my eyes spike with tears. I hate feeling weak, but I know it's just the alcohol messing with me. Nothing more. Not that stupid man or anything else to do with him.

Closing my eyes, I take a deep breath. *Screw him.* Damn all men and their inability to be faithful to someone who shows them an ounce of kindness.

When I open my eyes, I'm met with a night sky of blue eyes. That anger I thought I was familiar with isn't residing in his pupils. With that dirty blond hair stuck to his forehead, Harrison says, "It's not ending like this."

"What isn't?" I play dumb, hoping he doesn't see through my innocent act. I just need to get out of here with my heart and mind intact. *My heart? What does my heart have to do with this?*

"Us. You and I, Tatum. I should have fucking texted. Okay? Happy?"

I cross my arms over my chest. "Not particularly."

"Neither am I, so where does that leave us?"

"Stop asking me these questions like I have the answers." Raising my voice, I continue, "I don't. I don't know about you, us, or anything else happening between us other than I lowered my walls, and you trampled your way inside only to turn around at the first sign of a hot woman, or two, hitting on you." I mumble, "God, why am I even arguing with him?"

I storm down the sidewalk, pulling my phone from the pocket on my belt to order a car. My pace doesn't break as I head toward the corner, refusing to waste my time on that man. I've been hurt before, and I'm not going down that road again. I play hard to get better than I'll ever be the easy catch for many reasons. Seeing Harrison flirting with those women the first chance he gets is one of them.

"Hey!" His voice hits my back and grabs every other person's attention in the vicinity. *That's not embarrassing at all* ... "Tatum."

The interesting part is that he doesn't seem to be asking but demanding. That's not going to end well for him. Not that the night was a cakewalk prior. I whip around and plant my hands on my hips. "Don't you ever speak to me that way. Do you understand, Decker?"

"I understand that you're taking your anger caused by every guy who ever did you wrong out on me. And I'll let you, but you know what, Devreux?"

"What?" Bitterness coats my tongue, but I don't shy away from the confrontation. I was so stupid to think he could change or that he was different. He wasn't four and a half years ago, and he isn't now.

"I'm not going to dwell on this or continue wondering how I can get in your good graces. You're a beautiful woman, but in one night, I saw beyond the skin-deep shield you hold up to the world to protect yourself. I saw someone special, not because of her beauty but her heart."

A car honks to my left that matches the description on the app, but his words cause me to hesitate. I turn back to him and take a deep breath. "You can run away, but I've seen you, the real person inside," he adds.

"And I just saw the real you inside." I walk toward the car and dip my head toward the open window. "Tatum?" the driver confirms.

"That's me."

I open the back door and look back to find Harrison still

standing there as if we're going to hash this all out and be besties. I'm tempted to leave without another word. Unlike him, I thought we got closure on this, on us, years ago. "We can play games all night, kid ourselves for another four-plus years, or wonder what went wrong for the rest of our lives, but one thing remains, Harrison," I say.

His arms fly from his sides. "What?"

"If I was so special, you would have called." I get into the car because that feels pretty damn final to me and more than I've ever given any other guy.

When I shut the door, I sit back, not afraid to look out the window as the car pulls away from the curb. It's good to see your endings—helps to cope with the loss in the aftermath—but the way he watches me doesn't give me the satisfaction I thought I'd find.

Instead, I feel empty inside.

I hate him for that, for causing me to feel the guilt as it races through my veins, for the disappointment I'm all too familiar with, and for making me second-guess myself. "Stop the car."

We reach the end of the next block, and the car slams to a stop. Unable to get closer because of cars blocking the curb, the driver jerks his head around. "What is it?"

"I'm sorry. I need to get out."

He rolls his eyes, his gaze returning to the rearview mirror. Cars are blaring their horns at us for stopping in the lane. "I'm giving you a lower passenger rating for this."

"I'll take it. I'm sorry." I pop open the door and get out, squeezing between two parked cars. Once I reach the sidewalk, I start walking back to the bar where I left Harrison. I don't know why.

Why do I care?

Why am I doing this?

Why do I feel bad?

Why am I anxious to get to him?

I was practically born in designer heels, but I really wish I had on sneakers as I hurry upstream through the crowd that feels determined to keep me from reaching him. I walk faster, then slowly jog, my heart racing along with the thoughts of wondering what the hell I'm even doing.

Chasing guys isn't something I ever have to do.

I'm not even sure what I'm going to say to him.

Pushing my injured ego aside, I'm willing to start over. I won't hold a damn thing against him. This time.

I'd do it for real this time.

We can be friends.

Friends.

That almost sounds believable.

Being friends with him might be interesting because I don't have guy friends. Usually, it's for a reason, but maybe he'll be different if he's just a friend, and all the sexual tension between us will disappear. *Sexual tension? What the hell?*

A guy rushing in the opposite direction hits my shoulder, sending me back a few steps and wobbling. I catch myself, along with my breath, and then run as fast as I can while dressed in a short skirt and these damn high but stunning, heels. I'd take them off if I weren't well aware of the grossness on New York's sidewalks.

Just past the entrance to the bar, I stop, my chest rising and falling with heavy breaths as I stare at the spot where I left him. I look back at the door and then to the curb where cabs and cars pick up and drop off passengers.

A heavy exhale escapes me as defeat sets in, smothering the excitement that had been building like this is some dumb love story.

What did I really expect?

That he'd still be here like a fool in the middle of the sidewalk waiting for me to hop out of a car two blocks down and run against the current to get back to him? *As if.*

Who's the fool now?

That'd be me.

5

Tatum

MY STOMACH VIBRATES.

Ugh.

The stupid sensation won't go away even when I roll over. I can still feel it through the mattress. With my eyes closed, I rub my hand under the covers until I find the annoyance—*my phone.*

It does this most mornings like I don't have anything better to do than sleep. Beauty doesn't happen naturally. Stupid alarm. Sure, I'm to blame for setting it, but a good eight to ten hours is necessary, especially after a night of drinking.

My heart thumps in my chest as memories of last night come to mind. A certain man not standing where I left him causes a pang right after. I open my eyes and tap on my screen, shutting off the alarm.

Staring up into the darkness, I lie in my king-sized bed fit for a queen. Pillows, a fluffy down comforter, and the best sheets money can buy surround me. This is a life of luxury, one that usually makes me smile.

So why do I feel sad?

Reaching over, I hit the button built into the nightstand. The blackout shades start a slow ascent, and the sun invades my bedroom, the bright light burning my eyes. Grabbing a pillow, I pull it over my face and groan.

I can call in sick or just tell Natalie I want the day off. She'd understand. She always does. She's never been one to put on pressure or demand more than she feels she can.

Spoiler alert: She can. As the boss, she can demand that her employees show up for work.

With enough time to get ready and one other activity, I have to decide between coffee at a café, a workout, or a nap. Sighing, I throw the covers off and get to my feet. *Workout it is.*

I grab my workout clothes, thinking it's the best weapon against fighting this bad mood I can't seem to shake.

Thirty minutes later, I'm looking around the gym, wondering why it's so packed. Don't people have work to do or something else at 8:30 in the morning? I've had to wait to use every machine this morning. Wrapping up on the treadmill, I hit my stride on the third mile—my pace faster than usual and on a decent incline. The endorphins were good for my attitude because I'm feeling much better now.

"Tatum?"

I glance to my right at the man staring straight at me. His face is familiar, but I can't quite place him. At least he's cute. I pull my earbud out on the side where he is and slow the treadmill to a walking pace. With my hands on my hips, I try to steady my breath. "Hi?"

He picks up on the question without me having to ask, and replies, "Elijah. Elijah Morris. You helped me with—"

"Your proposal." Snapping, I point. "I remember. Your father connected us."

"Yes, he loves to spoil my mom."

"As he should." I punch stop on the treadmill. "Your proposal, that must have been, what? Two years ago? I guess you're married and living the life these days."

Still walking next to me, he looks through the window ahead of him and shakes his head. "Actually, the wedding never happened." He ends his treadmill session and slows to a stop on the belt. Gripping the sides, he looks at me. "She cheated on me with my cousin the night before the wedding." Wow, that's a bitch. *More accurately, she is.*

Cheating is the lowest. It's happened to the best of us, though—me and Natalie included. Elijah always seemed like a good guy, so offense fills me on his behalf. "I'm sorry to hear that."

"My mom had a sense about her the moment they met, not a good one. If you know what I mean."

"I do." My answer makes me cringe right after. I mean, someone telling you they got screwed over on their wedding day probably doesn't want to hear those two magical words . . . wait. *What? Magical?* I shake my head and inwardly roll my eyes at myself.

He continues, not noticing my crazy or maybe just polite enough not to point it out, "But sometimes we get caught in the moment more than the reality of what's right in front of us." Shifting to face me, he adds, "I was thinking we could go out sometime."

"Me?" I ask, not seeing that coming. "Ah. I get it. I'm right in front of you. You took that as a sign."

Shrugging, he says, "It couldn't hurt to find out."

Hurt. I don't get hurt too much, but disappointment finds me easily when it comes to men. "I appreciate the words of wisdom and self-realization, but it's not wise for me to date clients."

"I'm not one, not anymore."

Laughing, I waggle my finger. "I see what you did there, but I think we should keep things professional." Turning back to my machine, I punch it up a level to start walking again. "You're attractive, and I'm sure you can date whoever you want. You should play the field, recover from the breakup, and then find your co-signer for a property out in the Hamptons."

"That's a very specific dream, but I'm more interested in this weekend and spending time with you." *Ah. He's still playing the field and trying to play me.* Although I didn't need the confirmation to see through the situation, he has me thinking about my own goals. I hit the next level on the treadmill.

Working with my best friend has been amazing, and making her dreams come true has been rewarding. But am I settling when I'm actually working *for* her and more focused on her dreams than my own?

Here I thought being twenty-six, being able to do whatever I want and living on my own in New York City was a dream come true. A lot of my friends still live at home.

Home.

At what point does it switch from your parents' home to your own? I thought that's what I had, but maybe I don't. Not yet. And what dream of mine has come true?

Is it really an accomplishment that I can stay out as late as I want and sleep in on the weekends? I have no obligations or commitments other than showing up for work by ten in the morning. I live life on my terms. Shouldn't that be enough? *At least, for now?*

In college, I wanted to conquer the world and do something that mattered. I never had an interest in the shipping industry of the family business anyway. I wanted to make a difference somehow, forge my own path, and break away from the legacy of the Devreux name.

What happened to that girl? My actions—wild to the core, a party girl, a socialite—used to be motivated by getting my parents' attention. Though when I got out of hand, my parents didn't ground me. Instead, it was Natalie who talked sense into me. Tried and true, she was always there no matter how I behaved.

But that's not her job anymore. Maybe it's time I grow up and reevaluate my goals. Or set some in the first place. She's now Mrs. Christiansen, but I'm still just me.

Alone.

For Natalie, baby makes three. Where does that leave me?

Alone.

I like my morning routine, but it might be nice to wake up next to someone every now and again. I need to think bigger, and now more than ever, I need to think about the future. I need to focus on myself.

I need to make a change, get off this hamster wheel routine or the treadmill to forge my own path. I love my job, but I need to grow it and make it mine.

"Tatum?"

"Huh?" I'd almost forgotten about Elijah. Elijah's cute and all. His ring in a candy box proposal was sweet, but he's not my type.

"What level are you going? I can set mine to match." He points at the display screen.

"Match?" I sound like an idiot, but—*Oh!* "The treadmill. Match? I don't want to match. I want to stand out. To level up to my full potential."

His head jerks back. "So twelve?"

Not sure why he seems shocked, but I don't have time to overanalyze it. My head is spinning with bigger plans than where I am now . . . in life or at the gym. "That's it! I don't want to be a ten. I want to be a twelve."

"You already are. I was intimidated to even come over here to talk to you." That makes me smile. Maybe he was sincere earlier.

This isn't about being single or keeping up with my best friend. This is about developing into the person I'm meant to be. My feet land on the rails of the treadmill, and I punch stop. "I'm sorry. I need to go." Jumping off the treadmill, I'm a woman on a mission. "See you around, Elijah, and let me know if you need our gifting services again." I head toward the dressing room.

"I will," he replies, confusion ringing in his tone. "See you around."

WALKING into the bright and airy SoHo office, I'm greeted by Renee, our reception assistant. "Good morning, Tatum."

"Good morning. Is Natalie in?"

"She is."

"Thanks." I round the corner and head straight for Natalie's office, which is in the corner next to mine. I say hello to a few of the staff on the way but waste no time. Pushing into her office, I lean against the door. "I had an epiphany."

She peers up with a raised eyebrow. "Care to share, or are you going to hold that dramatic pose all morning?"

"Holding the pose. How do I look?"

"Gorgeous, darling. Want me to take a pic?"

I start laughing and shut the door. "No. I was only doing it for effect." I sit across from her and add, "I'm more than a sidekick."

"Sidekick? Who called you that? If anything, I've always been *your* sidekick."

"Precisely. Not that you're second fiddle or anything, but I'm the one who was out there—"

"And I was the one reining you in."

Grinning, it feels like old times with her, the days when we were younger and a lot more naïve. We spent every minute together as soon as we got out of school and in the summers. We've not quite captured that feeling in a while, until now. "It's like you can read my mind."

She shrugs as if that's a given and begins straightening her desk. "We're besties for a reason."

"I love you, Natalie."

Her gaze flies up to meet mine. "And I thought the entrance was dramatic. I love you, too, Tatum," she replies, giggling. "Now, what's going on with you today?"

"The baby. I've been thinking a lot about this."

A low gasp is heard, and then she leans forward conspiratorially. "I'm so glad because I can't think of anything else."

Reaching across the desk, I cover her hands with mine. "I'm here for you. This is incredible news, and I don't want to miss anything."

Tears well in her eyes, and she attempts to blink them back. It's not working. It never does. You would think we'd always be wearing waterproof mascara. One day we'll learn. I'm quick to grab a tissue from a box behind her so she can dab the corners of her eyes before the tears mess up her makeup.

"Thank you," she says.

"You're welcome." Standing up, I walk to the window to peer out. When I look back, I ask, "Do you have names?"

"Oh my God. Now you're reading *my* mind." She bursts out laughing. And then she pulls a pad from her Louis Vuitton and drops it on the desk. "I have a small list started."

When I glance over at the pink pad, my eyes go wide. "Small? Santa's list is shorter." She snort-laughs. I grab the pad and then shoot her a glare. "Rufus? I'm nixing Rufus. Nigel, Cook, and Devon are gone as well."

"What's wrong with Devon?"

"Devon Spears?" I reply as if she should remember this as clearly as I do. "The jerk sophomore year in high school?"

She cups her forehead as recognition fills her eyes. "I forgot about him. Definitely cross that name off the list. He was a total asshole. He told his brother, David, a senior, that I wouldn't put out, so he shouldn't ask me to prom."

"But you didn't put out in high school."

Her eyes slide to the monitor in front of her, a sly smile working its way onto her face before she giggles. "Good thing he didn't take me to prom then." She types something and then turns back to me. "At this rate, you'll have a name narrowed down in no time."

"Happy to be of service." I take a pen from her desk and start scratching through more names. "It's too early to know if you're having a boy, right?"

"Too early, but I don't know," she says, rubbing her flat stomach. "I feel like I'll have a boy. Nick has a brother, and I have a brother. It seems to be leaning that way with all the evidence."

"Sounds like you beat the odds. Anyway, I need a girl to spoil rotten, take shopping, and leave my wealth of designer wardrobe to one day, like my bag collection."

Her fingers were poised over the keyboard but never

land. Instead, she turns to me and lowers her hands to the desk. "As much as I'm already envious of a girl I don't have, you act as though you'll never have kids."

I realize kids aren't something I've thought about in a realistic way. "I've not been in a serious relationship in years. Not that I need a man, but I can't say I want kids anytime soon. What would I do with a baby?"

Exasperated, she rocks back in her chair. "What am I going to do with you, Tate? You love a baby and raise it."

I plop down in the chair again. "You make it sound so easy."

"I know it won't be, but I think our instincts will kick in. I also have a stack of books as tall as my bed to study in the next seven months."

"You're fifty steps ahead of me, friend." I return her newly revised list to her and set the pen on the glass top desk.

Laughing, she studies the list. "I'm not going to be one of those people forcing others to join me for this ride." Her eyes return to mine. "Having a baby is something Nick and I talked about for the past year. We weren't trying, but since we weren't using protection, I guess you could say we weren't not trying either."

"So, what you're saying is this baby is a double negative?"

Horror squeezes her face. "What? No, I didn't say that." Two protective arms cover her stomach again, her instincts already kicking in. "This baby is a double positive." When she grins, the tension releases from her shoulders.

"I'm only teasing. As for my epiphany . . ."

"Yes, back to that."

I'm so excited I'm literally on the edge of the seat. "I want to take more of a lead at STJ. I assume you'll be slowing down a bit since you're growing a baby and eventually need some time off. When that happens, I want you to know the company will be fine."

"You've always been a good partner."

"Emotionally."

"And you're a hard worker. You helped me build this business. If not for you, I'd be wrapping stuff and hoping I'm leveling up for the clientele."

"And you think I help do that?"

"I know you do, and this conversation is one we need to have. I suspect I'll be away from the office more, especially after the baby is born. What are you proposing?"

Sitting back, I reply, "When I was on the treadmill this morning, the words level and match came up."

"Out of thin air?"

"No, Elijah Morris, a former client, was chatting me up. Fiancée did the deed with the cousin, and he's now single. Poor guy." I give him a moment of silence and then add, "He asked me out, but that's neither here nor there."

"That's terrible. Not the asking out part but the fiancée doing the deed with the cousin. Also, why is asking you out neither here nor there? If I remember correctly, he's quite cute, great job down on Wall Street, and his dad is one of our top-tier clients."

"I want to be a twelve. Not in looks or personality. *In life.* I believe in your dream, and it's become mine without me realizing it. Until now."

Looking pleased, she reflects the excitement I feel inside with her graceful expression. The same hope I feel lies in her eyes. "Do you have a plan, or is this the start of the conversation?"

"A little of both. What I was thinking is that I could reorganize the company." I roll my hand in the air as a thrill zips up my spine. "We can have levels and reps. You and I could work exclusively with the top-tier clients. We have Phoebe training in the mid-range."

"Which is?"

"The fifty to one-hundred-thousand budget range."

"I think we'll need to add to that range. It's been popular this last year and a little easier, time-wise, for us to pull off."

"Agreed. It's more about the gift than the production in that range, making it less time-consuming and a quicker turnaround from the larger setups. I think we can even divide the under fifty budget into two levels, hiring maybe two or three people to train in that range. I want to go over the numbers once more to confirm, but those were the fastest growing areas of the business in the first quarter."

"We turn away potential clients every day due to lack of time, so this would solve that issue to an extent. I just have one question."

"Which is?"

She stands and holds out her hand. "When do you want to start?"

Shaking her hand, I stand as well. "Right now."

"You've got yourself a deal."

6

Harrison

MORE FLOWERS ARE NEEDED, ACCORDING TO NATALIE, SO I'VE been sent to the shop around the corner to buy them.

Just as I step onto the stoop, a car door opens at the curb, and a tan, lean leg and red heel lands on the sidewalk. My attention is fully captivated, and I angle to get a better look.

The top of a blond head is seen first, and then Tatum and her curves follow. She tells the driver, "Thank you," before noticing me.

After the other night, she's not someone I can tango with any longer. I shove my hands in my pockets and lower my gaze to the steps beneath my feet as I travel from the stoop down to the sidewalk. I don't bother with niceties. We're long past that. I head in the direction of the shop I've been sent, putting my thoughts on the errand ahead instead of on the woman behind me.

"Harrison?"

I stop one brownstone down, debating if I should even

try. I received her message loud and clear when she left me the other night.

Guilt tweaks in my bones. My mom raised me to have better manners. My dad told me to confront life head-on. *Life. Tatum.* Kind of the same thing right now.

"Please?" she adds. When I turn around, my eyes meet hers, and that plea is still wrangling her expression. "Can we talk?"

"About?" I ask, allowing my gaze to dip down. Dressed in a strapless, fitted black top and a full skirt that hits just at her calves to match, she looks so fucking gorgeous that it pisses me off for some reason.

She comes closer with a box in her hands and a small red bag dangling from her elbow. Her hair is pulled back in a sparkling clip on one side and falls in soft waves on the other side of her face. Her bold red lips don't compete with the faintest of pink on her cheeks that could be mistaken for her blushing instead of makeup. But it's her eyes.

Always those eyes that hide a million secrets locked inside. She's hard to look away from, but I force myself to the trees lining the streets until she says, "The other night . . ."

On the end of an exasperated sigh, I say, "I don't need to relive—"

"I know, and I'll respect your wishes and won't go over the details, but I need you to know that I came back."

"You came back where? When?"

"When I left in the car, I had the driver stop the next block down. I came back for you, Harrison, but you were gone."

Pulling my hands from my pockets, I work through her words in my mind as my body straightens. I'm lost on the change of heart, or is it a revelation? "Why?"

"Because I wanted you to know that I'm sorry."

"Why?"

I mentally scold myself for sounding so dumb. I'm not sure what it is about Tatum Devreux that makes me go stupid, but I really need to get that under control.

"I've pinned a lot of hurt on you, and the fact is, I need to take responsibility, too. I could have called you, Harrison. I should have." As I stand in my victory for winning the verbal battle, her shoulders sag in defeat. I take the box from her because it's starting to look heavy, thinking that might be weighing her down.

There's no change in her body or her stance. "Thank you," she whispers. I know what she means. It's for the box. But she adds, "I wish I would have called you."

Talk about a victory. I'm tempted to do a lap to celebrate, but not when it comes at the expense of her happiness. I hate that we keep getting locked in this weird purgatory state. "You mean that?"

She smiles, and I thought I knew what victorious felt like until then. This is a gold medal win, selling my first house celebration, losing my virginity . . . okay, we won't go that far, but it feels pretty damn good to see her smile because of me. *For me.*

Nodding, she says, "We said we would start over, but this time, I really mean it. If you'll give me another chance."

"You don't even have to ask. I'm not one to hold grudges."

"I'm the worst about grudges, but maybe that's something I need to improve as well." She looks back at the front door and then to me again, and asks, "The party hasn't started, and you're already leaving?"

"Flowers. Natalie wanted more, so I told her I'd go to the

florist around the corner to get them." Checking my watch, I say, "I should get going. They're closing soon."

"I can go with you?" The question isn't missed in the offer. "I just need to drop off the cake."

"It's cake?"

"The bakery was in a fender bender on the way over, and it messed up the cake. I offered to find another, and there's this great bakery by my apartment."

"That was nice of you. Saved the day."

Her cheeks pinken, and she says, "I forgot my cape."

"If you're still interested—"

"I'm interested."

I chuckle. "I'll take this inside then and be right back." I head up the steps. The catering company bustles around the kitchen, so I set it down and let them know before ducking outside. Natalie is working with the party planner on the table set up on the lawn, one long table with centerpieces of flowers running its length.

"Tatum brought the cake. I left it inside," I say.

"Great." Looking behind me, she asks, "Where is she?"

"She's going with me to the florist."

"She is?" Natalie asks, her eyes wide in surprise.

"She is."

"Okay." Her grin says it all, so I leave before any teasing begins.

I open the front door to find Tatum standing on the top step waiting for me. *For me.*

Holding out my elbow, I ask, "You ready?"

"Absolutely." She takes my arm as we descend the steps together. Her touch is missed when we reach the safety of the sidewalk, but I'll keep that to myself.

"I love this flower shop. They have such gorgeous arrangements. Did Natalie place an order?"

"Yes. I'm just the muscle."

"Don't sell yourself short. You've got a great ass, too."

"Didn't know you noticed."

She flips up the back flap of my black suit jacket. "You can't hide that goodness."

I don't know what's come over her, but she's giving me whiplash. "Have you been drinking?"

Whacking me on the arm, she laughs. "No. I'm just trying to be more open, friendlier, and say what I mean. No boundaries. Basically, telling the truth and seeing where it takes me."

I realize I'm going to like this new start to our relationship. I open the door for her. When she passes, I smack her ass. "Yours isn't so bad either."

The thrilling allure in her eyes has me wondering how I'm going to survive if flirting will be a regular thing between us. As for boundaries, there doesn't seem to be any.

Fuck. She's going to do me in.

Open. Fun. Willing. Sexy.

She's everything she was back in Catalina.

I start moving a lot faster, thinking it's best to get back before we get in any deeper. Our arms are full of bouquets when we return, and the decorator and her assistant get to work on the arrangements. Natalie is still in a robe with curlers in her hair, though her makeup has been done. She has a bottle of water, and Tatum grabs a glass of champagne before they head upstairs together.

Guests begin to arrive for their wedding anniversary celebration, filtering through with a quick stop at the bar before dispersing around the living room and outside. I order my usual and head to one of the couches set up on the lawn.

I barely have time to sit before I'm standing to give Nick's mom, Cookie, a kiss on the cheek. "It's good to see you, Mrs. Christiansen."

"Stop that. You're a grown man. Call me Cookie." Taking me by the shoulders, she admires me before saying, "I haven't seen you for what feels like years, Harrison. Ever since the boys moved to New York. Still driving all the women wild?"

"I try my best," I reply, thinking about the sexual drought of the past couple of months. Shaking Nick's dad's hand, I add, "Good to see you, Mr. Christiansen."

He's a lot like my dad, preferring the formality, unlike Cookie. "You, too, Harrison. How's the real estate market in New York?"

"Gangbusters. I haven't sold anything yet since I just got my license, but I have three offers in, and I'm starting the search on a ten-mil deal."

"Impressive. I bet your father is proud."

"He will be." My dad is not the warm and fuzzy kind, but you know where you stand with him. I exceeded his expectations in LA after years of busting my ass, but now it's time to repeat the process here in this city.

"Are you dating anyone?" Cookie asks. *One-track mind— love.* Guess there could be worse things to bide your time.

She loves to dabble in matchmaking. Nick and Andrew are proof of her skills. Do I want to be next? Tatum steps outside, already engaged in an exchange with Natalie's brother, Jackson. She laughs, and then they embrace. My eyes return to Cookie. "Not right now."

"What do you say I look at your stars and sign? You don't have to follow any rules, but sometimes, it's good to know what the universe has in store for you."

"If the universe can tell me my fate, I'm all in."

Cookie's practically a second mom. She already knows

when my birthday is, and I'm sure my sign. Nick and Andrew called her New Age beliefs nonsense, but I'm game. "I'm not looking for love or anything like that. I'd rather keep this focused on my professional life."

"I don't decide what information is returned, Harrison. I just try to decipher it."

Corbin chuckles. "Ah. I see the Devreuxes are here." My ears perk up, and I follow his gaze to see a couple who I can instantly tell are Tatum's parents. Her mother has a similar shade of hair color as her daughter, and they share the same skin tone, eye shape, and high cheekbones. "I'm going to go say hi to Camille and Laurence," Corbin Christiansen says. He gives Cookie a kiss on the cheek and heads back toward the house.

Cookie says, "You're an Aries. Passionate and determined. Self-motivated and driven for success. You've always been those things. Even your wild younger years with Nick couldn't change your traits." Sipping her champagne, she then smiles. "Speaking of the female persuasion—"

"Were we?" I knew it was coming, but I still take two gulps for this part of the conversation.

There's an airiness to her laughter, a comfort found in the sound. I spent so much time at the Christiansen house growing up—eating meals, spending the day at their pool, hanging out with Nick and sometimes the whole family— that hearing her reminds me of home.

She taps my forearm with familiarity. "Oh, Harrison, you're so funny. As for a good match, I'd look for a Gemini. They go swimmingly with Aries."

"Why is that?"

"Compatibility, communication, and last but certainly not least when it comes to romantic relationships, sex. Aries and Geminis are perfect for each other. Of course, people fight their destinies sometimes, but if you follow your heart, it will never lead you astray."

"Cookie?" Natalie calls from the patio and waves her over.

Cookie looks at me and smiles. Touching my arm again, she says, "Good things are in store for you, Harrison. Just be open to the signs that lead you there."

After that conversation, I might now side with her sons and call it New Age nonsense. Signs and all those traits. With my eyes on Tatum, I drink up, realizing Cookie described the perfect woman. I'm not sure if that exists anymore.

Anyway, I prefer to control the situation. There's no way I'm handing it over to the universe and fate.

Tatum's laughter rings out like a bell.

Now there's a sign . . . a sign to leave her alone.

Cookie has me pegged all wrong. I like the women I date to be independent. That's much more attractive than clingy. Confidence is an aphrodisiac.

And those are definitely traits I see in Tatum. Although, it does make me wonder why she was so angry and determined to avoid me when I saw her two days ago. Despite her apology for lumping me in with other men and for not attempting to call me, I still want to sort through where we went wrong to see if we can get back on the right path.

And *that's* not normal for me. I've never wanted that with exes or women I've dated a few times and have always accepted the natural end of a relationship. If we detoured or veered off track, I had no problem walking away. Yet with Tatum, it's different and worth the effort. And I wonder if that's because of the glimpse of excitement I experienced earlier. *Her vivacity.*

Tatum and Camille head in my direction, but Nick and

Natalie gather the guests to sit since the food is about to be served. I walk along the long table set up in the garden, looking for my place card. Intrigued to see who Natalie sat me next to and near. I'm pretty easygoing when it comes to these types of situations, but when I see Tatum rush past me and covertly switch two cards, I'm impressed with her deviousness.

With Nick and Natalie sharing the head of the table, their moms are seated next to them and then Tatum and Jackson. Tatum is directly across from me. The sign would lead me to believe that Tatum and I aren't too far gone if she's sneaking around to sit closer.

The champagne glasses are already full. When everyone finds their seats, Nick stands with his glass in hand. "On this beautiful evening, I wanted to thank you for celebrating our wedding anniversary with us." He looks down at his wife, who's beaming up at him. "Destiny brought Natalie into my world—"

"Stumbling, actually," she adds.

A low murmur of laughter rolls across the table. He takes her hand. "Yes, she fell into my arms, and I couldn't dream that this beautiful soul would see anything in me, but she did." Speaking to her directly, he adds, "It took us three times to get things right, but once we did, there was no going back. I couldn't have dreamed of a better match than you. There's no one else I'd rather spend my life with. I love you, Natalie." He helps her from the chair so she can stand next to him. Leaning down, he kisses her. "Happy anniversary, baby."

Wrapping her arms around him, she stares into his eyes like he put the stars in the sky just for her. "Happy anniversary, my love." They kiss again. Then she turns toward the table. Waggling her finger, she adds, "Nick gave me this stunning ring." The last light of the sun hits the slim gold band of the ring on her right hand. The single pearl on top is elegant and so romantic.

She gives him one more kiss. "We're so happy to share this day with all of our friends and family. We also thought tonight with our parents here was the perfect time to announce we're having a baby."

The moms stand on either side to hug their child. It doesn't matter how old we get—that's what my mom tells me. The rest of us clap. Staying with them has given me the benefit of being an insider on the situation. As much as it's weird that Nick's going to be a dad, a little part of me is envious he's really kicking off the next chapter of his life while I'm still stuck in first gear.

I reach for my champagne and stand, ready to give the toast as Nick's brother and his wife, Juni, finish hugging the guests of honor. Juni's about to have her first baby, making Nick and Natalie an uncle and aunt. When they return to their seats, I hold up my glass. "To the soon-to-be parents. Congratulations!"

After taking a drink, I go around and shake Nick's hand. I drag him in for a hug, though. "Congrats, man. Couldn't happen to better people."

"Thanks, Deck."

I return to my seat and catch Tatum looking my way. I grin because why not? She's in a great mood. I'm in a good mood. We bonded over flowers and putting an end to the madness of holding grudges. Holding my glass across the table, I wait until she brings hers close enough to tap.

"Here's to new beginnings," she says.

"To new beginnings." *And reading the signs.* I keep that last part to myself.

7

Harrison

THE SECOND COURSE IS SERVED.

The mothers flanking Nick and Natalie have been gushing with excitement since the couple announced the baby. Jackson has talked Tatum's ear off, but I try not to be jealous. *They're old friends*, I remind myself.

He starts a conversation with his other neighbor, *finally*, giving Tatum and me the first chance to speak.

Tatum leans forward to whisper to me, "You look bothered."

"That's just my face," I reply, teasing.

"No, it's not. Maybe bothered wasn't right." A myriad of emotions flickers through her eyes as she studies mine. "I'm leaning toward jealousy."

Chuckling, I spin my glass of whiskey between my fingers on top of the pale pink tablecloth. "You tell me. You seem to know the emotion well, or is jealousy a reaction?"

"Why would you say that?"

I hold my hands up in surrender, but inside, I'm laughing. "I didn't know you had an issue with grammar questions."

"Stop being ridiculous." Not when it brings that pretty smile of hers to the surface. She's still laughing when she says, "I meant, why would I be familiar with jealousy?"

Finishing the amber liquid, I ask a passing waiter for another and then return my attention to the stunner sitting across from me. "No reason. No reason at all." My words contradict my true emotions. I was so fucking jealous of Jackson, but I'll never let her know that. Maybe I hid it as well as she did at the bar with those two women. *Basically, not at all.*

Flirting also seems to challenge our earlier agreement, but maybe we're just those kinds of friends as well. *Who says you can't have it all?*

As we eat, I keep catching the warmth of her gaze on me. She plays it off and is quick to look away most of the time, but she locks her brown eyes on mine every once in a while without apology.

Natalie stands after our plates are cleared, her glow filling the garden with the pure joy written across her face. She gently taps her spoon against the side of her crystal water glass. "We're having such a lovely evening with you that Nick and I felt tonight would be a good time to . . . well, I want to say something to my dearest friend." Her gaze slides to Tatum. "You're my sister and my best friend. I don't need an answer now, but I'd love for you to consider being our baby's godparent."

From the other end of the table, Camille Devreux barks with laughter until she realizes no one else has joined in. My eyes, like everyone else's, dart from her back to Tatum, who appears mortified by how she's shrinking in her chair. I'm not sure how to save her the humiliation, but if I could, I'd take it away completely.

I do what comes naturally and stretch a leg across the divide under the table until my shoe touches the tip of hers, wishing it was our hands. Staring into the eyes that remind me of the Catalina cliffs at sunset, I try hard to decipher what's going on in her head. The strength I hoped to give her can't compete with the plea shaping her expression.

The uncomfortable silence grows until Natalie reaches across her mother's place setting without a second thought and takes Tatum's hand in hers. "There's no pressure, but we want you to know that we trust you and love you."

Tatum swallows so hard that I can hear it sitting across from her.

"I love you, too," she whispers.

Nick doesn't stand, but he does say, "Harrison, Natalie and I would be honored if you'd consider also being our kid's godparent."

"What? Me?" I don't make a scene like Mrs. Devreux, but I swear I don't hear him correctly. "You want me to take care of your kid in case of an emergency?"

"You and Tatum," Nick says. "Something for you to consider."

What the fuck is he thinking? This is insane.

Tatum scoots her chair back from the table. "If you'll excuse me."

"Would you like me to come with you?" Natalie asks.

"No. Enjoy the party."

As forks clang against china and the low rumble of conversation picks up again, Tatum walks up the steps of the deck and into the house. I look at Nick and then Natalie.

"Thank you." Nick nods once, and I add, "I think I'm going to check on her."

I cross the deck and am inside just as the waiters begin bustling around the table again. "Tatum?" I look toward the kitchen and peek into the front room where the bar is stationed. When I don't find her, I check the downstairs bathroom, which is empty.

Taking the steps by two, I rush up to the second floor and find her in the nursery. I knock lightly on the door, not wanting to sneak up on her. Tatum whips her head to the side, her arms crossed over her chest, and tears in her eyes. "My mom is right. What would I do with a baby? I can barely take care of my own life."

I understand her shock. "Andrew's the most responsible person I know. Why the fuck would Nick think I'm more suited for the job?" Just inside the door, I add, "But they know us. They know we'd love their baby like it was our own. I'd raise this kid to know everything about Nick, and you'd teach them everything about Natalie while giving them enough love to hopefully fill any voids."

She gently swipes under her eyes before the tears fall. "Did you know about this?"

"No. I didn't see this godparent thing coming." I chuckle humorlessly. "I'm not sure what to think, but what I do know is that our best friends trust us with their kids." When I smile, I feel the honor bestowed upon me mixed with the disbelief of the situation.

A smile appears, and she sniffles. "Crazy. But what you said . . . that was beautiful, Harrison. If the unthinkable happens, we'd love their kids like our own."

"We would." I move inside and look out the window down at the dinner party below. "You don't have to say yes. It's just something for us to consider."

She joins my side, resting her head against my arm and staring out the window as well. "My mom laughed at the thought of me taking care of kids."

"Sounds like your mom doesn't know the woman you've become."

Her arm slips around my back, and I slip mine around her. "Why do you say such thoughtful things when I don't deserve them?"

"Who says you don't? We all have good and bad days. It's hard to remember the good sometimes, but we shouldn't hold a bad one against someone for life."

"Be careful, Decker, or I might think you have a heart."

"Ugh." I hold my hands over my heart like I was just struck. I chuckle to myself, a low rumble remaining in my chest. "Don't go telling the ladies, or you'll give me a bad rep."

"Don't worry. Your bad rep"—she taps my chest—"and your heart are safely intact." I can feel the lift of her cheek against my muscle.

The sun has set behind the back neighbors' townhome, and the string lights draped over the yard are like stars we're looking down on. There's enough light from the hall for us to see our surroundings. Even the little luminescent stars outside feed light inside.

Tatum's frame fits against mine, and I wish I could make her happy like she was when she arrived. I have no idea about the history between her and her mother, and I'm annoyed her father didn't bother to stand up for her downstairs, but I don't for one minute think she deserved the taunt. Natalie knows her extremely well, so if she believes she's the one she wants long-term in her baby's life, then everyone else should trust in that confidence as well.

This woman is good.

The fact that she's leaning on me for comfort means she trusts in me. I like her. And given the tips of her fingers are tightening against my side, I'm thinking she feels the same more-than-acquaintances vibe filling the air as I do.

When I look down at her, she looks up at me, her usually expressive eyes filled with restrained emotions. "You make me feel everything from happy to mad, but you also make me feel safe. I hate that you seem to be the only one who can do that lately," she whispers.

"It's trust. You may not like it. It may feel uncomfortable, but deep down, you know you can trust me." I turn to face her, wanting to look into the depths of her eyes to find the truth she can't hide.

Something heavy settles between us—a tension that isn't troubling—but makes my heart beat harder against my rib cage. Her chest rises and falls with deeper breaths. The smile I was craving a moment earlier doesn't come, but a lick of her lips has my locking my gaze on the little teasing.

When she cups my face, a million thoughts run through my mind—are we going to go down this route again, or is it better to play it safe and stick to being friends? Although I'm pretty sure she's about to kiss me, I can't let that happen without telling her the truth. "I went back inside."

The grip of her hands softens, and I could kick myself for letting the moment slip away. "I don't understand."

"Thursday night. You said you came back for me. I went back inside the club."

"Oh," she replies, seeming surprised. Her hands lower to her sides, and she takes a step back. When I lose sight of her eyes, and her arms cross over her chest, her walls start to return. "I guess shame on me for thinking that something was building between us."

I step closer and tilt her chin up with two fingers. "It

was." Before she can ask the questions populating her mind, I continue, "I went to say goodbye to the guys and thank Kaz for the tickets. I went back in thinking I would have another drink and that would help get you off my mind."

"Did it?" Her tone turns harsh, her eyes cold. She jerks her chin away, and asks, "Or did someone?"

"Alcohol can't keep you off my mind, and no woman has captured it like you have, Tatum."

"See?" she asks through tight lips with aggravation in her tone. "There you go again, Harrison. Why do you do that?" When her hands reach out to push me away, I grab hold and keep them pressed to my chest. "I don't want to fall for you again. I did that once, and it didn't end well for me."

"You didn't fall for me. You had a good time one night, but what scares you more, Tatum? That you might fall for me or that you might like it?"

Her hands stay firm against me. "I don't understand the difference."

"Then give me a chance to show you. We might be good for each other."

"We might be bad."

I smirk. "We were always bad, but I haven't lost all hope just yet."

She closes the gap, her shoes between mine. "What makes you so confident?"

"I know a good thing when I see it."

"And you see the good in me, Decker?"

Our breaths begin to mingle when I angle my head and whisper against the shell of her ear, "So much good."

"What if . . .?"

"What if?" I whisper, matching her tone.

Tilting back just enough to look me in the eyes, she cups

my cheeks again. "What if we had another night together. What would you do?"

"I wouldn't waste a single second of it."

"Then don't." Her lips crash into mine, and when I take her in my arms, I won't let this second chance get away.

8

Tatum

Breaking the rules never felt so good.

Or maybe that's Harrison's lips on mine that feel amazing. God, how I missed this. Him. He makes me feel like he's been craving me more than the air he needs to breathe. "Harrison," I say, not sure why I'm even saying it but feel it purr through me again.

His hands run down my ribs to my hips and then up to my waist as if checking that I'm real. Pulling back, he looks into my eyes, breathing heavily. "What are we doing?"

"I don't know." I run my hands over his jaw, feeling the rough edges of a recent shave. I'm famished for his touch, to feel like nothing else matters and lose myself in the abyss of the bliss he brings my way, even if for just a short time.

He says, "We should—"

"I don't want you to stop."

This time when he kisses me, the backs of my thighs hit the windowsill. When my back reaches the glass, he pulls me forward and takes my hand. "My room on the top floor will be better." We're fast out the door.

"I know it well. I've been in that bed many times."

He comes to an abrupt halt on the stairs. "What?"

Then it dawns on me how that sounds. "Oh God, no. I meant, I sleep there when I stay the night. I've not had . . ." I whisper, "sex or done anything else with someone in that bed other than wearing face masks with Natalie."

Confusion digs into his brow but then disappears. "Good enough."

We continue rushing up the stairs when I slow, bringing him to a stop this time. He looks back, his hair already a mess and falling over his forehead. My stay-all-day lipstick didn't live up to its promise, so I reach up and run the pad of my thumb over his lips.

He kisses it. "Are you okay?"

"I am." He's so handsome with his endearing eyes, that strong, sharp jaw, and the straight bridge of his nose. Why am I stopping this from happening? Why do I torture myself for no reason? *Oh right* . . . "The party."

"Right," he says with a sigh, his lids dipping closed. Running his hand through his hair, he takes three steps down, giving me the advantage. Releasing my hand, he takes hold of my waist again. "I don't want to lose this . . . whatever it is between us."

His words play my heartstrings like a violin. I suck in a staggered breath as fear creeps in—the thought of being hurt, the unknown, and the disappointment that followed a perfect night in Catalina, and what might have been tonight. I swallow it down, deep inside me, refusing to let it get air.

Taking a step down, I wrap my arms around his neck and kiss him again. It's not hurried or a goodbye, an end, or a kiss-off. It's true and full of the feelings that I like better—

the good ones that feed my ego and my well-being. "Would you like to come to my place tonight?"

A wry grin wriggles into place. "Yes."

To the point. Much like Harrison Decker. For someone who I've overheard being called a shark in business, that's not what he's been with me. Not tonight, at least. "Then it's a date, the kind with benefits."

His deep chuckle fills the staircase. "We should get back."

"I don't want to make a spectacle. One's enough for tonight." I nod toward the top of the stairs. "And you should probably wipe my lipstick off your mouth."

"Probably a good idea." Rubbing his fingers over his wry grin is something I could watch all night, but I tear my gaze away and start down the steps as he heads in the opposite direction.

Standing on the landing, I ask, "Harrison?"

He stops at the top and looks back over his shoulder. "Yeah?"

"Thanks."

It's not a grandiose reaction, but it doesn't need to be. A gaze is exchanged, but he doesn't ask what I'm thanking him for or to explain. He just accepts the offer with mutual understanding.

I straighten my skirt in the downstairs bathroom and then reapply my lipstick. Grabbing a vodka soda from the bar on my way outside, I catch my mom's eyes on me first, a sinking feeling dragging the high I was riding down with it. Then I see everyone else looking. *Great . . .*

Typically, I'm the one on top of the bar getting attention, but this isn't the limelight I desire. My mom gets up and meets me as I make my way back to my seat. "I didn't mean to hurt your feelings, darling."

We step off to the side for any bit of privacy we can get. Though my stomach isn't thrilled we missed the main course, I'm relieved when the other guests are served dessert. The chocolate cake is just the distraction I need to deter their attention away from me. "I don't know why you'd humiliate me like that, but this is not a conversation we can have right now."

"I was taken by surprise."

"Imagine how I felt," I snap. I'm never rude to my mother. Even through my rebellious high school days, I still managed to give my parents the perfect grades they expected. Now I know where I really stand in her eyes.

"We can meet for brunch tomorrow to have this discussion. Just not here," I say under my breath.

She narrows her eyes a little but then agrees. "Brunch at Bistro 55. Eleven thirty." At that, she leaves and walks back to the table, but I don't miss the roll of her eyes toward my dad. *What was that for?*

I return to my seat just as Harrison sits down across from me. So much for timing. Who really cares? No one, most likely.

When I look up, I'm met with Harrison's strength and a smile filled with confidence—not the arrogant kind, but the one he's willing to share with me. He's right. I shouldn't feel embarrassed or ashamed. I turn to Natalie, who gives me the same grin. She trusts me with her child's life. She sees something in me that I can't. Maybe it's time I tried.

"Try the cake. It's divine," Natalie's mom, Martine, says sweetly.

"Excellent idea." Chocolate's always been a weakness of mine. Taking a bite of the decadence, I close my eyes as the sugar coats my tongue and softly moan in delight. I open my eyes to find Harrison's glued to me, his lips parted, and if I'm not mistaken, the little chocolate on the side of his lips I wouldn't mind licking off for him.

Leaning forward, he whispers, "We can skip dessert . . ." He signals toward the exit just in case I didn't get his intention by "we can skip dessert."

I start laughing but am quick to cover my mouth with the back of my hand. "What kind of maniac skips dessert?"

It only takes one bite before I sink into the seat to let the sweetness take over. "This cake. It's orgasmic."

"Orgasmic?" Cookie asks. "Well then, I might need another piece to go," she says, digging her fork in for a second bite. "For later."

Nick sighs heavily as he sets his fork back on the table. "No, Mom. I can't. I know you want to treat Andrew and me as the adults we are, but I just don't think I can listen to sex talk around you."

Natalie starts laughing, then Martine, with many others joining in, almost like the earlier incident never happened. *That's how I like it best.*

When guests begin to leave, and others enjoy an after-dinner digestif, Natalie takes me by the hand and pulls me to a corner of the dining room. "Marcelles opened spots for their next cooking class. I was thinking it could be something we do together," she says.

"You don't want to take it with Nick?"

"I figured Nick wouldn't be upset since he'll benefit from the outcome. But more so, I thought it would be something fun for us to do together that's not work-related. It will give us a guaranteed weekly date. I miss just spending time with you."

She's right. We haven't been going out much, and now I know why—the baby. But also, work has picked up year over year. That's why I need to get to work on this new plan. As for downtime, I may see Natalie almost every day, but I still miss my friend. "I'm really great at ordering food, but maybe I could learn a new skill and cook instead." I wink.

"We can cook together, too. Maybe have a regular dinner—"

"Let's slow down," I say, my hands flying up. "At least until after the first class."

Holding her stomach, she giggles. "Good idea. I might have good intentions, but no promises it tastes good."

"Natalie?"

Her mom calls her from the entryway. She gives my hand a squeeze. "I need to say goodbye, but I wanted you to know that I'm happy for you and Harrison."

"What are you happy about?"

She holds a finger to her lips. "Don't worry, I don't think the others noticed, but Nick and I saw you in the window."

My legs hitting the sill, my back to the window. I cringe as a second wave of mortification rolls over me. I swallow. "I'm sorry. He—"

"Natalie, I'll call you," Martine says.

"I'll be right there," she calls back. "It's okay. I just wanted you to know that I'm glad it seems you've made up. *Literally.*"

I restrain my laughter, but a giggle comes out. "Thanks for putting it so . . . nicely."

Natalie's in her mom's and dad's arms, both of them hugging her. I'd almost forgotten my parents and her dad were here. They tend to sneak away to talk business when they get together. As if me mentioning him in my head made him magically appear, my dad comes in through the butler's pantry. "I've been looking for you, sweetheart."

"I've been around," I reply.

He comes straight for me and gives me a hug. "Are you doing all right?"

I put on my best stiff upper lip, just like they taught me. "I'm fine. No need to worry."

"I do anyway." His softer tone catches me off guard.

Suddenly feeling every bit his little girl, I rest my head on his shoulder. "Thanks, Dad."

My dad kisses my head and then heads for the door. "Love you. Call me soon."

"I will. Love you."

After they leave, I grab my bag and head for the door. Just as I reach my best friend, Harrison comes from the living room. "You weren't sneaking out, were you?"

"No. I made quite the show of things tonight. So why would I bother sneaking around now?"

Always ready to laugh, at least my jokes land with him. "That's good to hear."

As if Nick appears out of nowhere, Natalie turns back to me while resting against her husband. His hands slide around her waist, resting on her flat belly that will soon be much bigger.

It's not envy.

I'm not ready for the baby stage of life yet, but maybe my own person to rest against wouldn't be so bad.

"In regard to being godparents, we took you both by surprise, but please don't think we made our decision lightly," Nick says.

Harrison stands next to me, and for a moment, our hands brush against each other's. It's the lightest of touches, but it makes me feel like we're a team. "I won't speak for Tatum, but it would be an honor."

"You're a good man, Deck." He and Nick do that man-hug thing guys do—a shoulder bump, a pat on the back, lots of self-congratulatory talk.

Wiping a tear, I find it's heartwarming to witness. I want that. Not the man-hug thing, but to be a part of something amazing that will always bind me to my best friend. "I'm in." The words come out too fast to take them back. Not that I want to, but I probably should have given it more thought.

"You are?" Natalie asks, her eyes welling with tears. Joy lifts her expression as she rushes to hug me. "Thank you, Tate."

"Our kid will be lucky to have you," Nick says.

"Thank you."

As other guests come toward the door, Harrison says, "I'm going to see Tatum home."

Knowing they saw us earlier, I feel my cheeks heat. Blushing isn't something I normally do, but here I am, acting like a schoolgirl. We say our goodbyes, and then Natalie says, "Thanks for taking care of my best friend."

Harrison looks back. "My pleasure."

The door closes as we walk down the steps. "I'm hoping it's mine, as well." I click my tongue and give him a little wink.

"Don't worry." We reach the curb, and he opens the door for me. Just as I start to get in, I stop to say—but he kisses me, stealing the words right off my tongue. "I've waited what feels like forever for this night. There's no way I'm leaving a single inch of you untouched or wanting."

There's not much left to say, except, "How fast can we get to Tribeca?"

9

Harrison

Apparently, one *can* get from the Upper East Side to Tribeca pretty damn fast when a large tip is involved. Who knew, considering it's Saturday night? Helps to have a local calling the shots. And call the shots she did anytime traffic slowed. He finally gave in and just listened to the lady.

Smart man.

She was right, but that doesn't surprise me.

Her building, on the other hand . . . *Holy. Shit.*

Pure money. I'm still learning about Manhattan real estate, but damn, even I know nothing's worth less than a mil in this place. And that's probably a basement apartment with no windows.

Location.

Location.

Why is she located so far from me in this elevator? Just the way she looks at me has me hard. *Fuck*, let's be honest. She doesn't even have to look at me. The tips of her fingers teased my leg in the back of the car. The kisses she placed on my neck when the driver was too busy to notice in the mirror had me squirming.

I was good, keeping my hands to myself, but these last few flights are a struggle. She's so sexy I could devour her whole.

I'm still hoping to actually . . .

The elevator dings when we reach her floor, and she says, "Almost home," like she's talking to anyone she knows, not the guy she wanted to have sex with in the middle of a dinner party earlier. Please don't let things have cooled. It's a vicious cycle we're caught in. I'm starting to think we have the worst timing ever.

Her door is at the far end of the hall. Judging by the spacing of the others in the hall, the apartments are bigger than the average New York City dwelling.

The black lacquered door stands out among the neighboring wood tones, each resident's personality already on display. Tatum's doesn't just stand out because of the color, but the design of the panels reminds me of the high-end shops of 5th Avenue.

I'm not used to silence, but she owns every second of it, comfortable in the quiet. Growing up with two brothers and a sister meant the noise levels at my house were always high. It was nice to escape to the Christiansens' house, where the energy was more laidback.

"Do you have siblings?" I ask, cracking that silence in half.

With a key in the lock, she turns back, curiosity filling her pretty eyes. "I'm an only child." A smile appears, and it's nothing less than entertained. "Such an odd question at this juncture in the night."

"Why don't I know more about you?"

"Guess we never delved that deep into our lives because you were busy delving deeper into other things."

"Mainly you." I shrug. "Can't resist a perfect setup."

"What can you resist?" she asks, her breathing becoming heavier.

The door is stiff when she tries to open it, so she hip bumps it, and it swings inward. "Sometimes, you just need a solid thrust." Her chest rises and falls as if my mere proximity to her is a turn-on.

I'm never going to last with this siren. Not only did I never think we'd be this close to having sex again but that trust she showed in me earlier blankets her eyes now as she welcomes me into her world. The sight of her practically purring for me has my body on high alert and begging for more. I move in, boxing her with my arms on either side of her head. "You found the man for the job."

She runs the tip of her finger over my Adam's apple and continues lower until she reaches my chest. "What am I to you, Harrison?" she whispers. I try to wrap my head around the question. She might need a different answer than what she is to me.

She's the forbidden fruit.

A decadent dessert.

The finest whiskey. *A piece of chocolate you've only experienced once but have been searching for ever since.*

And that's the truth of it. I've never wanted anyone as much as I want Tatum Devreux. This torture has continued for a million reasons, but both of us seem to finally be headed in the desired direction. I'll let her lead, play the games, participate in the Q & A's if it gets me more time with her.

"You were never a one-night stand, not to me."

The answer appears to satisfy her as the corners of her

mouth tip upward. Fisting my shirt, she tugs me closer and then kisses my chin. "It's sad we ended up that way."

"Then let's write a new ending." I cup her face and kiss her hard.

Her lips are plush and accepting, her fists holding me just as tightly. Turning, she pulls me into the apartment and kicks the door shut. Our lips part, and she takes a deep breath of air.

She spins away from me, locking the door, and then walks deeper into the apartment. "Are you going to keep me waiting?" she teases, glancing back at me over her shoulder.

"No. Just taking it all in."

I follow her into the dimly lit living room. It's not what I expected for Tatum. Her style is typically fashion-forward and tending toward the dramatic, so I imagined stark walls and furniture that's slick in design and cutting-edge modern.

Considering it's a corner unit with windows wrapping around that sharp edge, the décor lies in contrast. An exposed brick wall with a fireplace, inviting wood floors throughout that inspire me to see where they lead down the hallway, and large, black-framed windows give warmth to the space. The age and character are what I imagine in old New York City apartments and see in Nick's brownstone. Not what I expected from a mid-rise skyscraper built in the past twenty years. "I like your place."

"Thanks," she says, biting her lip when her gaze scans my body. "I almost forgot my manners. Whiskey and Coke?"

"Sure."

"I think I'll join you. Feel free to snoop."

The heat isn't lost. It's still simmering beneath the surface, but all good things come to those who wait. *So I wait.*

Standing at the window, I look at her view of the street while noting we're high enough not to hear any traffic. Not a lot of privacy, though, considering she has windows everywhere. I hear the clink of ice hitting the bottom of the glass, the air escaping the bottle of soda, and then the fizz as it's poured. "Do people in Manhattan ever close their windows, or they just get used to living in a fishbowl?" I ask.

"The latter. Most probably don't even have blinds or curtains. I do in the bedroom but not out here. Why? Do you feel like people are watching you?"

"Kind of."

I feel her next to me, standing so close her arm is against mine. She hands me one glass, keeping the other and taking a sip. Her eyes return from the distance to peer up at me. "What should we toast to?"

Leaning the edge of the glass to hers, I reply, "To tonight."

There are no words spoken but a silent understanding, making me realize we do that a lot for two people who apparently can't read each other. Taking a gulp, I return my gaze forward. "It's a nice view."

"An exhibitionist's dream come true." There's no glory in the words, almost as if she doesn't relate. Anymore . . .

I glance down at her as she sips her drink. "I didn't know you liked whiskey."

She smiles, the heat of the alcohol reaching her cheeks. "I don't, but I liked the way you tasted earlier." Seeming to catch herself, she laughs lightly. "Maybe I like whiskey, or maybe I just like the taste of you." There's no follow-up shrug or deflection. Tatum stands there, owning her likes and dislikes without regard for judgment or fear of rejection.

I couldn't turn away from her if I wanted, so she's righteous in her stance. Angling closer, I tilt down and kiss her on the forehead. It's not steamy or frenzied, but it fits the moment.

Finishing her drink, she saunters back into the kitchen. When I turn back, she's grabbing two bottles of water from the fridge. "We didn't eat much. Are you hungry?"

"Starving."

She laughs. "Let's get you fed then." Pulling a binder from a drawer, she leans against the counter and starts flipping through the pages. "You can have anything your heart desires."

I come up behind her, not subtle, and slide my hands around her waist. There's no tension in her body, and when she tilts her head to the side, she gives me full access to that graceful neck of hers.

Simmering.

Her body vibrates with untamed energy, her breath laden with need just from the simplest touch of her body and kisses placed sparingly on her neck.

She inhales another jagged breath. Like a mouse, she taunts me, keeping the one thing we want just out of reach. "I thought you were hungry?"

"I am." I reach over and close the binder, preferring her hands on me instead. Unlike a cat, I don't play with my prey. "For you first. Food later."

Spinning in my arms, she wraps hers around my neck. "Why do I have a feeling that by later, you mean tomorrow?"

I lean in again, this time nuzzling her ear and placing a kiss just under her lobe before whispering, "Because you and I both know we're going to be too busy to bother with—"

"The essentials like eating and—"

"We can shower together." *Kiss.* "Eat together." *Kiss. Kiss.*

"Have sex again, and then—"

"Repeat." Looking into my eyes, she studies my reaction as if I scare easily.

I kiss her lips so softly that a breath breaks us apart. "You don't have to play hostess. I want you, Tatum," I say against her cheek as I rest my forehead to hers.

A soft sigh is followed by the whisper of a question. "Why have I been fighting this so hard?"

"Because you're scared of the possibility of us."

"I'm not scared," she says with a tremble in her tone. She exhales and then smiles, an assurance taking over. "I just don't understand where this could possibly lead tomorrow when we live across the country from each other."

"We don't."

"Currently. One day, you'll return to LA. You might already have your one-way ticket home."

I caress her cheek, thinking her tough exterior wasn't built on gentle touch. It's not taming her wild side but embracing the softer parts of her. "I'm here now."

"You say that as if the hero has entered the story and will save the day."

That mouth. *Fuck, that mouth.* I kiss her, embracing her lips with mine, our mouths open and our tongues tangling together. This time, I take charge and pull back under panting breaths. "You don't need saving, baby. You just need someone else to keep the world from weighing you down for a short time."

"Oh, yeah? How do you expect to do that?"

Running my hands over her rib cage, I continue lower. I like the feel of her in my arms again, being close, and the anticipation of what's about to happen. The thin material of her black top allows me to feel the side curve of her great tits. "By making you forget you have to. Just for the night."

She leans against me, and her hands slide under the sides of the jacket, lowering to my ass. Giving me a good squeeze, she smirks. "Mmm." Her moan travels straight to my groin and hardens for her to feel instantly, and she does like she fucking owns my cock. She's owned many of my thoughts over the years, so I admit she owns my dick as well. "How do you feel about mornings?"

"With you, I'm willing to find out." I scoop her into my arms under the melody of her laughter and cut through the living room.

"Last door on the right." *Always giving directions.*

I fly down the hall, not only tired of playing these teasing games but ready to see her naked again. Many nights have been sweat out to the memory of her body writhing under mine, her lips wrapped around my dick, and kissing her sweet pussy until she came so hard that management was called. *Fuck me.* I need to be inside her again.

I'm stopped the minute I enter her bedroom.

"This is where you sleep," I say like a dumbass.

She laughs again. "Yep, this is where the magic happens."

A growl rips through my chest as the thought of magic with anyone else happening with her brings back that earlier reaction—jealousy. I have no claims to stake. She's her own woman, but I don't need to hear about other dates. She lifts and kisses my cheek, and then says, "If it makes you feel better, by magic, I meant my beauty sleep. It takes magic to make me look like this each day."

"I beg to differ. I've seen you with nothing but the sunrise drifting across your skin, a vision of beauty I'll never forget."

"You don't have to beg." The smile softer now. "And stop being so nice."

"It's the way I'm built."

Trying to squeeze my bicep, she fails, and says, "I've always appreciated your build." I set her down on the bed and spin her until the heels of her shoes are against my chest. "Ooh!"

No fucks are given about dirtying my shirt. The view is killer. In the low light supplied by a lamp on the nightstand, I unbuckle the strap wrapped around her ankle and slip the shoe off, dropping it on the floor, and then repeat with the other.

She props herself up on her elbows, watching every move I make.

We might have chosen a different topic of conversation to travel, but going back to the thought of her with someone else, I say, "We've lived our lives, but in here, when we're in this bedroom, or any other, together, it's only us." Running my hands up the sides of her legs across her smooth and tanned skin, I keep going until my hands disappear under her skirt. Under her heavy gulp, I part the softness of her inner thighs. Her mouth opens, and her teeth dig into her bottom lip. "Okay, baby?" There's only one answer, but I volley the power into her court.

"Okay." She spreads her legs wider, allowing me to go higher.

"Good girl." I know how to tease to please a woman. Greeted with lace at her hips, I wrap my fingertips around it and pull down until she's freed from the delicate fabric.

I may not be able to see her sweet spot, but I can stroke the soft skin. "What do you want, Tatum?"

Lying flat, she'd let me do anything I wanted, judging by the trust residing in her eyes. And I just might. But then she says everything I've been waiting to hear for years. "I want you, Harrison."

10

Harrison

"WHERE DO YOU WANT ME? BE SPECIFIC," I SAY, SLIDING MY finger through her heat, her body already submitting to mine. Coating my finger in the lightest essence, I bring it to my mouth to taste. Her eyes are fixed on my lips, so I take it in and suck it clean.

Pleasure lifts the sides of her mouth, and she replies, "I want your mouth on me. Down there." She lifts her skirt, confidence filling her expression. Another challenge laid down as if I won't jump at the chance to savor her again.

Tugging off my jacket, I let it fall to the floor as I drop to my knees, not wasting any time, and duck under her skirt. The room is dimly lit, but under the thick fabric of her skirt, there's no light at all. I don't need it, but I wouldn't mind seeing her up close again.

I rely on my other senses and lick her lower lips like a melting popsicle. Despite the cavernous feeling of her skirt wrapping around me, I'm privy to her moans and can feel her body wiggle as her legs open wider, welcoming me in.

When my tongue plunges into her entrance, her knees grip my shoulders, and her back arches off the bed. The pressure of her hand on my head is felt as she holds me there. "Don't leave me, Harrison . . ."

I don't stop, though the words get stuck in my head. *Why would I leave her? Why would that even cross her mind at a time like this? Who the fuck is leaving her unsatisfied?*

The pressure intensifies, and she continues, "So good. Don't stop. Yes . . . yes . . . so good."

Picking up the pace, I fuck her with my mouth and then add a finger into the tightness of her swell.

The need to come is building, and my erection seeks relief against the bed, though it does nothing to satisfy my urge to be inside her. Distracting myself from my own needs, I take advantage of the time to reacquaint myself with what turns her on.

Hot breath makes her moan.

A flat-tongued lick has her panting.

A good old-fashioned finger fuck has her squirming on the bed.

I use one hand to pin her down and then add another finger when she begs for more, faster, harder.

Tremors rip through her body like little earthquakes. I stay steady until her body tenses and tightens around me. My name was rattled off at the peak of her orgasm and then mingled with breathy cursing as she melts into the mattress before me. "Oh fuck, yes. God, yes."

Pulling back, I watch as she comes undone, and it's a beautiful fucking sight to behold.

When her breathing steadies, I flip the skirt off my head, and it flies over her face. Tugging it back enough to reveal her beauty, I then drop my hands down on either side of her head. "You have a dirty fucking mouth, baby."

"Only when it comes to you."

"Speaking of coming." I kiss her—heated more than before and hard as I take control of her tongue. My hips push against the apex of her thighs, and I grind against her. "See what you do to me?"

"I don't want to see. I want to feel you inside me."

Fucking hell. She's going to kill me dead with her words alone. "I want you naked on the bed. Or bent over the dresser . . . in the living room. Your choice, but you only have until I'm naked to be ready for me."

She scrambles to her feet. With her back to me, she twists to unhook the fasten on the side of her skirt. That puddles around her feet as she starts on her top, unzipping the side and pulling the body-hugger down before stepping out of that as well.

My pants are hanging open, and my shirt is almost unbuttoned when she pulls the clip from her hair, and it cascades past her shoulders to her back to hang with the rest. Her ass is round and smooth, drawing me closer. I grab her cheeks, and she stills. Glancing at me over her shoulder, she says, "Patience is a virtue."

"I have none when it comes to you."

A sneaky grin slides across her face before she leaves me with an erection aching to be freed. I finish undressing, trying to decide how I'm going to take her first. She crawls onto the bed, flaunting her ass, so I ask, "Is that an invitation?"

Slipping her feet under the covers, she doesn't scramble to hide her body but taunts me with the sight of it before tempting me to rip these covers off the bed entirely.

I take my time and walk around to the side of the bed, my dick hard and my eyes never leaving hers. I'm about to climb into bed next to her when my stomach plummets. "Fuck."

How is this possible?

Why would I be so dense?

"What's wrong?"

I haven't been carrying protection around Manhattan. I had no reason to. It's not like I'm fucking every girl who asks in LA, and believe me, they ask and often. But I'm usually prepared just in case. "I don't have a condom." I'm finally with the girl I can't stop thinking about, and I'm blowing it. "Do you have one?"

"Those went bad a long time ago." Unfazed to the panic I feel inside, she rests her hands behind her head. "How long has it been?"

It's not that I've been with so many in the last year. It's that they weren't memorable enough to recall on demand. "Four months, maybe five. I never went without a condom." I don't even know what I'm saying. I mean, it's the truth, but why does that matter now?

"Eight months for me," she offers without missing a beat. "I threw out the small stash I had after a bottle of champagne and a broken date two months ago. I swore off men that night. But here you are, and neither of us is prepared. Go figure."

"Yeah, go figure." My dick never falters as we wait for her to determine our next step. "I'll run to the store." I turn to grab my pants, but she sits up in a panic.

Grabbing my hand, she says, "I'm on the pill."

"But we need—"

"It's okay. I trust you, Harrison." She pulls me close enough to encourage me into bed with her.

I don't know what I'm doing, but I don't want to stop, not

with her. I will, though, if that's what she wants. She kisses me, giving me every reason to believe her words.

Cupping my face, she kisses me again before we fall between the sheets. Holding her in my arms, I settle between her legs as her body blooms under my kisses. I can't blame the alcohol, only myself for what I'm about to do. And although my mind has a million thoughts zipping through it, my body knows what it wants. *Her.*

So I won't tell her no. Nor will I deny her pleasure. Her pleasure is ultimately mine.

When she moves on top of me, I push everything out of my mind except for what's right in front of me, on top of me, and around me. Staring at her tits and curves, her smile, and the mischievous glint in her eyes.

This isn't how I thought we'd start, but there aren't any complaints from me. Tatum lifts and then slowly slides down, her heat engulfing me and causing my eyes to close. "Oh fuck."

Heaven.

Hell.

And the purgatory between.

I'm caught in every emotion and state of being, lost inside her, no barrier between us, as she begins to ride me. "Look at me, Harrison," she commands. Her words come out as if the demand itself stole her breath away.

Opening my eyes, I watch as our bodies move, as they remember the way they once danced. I move to feed the deep-seated tightening inside, but the craving can't be satisfied. So I grab her hips and start fucking her.

When she puts her hands on my chest, I drive into her. She comes down and bounces on my lap before hovering over me, our eyes locked on each other's. "Slow down," she says, her voice low in the dimly lit room. "I don't want to rush."

Reaching over, she pushes a button, and the curtains begin to close. Here I thought we were about to give New York more of a show than we already have. I pull the covers to my thighs, exposing her bare body for only me to see. I worship at her altar as I give her everything I can when inside her and the passion she deserves with every kiss that's pressed to her lips.

Her head tilts back, the tip of her hair wading across the tops of my thighs. When she's leaning back, her tits are perky, the nipples perfect pink buds begging to be . . . I reach up and run the pad of my thumbs over each one until they perk and harden.

When her hands land on my legs and those tits are paraded in front of my face, I cup them and then bring one to my mouth, flicking it with my tongue. I leave it wet and wanting like her and move to the other to do the same.

Though she's settled on top of me, there's no less a frenzy of feelings and touches shared between us. Starting a slow but steady rocking action, she feels too good to last long.

The scorching heat of our bodies' connection is intense. I take a deep breath, everything feeling more than it ever has before. The barrier of a condom was black and white to the technicolor of being bare.

Gripping her hips, I thrust up, moving in and out as I hunt for the release that will send me over the edge. I watch her tits bounce as I fuck the breath from her, getting off on how much she's turned on. "You're so goddamn beautiful."

The tips of her fingers sweep across my forehead, pushing my hair to the side. "You're only saying that because you're inside me right now."

"I wouldn't say it if I didn't mean it." My words are spurs that get her moving to the pace she was begging from me earlier—*faster, harder* . . .

"I'm going to come again," she exhales on a harsh breath, her eyes still latched to mine.

The climb to the edge is exhilarating, and my body pulses in anticipation. I'm close, but I want to watch her fall apart again and feel her succumb to the bliss while riding me.

Bringing her closer, I wrap my arms around the small of her back, and we rock together until her breathing deepens and her eyes close from the lust. Her mouth opens, and, "Harrison," tumbles from her lips as if I'm her savior.

When I feel the quakes building in her body, and one begins to erupt, I pull her close and begin kissing and sucking on her neck. "Yes, baby. Come for me."

Control was lost already, and her arms tighten around my neck to relish in another orgasm. "Yes. God. Yes!" Trembling around me, she squeezes my dick until I can't stave off my release any longer.

Letting go, I move my body on instinct, my willpower lost in the throes of her passion and soft mewls as she comes down. I fuck until part of my soul goes missing, seeking to reclaim its other half. I swear angels sing when the torture that had been packed into a compartment years ago is released. "Oh fuck."

She slams onto me one last time before I hold her in place like the last puzzle piece that completes the big picture. I'm emptied of anything of value—my energy, soul, and heart if I'm being honest. I rest back and try to catch my breath. "You . . ." Through panting breaths, I confess, "I knew what we had was special." I cup her face, a sheen glistening across her cheeks and chest, her skin, and a thrill still so striking in her eyes. "You're incredible."

Laughing softly, she says, "I might have missed you more than I realized." She leans down and kisses my temple. The tip of her tongue dips out and swipes the salty sweat from my forehead.

"Might have?" She begins to wriggle away, so I catch her wrist, looping my hand around it gently. She's free to go, but I like that she stays. "I'm really great at accepting compliments. You should try me and say what you mean."

"I just bet you are." Kissing my shoulder, she lingers before facing me again. "You were better than memory serves, and I have incredible memories of that night."

A smirk would be justified, but I grin instead, feeling this moment with her deserves something more befitting. Lightly pinching her chin between my fingers, I say, "It was one of the best nights of my life."

"Harrison?" she whispers, her gaze lowering between us as if I've gone one step too far for comfort.

"Don't lock me out. I'm not asking for anything." When she looks up again, I swear water shines in her eyes. The last thing I want to do is make her cry. "I just wanted to get that off my chest."

"I didn't take you for the sentimental type."

This time, I do smirk because fuck, I'm now deep in the feels. "Me either." I chuckle, keeping it inside because I prefer to hear her laughter, which is softer in the afterglow.

"Thank you."

"You're thanking me for sex?"

The corner of her mouth rises up on one side. "I'm thanking you for tonight." She slips out of bed, and adds, "I'll be back."

Most women snuggle against me, wanting me to stay.

Some even beg or coerce me into it. My guilt gets the better of me sometimes.

The one woman I wouldn't mind trying to cling to me has no interest in such things. She disappears into the bathroom, leaving me lying there alone with my thoughts. With my arms spread wide, I take a deep breath and slowly exhale. When I'm with her, the mental gymnastics easily competes with the physical demands. I could lie here and go through every conversation we had to try to figure out where I stand in her world, but I'm exhausted and decide to give it a rest for now.

As my lids grow heavier, my muscles relax against the mattress. Trying to force myself to stay awake, I turn toward the closed bathroom door, and call out, "All okay in there?"

"All good!" she calls back.

I give in and close my eyes, unsure how long she's planning to be gone.

The scent of soap and sweetness fills the air just as a warm hand grazes across my chest. A kiss to my cheek has me not only opening my eyes but reaching to hold on to the softness of her skin.

The lamp is now off, inviting darkness to stay. The night might be owning the space, but I see her. I see her bare before me in every way; her face is clean of makeup, and her hair is hanging over her left shoulder. Turning to catch her lips with mine, I ask, "What took you so long?" My voice is gruff with sleep.

Running her hand over the scruff of my face, she whispers, "Just that magic I spoke about earlier. Do you want to stay?"

A smile creases my cheeks. I'd already planned on it since I fell asleep, but knowing she wants me to has me feeling like an Olympic gold medalist. "I'll stay." Can't sound too eager, though. Wouldn't want to feed the ego she wears like armor. I like when her defenses are down, and I get to spend time with the woman she really is instead of what she wants the world to believe.

When she lies next to me, we stare into each other's eyes. "If you need to use the bathroom . . ."

"I'll be right back."

She nods, and then her eyes close just before I slip out of bed. I don't take long in the bathroom and even score a little finger scrub with toothpaste to clean my teeth and have fresher breath. I splash water on my tired face, dry my hands, and then run my hands through my hair. I'm not sure if she's up for more fun, but I'm not opposed to as much action as she craves.

Taking a second, I push my palms down against the marble counter. The exhilaration of getting what you want after so long and then having her like no other woman I've been with—no barrier between us, just pure heat and lust, desire and Tatum—causes my heart to beat hard in my chest. "Fuck." I squeeze my eyes closed and try to calm back down before returning.

I look at myself once more, push my hair back, and return to the bedroom only to find her asleep. Guess I got my answer regarding the rest of the night.

I slip under the covers. Clearly, she's a woman used to sleeping in her own bed by how she sleeps in the middle of it. I keep my chuckle under wraps and then move next to her. My eyes slowly adjust to the dark again, and I can just make out her delicate features. She's a stunner with makeup, but without, she's truly breathtaking. I can't believe I'm the one who gets the privilege of seeing her stripped down to nothing.

So fucking lucky.

I take my watch off my wrist and set it on her nightstand next to a book and an alarm clock. Though she's facing me, I pull her close, leaving no room between us, her breathing remaining steady as she stirs and readjusts with her head resting on my shoulder.

In the quiet of the room, I can only hear the matching cadence of our breathing. I realize I don't mind that she fell asleep since I get to hold her like this. I kiss her on the top of her head and then fall asleep.

11

Tatum

I shouldn't like a strong arm around me like I'm captive to this bed.

But I do.

Or maybe it's just him that I like so much. He's so warm, and I can't resist staying curled up against him as though I've been left out in the cold too long. *Huh. Wonder if there's some truth to that.* Something to ponder when I'm fully awake.

For someone who *can* sleep in, I see this time of morning too often. To-dos and random stress, even loneliness creep in at the most annoying times of the day.

Judging by the faintest light of the sunrise I spy through a crack in my curtains, I'm guessing it's around five thirty or six. *Go to sleep, Devreux.*

That's not what has me awake, though. Loneliness is the furthest thing on my mind when it comes to Harrison Decker being in my bed.

I wish I could see his face, but I'm too content to make

the effort to turn around. *Sigh.* I close my eyes, dearly wanting to accept this moment for what it is.

Comfort.

Warmth.

Shelter.

~

COLD AIR ROLLS over my skin, leaving goose bumps in the wake. I tuck my arm under the covers and tug them higher. Rolling to the other side, I catch a whiff of something in the air.

Coffee?

Bacon?

Harrison?

Harrison! I open my eyes in a flash when last night finally returns to the forefront of my mind and find the bed empty beside me. Flipping the covers off, I get to my feet and grab my robe from the chair where I left it draped. The silky material slides down my arms, and I fasten the belt around my waist. I reach the living room when I'm pulling my hair out from the collar and freeing it to lay on top.

Judging by the sunlight flooding the apartment, morning is in full swing. As is Harrison cooking at the stove. "What are you doing?" I ask.

He looks back over his shoulder. It's then that I regret not taking the time to appreciate the sight of him prior to disrupting him. "Good morning, sunshine. You hungry? We never did get around to eating last night."

Resting my middle against the counter of the peninsula, I ask, "Did I not satisfy your appetite?" I don't know why I lick my lips. *Gah.* He gets my feminine wiles going. It's probably how sexy he looks shirtless while holding that spatula in his hand. The black thigh-length briefs don't hurt either. The way the waistband clings to that V of his lower stomach like I did last night . . . yeah, I bite my lower lip and admire him while I can.

"More than, but I need nourishment if you intend to wear me out like that on a regular basis." When he turns his attention back to the food he's cooking, I brace myself as the words *regular basis* sound like he's moving in. I know he's not. He lives in California. That's his home. But I'm not used to someone speaking so carefree after one night. Two, if we count Catalina, and we always do.

Let it go, Tatum. It's not a proposal but just an innocent turn of the words.

I let that phrase take up space in my subconscious and focus on the here, the now, and that glorious ass of his. *Oh, good Lord.* That ass . . . I grin, remembering how incredible he looks naked. Not that the briefs leave much to the imagination.

Releasing a deep breath, I realize my body is loose and tired like after a really great workout. I've not felt this carefree and relaxed in a long time. "So what you're saying is we eat and then return to the bedroom to finish our meal?" I thumb over my shoulder, not worried one bit when the top of my robe slips open.

His gaze plunges from my eyes to my chest, and he has no shame in staring, taking full advantage of the situation. I could close it again and tighten the belt, but what's the point? I like the way he looks at me like it's the first time all over again.

He chuckles, pulling the pan to a different burner and turning off the stove. "That's exactly what I'm saying, baby."

Baby sounded different in the heat of the moment than in broad daylight. Am I a cute nickname kind of girlfriend?

Girlfriend? Clearly, having sex for the first time in forever has scrambled my thoughts and better judgment. He says, "I'm going to feed you first, and then I'm going to ravage your body for the rest of the day." Two plates are on the island, and he puts scrambled eggs and bacon on each, right next to the sliced tomatoes.

"Where'd you get the plates?"

"The cabinet over by the fridge."

"Huh?" I don't think I've ever used them. Maybe once, but it's been longer than I can remember.

Looking up with a plate in each hand, he asks, "What do you mean?"

I shrug. "I don't cook." Suddenly feeling self-conscious, I add, "Much."

No judgment crosses his expression, but a smile does. "I eat out a lot because of my job, taking clients out and that kind of thing, but there's something different about a home-cooked meal that has my heart."

Is he dropping hints for me, or is this just casual conversation? "From what I remember, you like scrambled eggs."

"I do." I move into the kitchen and take a plate from him. "Thank you. Do you know where the silverware is by chance?"

"For real?"

Laughing, I pass behind him and smack his hard ass. "No, I do know where that is." I pull open the drawer and hand him a fork.

"You had me worried."

"No need. I know where the basics live, or at least, what I use." I hip check the drawer. "Want to eat in here or in bed?"

He starts for the bedroom. "Bedroom's good."

"I have to agree." All the more so when he's in there with me. Wait . . . *what?* My heart starts racing, and my feet stop just as he disappears inside the room. No. This is not going to become a regular thing. I'm a layover at best for him, someone to hook up with while he's in the city, and then what? He goes home. *Oh my God.* I didn't even ask him if he has a girlfriend.

The lighthearted feeling disappears as I head down the hall a little slower, more hesitant, cautious this time. *What am I doing?*

Harrison steps out into the hall sans plate. "What are you doing?"

"I was just asking myself that same question."

"I had a feeling, but maybe we can hold off on the doubts and questioning what happened last night until after we eat. We'll have clearer heads on full stomachs," he says.

"Keep it light." I can't. I know I can't. I ruin everything by asking too much and too many questions.

"Probably best, for now." He signals into the bedroom before he turns to go.

I follow him in. He sits on the same side of the bed he slept on, leaving room for me. Actually, leaving me most of the bed and the middle for me. I can't say it upsets me. It's quite sweet. I go to the other side and climb onto the mattress while balancing my plate in hand.

Leaning against the headboard, I cross my ankles and take a bite. Doing anything I can to pretend to be as happy as I was five minutes ago. "Thank you for cooking for me." *Yikes, that sounded so formal.*

"My pleasure."

Half his plate is already emptied when I've only taken a few bites, my appetite waning. "Would you like mine?"

"You don't like it?"

I glance at his plate and back up at him. "I do, but you look hungry."

"Thanks, but this will hold me." His laughter fills the space. What he said wasn't a joke, but it's funny that he cracks himself up. I can only imagine what's going on in his head.

After pushing my food around on the plate, I ask, "What are your plans for the day?"

"Not sure."

"Are you going to see your girlfriend?" I accuse, the words bursting from my mouth like a bad case of food poisoning.

"What? What girlfriend?" His plate is discarded to the nightstand, and he stares at me like I grew a third eye. "What are you talking about?"

"You were right. We don't know anything about each other." Throwing my hand in the air, I angle it toward the door. "You could have a girlfriend back in California for all I know." I shrug. "How would I know? How would she know that you just slept with me? God, I hate cheaters."

Grabbing hold of my hand, he brings it between us, still holding it in his. "Slow down, Tatum." When the anger I spun up inside like a hurricane begins to lessen, he says, "I don't have a girlfriend. Not in California or anywhere else. I'm single. What I told you last night is the truth. I haven't been with a woman in five months or more. I haven't been serious about anyone in over four years. So I don't know where this train of thought came from, but you can ask me anything, and I'll tell you the truth."

My heart is racing again but for different reasons—him —and his honesty. "I'm sorry."

He looks down at our clasped hands, and asks, "Don't you think Natalie would have told you if I had a girlfriend?"

"Stop being logical. My mind went into a momentary tailspin." When his gaze meets mine, I add, "I'm not always loveable. Being burned time and time again does that to someone."

"I'm sorry you've experienced that, but I'm not looking to burn you. Last night was good, don't you think?" He pulls my hand to his mouth and kisses it.

The feel of his lips against my head brings a sense of security, safety found in the truth of his words. *Temporary.* I have to remind myself not to get invested. "It was, but—"

"Let's save the buts for another day." Lying back, he rests his head against the headboard while still holding my hand.

Why can't I enjoy what this is in the moment instead of worrying about what's next when it comes to us? The past might be the best indicator. I silence my fears instead of voicing them, willing to try anything to live in the right here and now like him.

I lie next to him at first but eventually move in and cuddle. His arm wraps around me, holding me close, and then he kisses my head. It's easy to lose track of time with him.

Not sure what time of day it is, I glance at my clock on the nightstand. 10:15.

"Oh, shit." I jump up, scrambling to my feet. "I have brunch with my mother today."

"What time?"

"Eleven thirty, but it's a cab ride back to the Upper East Side." I cut across the room to my main walk-in closet. "She gives me the hardest time if I'm even a minute late or have a hair out of place."

"How will it go after yesterday?" Harrison asks.

"It will be fine. We'll talk about what happened at dinner last night in passing, and she'll move on. Nothing new. I'll be fine. I'm used to it."

"That doesn't sound healthy."

"Healthy," I say, laughing humorlessly. I come out with a dress and my undergarments. "It's sweet that you think it should be. Every family has its difficulties, Harrison. I'm sure my family's no different."

I think of Natalie. Her parents were there for me when mine were away for business or pleasure, sitting in the front row for us when we graduated and planning parties to celebrate our big days—sweet sixteen, high school graduation, and then a big dinner at one of our favorite restaurants after we graduated college. It took months to coordinate and make happen after we walked across that stage, mainly because it was hard to pin my parents down for a date. *Yet they could turn up for my best friend's anniversary party at the last minute.* Makes me wonder if that was only because Martine and John St. James were attending since they're best friends. A fly-in, fly-out visit to New York to see their friends sounds reasonable.

If only they'd do the same for their daughter.

"My family can be so annoying. I'm lost in the middle of this pack of kids. It's loud at the dinner table. Forget about being heard. The schedule conflicts—my sister's ballet, baseball games, missed plays, and award banquets. Hell, they forgot to pick me up after the regional championship one time. Simply slipped their minds because my brother had been in a car accident." He watches me pick out my jewelry. "Don't worry. It wasn't serious other than he took my dad's new Porsche out for a joyride and got into a fender bender."

"What happened to you?"

"They remembered around eleven that night when they did their nightly round of goodnights. It took them two hours to get across LA and two hours home. Not one word about my game. It was all about my older brother and that fucking Porsche." Seeming to catch himself, he chuckles. "Despite how I sound, that stuff doesn't matter now. I wouldn't trade my family for anything, not even for the Christiansens. Their family dynamic is great, but there's something to appreciate about the crazy of your own family. Is that what you're missing? The crazy? Or the stability. Most fall into one camp or the other."

"I'm missing everything. I was raised as a third adult in the house, a friend instead of a kid."

He angles his head and then gets up. Walking behind me, he slides his hands around me, and though my instinct is to slip out of his hold, I stay. He kisses my shoulder, his lips lingering, and if I had a say, I'd keep them there forever.

When I look up, his eyes are filled with a sympathy that makes me squirm, hating that he feels sorry for me. I say, "They're not bad people. Just preferring to jet set than sit home and raise a daughter. They gave me everything, more than I could ever want or need."

"Okay."

I don't look at him. He has no right to judge me when it sounds like his family has problems of their own. "Seriously. I got a custom-painted convertible for my sixteenth birthday and a blank check for each of my graduations. This apartment was for my twenty-fifth birthday."

"That's cool." His tone is so flat that I tense from the words he's *not* saying.

I head for the bathroom but whip back to face him before I enter. "You know what? I don't have to justify my situation to anyone, least of all, to a man I barely know, even if he was just inside me. I need to get ready, so you can see yourself out." I tighten my robe, fisting it closed at the top. "Maybe we'll see each other around." *Hello, salt. Hello, wound.* It's not so nice to see you again. *I hate how my defenses work against me as well. I may win this battle, but I'll lose him in the war.*

Standing where I left him, he narrows his eyes and shakes his head. "What the fuck just happened? And what do you mean by maybe?"

"Exactly how it sounds. You're busy building your business, and I'm busy building my career. Last night was fun, but we knew it was only temporary."

"Is that what we're doing, Tatum? We're walking away because you got uncomfortable over something that I had nothing to do with?" He clicks his tongue as if disgust covers it and walks toward the end of the bed to grab his pants.

"I'm just not going to be around today, so I thought you might have other plans as well."

With one leg in his pants, he slips his other through the other leg. A humorless chuckle comes before I'm met with a hard glare. He grabs his shirt, punching his arm like he wishes it was a wall. "Fine. Whatever you want. That's what you're used to, right? Getting everything you want from blank checks to three-million-dollar apartments? If that's not love, I don't know what is," he spits sarcastically.

His words smack me, a low blow not to only my heart but also what I thought was changing between us. Causing me to shift in the truth of the discomfort he mentioned, I say, "If that doesn't say it all, I don't know what will." I grab the knob of the door, ready to slam it but stay long enough to say, "Guess I should have seen this ending coming. Nothing changes with you."

"You're right, princess. I'm as steady, loyal, and reliable as they come. Not something you're used to."

I try to crush the metal knob in my hand, but when it doesn't give, I take a deep breath and shield my heart under a coat of mental armor. "You can see yourself out, and by the way, as a real estate agent in New York, it's four million in this market." I shut the door, locking it behind me. *Screw him!*

And to think I let him have sex with me without a condom. *Ugh.* I slam my fists against the door and slide my back down it until my ass hits the marble floor.

I let him get too close. That was my mistake. Now I'm stuck here waiting for him to leave. I don't know how long I wait, but I keep pressing my ear to the door, hoping to get some indication of when he's gone. The last thing I want to do is walk out to find him still here. I don't need his negativity in my life. I don't need anything.

Or anyone.

I especially don't need Harrison Decker, which is a shame because he was slowly becoming one of my favorite things. But just like everyone else, he chose to walk away. He chose to leave after I begged him last night to stay.

He might be right when it comes to me getting my way, but he's also wrong when it comes to my life.

I'm used to many things, and one of those things I'm most used to is being alone.

So much for steady, loyal, and reliable.

12

Harrison

"Tell her to come over here." I overhear Nick tell Natalie in hushed tones. On the stairs, their voices travel, reaching my ears.

Natalie huffs. "It's not that simple. I know her better than anyone. She'll put on a brave face and pretend it doesn't matter in front of you. But I know she's hurting inside."

I lean against the wall, not sure what to think or how to feel. I know they're talking about Tatum but have no idea what's going on. One of those is a lie I tell myself. I know exactly how I feel. I'm still reeling from that fight that came out of nowhere.

We were good.

We were fucking great.

Then she had to light a match and set us on fire again. After I got back from Tatum's, I went for a run on the tread-mill in the basement to burn through the restless energy I had coursing through me. It's not the same as running oceanside, but it got the job done. Until now.

I stop and listen, though I know better than to eavesdrop. There's just a niggling suspicion inside my chest that something might be seriously wrong.

Nick says, "She doesn't have to be guarded with me. I've been around long enough to know the truth. And I'll leave you guys alone. She's always welcome here no matter what happens."

"I appreciate that. It's just always been her and me against the world and . . . well, then came you and now comes a baby. She's not showing it, but I can tell she's now struggling to find her place. That's why I asked her to be a godparent. I want her to know she'll always be a part of our lives."

"Honey, you can be there for her, but if she doesn't want your help—"

"She does. But if I'm not there, it just proves her point. She's used to being left alone to deal with things on her own. If I were in her shoes, I'd be wondering if I have a place as well. I don't want her to wonder. I want her to know she has us."

"I'm happy to go with you," he says.

"No, it's fine."

Pushing off the wall, I come around the corner. They're quick to step apart like they've been busted by their parents. "At ease, soldiers."

Natalie hangs on Nick's arm. "We weren't doing anything sexual."

Grabbing her, Nick pulls her to his side. "Yet anyway."

She shoves him playfully. "No, don't trap me. I need to go."

I stand on the other side of the island and press my palms to the cold stone. "I overheard you talking about Tatum. What's going on?"

They exchange a glance, but then she turns to me. "Her mother didn't show up for brunch, so I was going to meet her at the restaurant." The same mother who humiliated her daughter and scheduled this brunch as an apology? *What the hell?*

Looking at my watch, I ask, "I thought that was more than an hour ago?"

"It was." Her tone is solemn as she looks down to put her phone in her bag on the counter.

My imagination starts to get away from me. I want to be wrong, so I ask, "She's been there alone this whole time?"

"Yes." Natalie swings her bag onto her shoulder and lifts to kiss Nick. "That's why I'm going to see her."

"I'll go." They both look at me as if I'm speaking a foreign language—heads tilted, confusion cinching their brows together. "I want to go," I add as if that will make them understand the guilt I feel for what I said to her this morning. We argued, but I can still be there for her in a time of need.

"I don't know, Harrison," Natalie says, slipping out of her husband's embrace.

"Did she say something to you?"

"Should she have?" she asks defensively, crossing her arms over her chest.

I exhale and run a hand over my head. "We had words this morning."

Without blinking, she looks at me with her mouth open. "I thought you were here last night, just sleeping in."

The tables have been turned, and now I'm the one who's busted. I don't have to justify my whereabouts to anyone and haven't in years. But as she said, Tatum's important to her, and I know her worry comes from concern for her friend. "I stayed with her last night. That was great. This morning . . . not so much. I'd like to go and talk to her . . . be there for her."

Nick eyes me, seemingly invested in Tatum's well-being. It's not like he hasn't known me his whole damn life. "Really?" I ask, annoyed.

He crosses his arms, and something appears to satisfy him. "I think you should let him go, Nat. It sounds like they have some unfinished business to take care of."

Natalie's gaze volleys between us a few times with a debate sparked in her eyes. "I don't know if that's wise since you had a fight with her as well. It's not dump on Tatum day."

"You've always been there for her, but today, I can be the one," I say. The words that came so naturally off my tongue sound strange to my ears.

The one?

What the fuck am I saying?

I barely stepped foot in Manhattan, and she's already written me off. That's my wounded pride speaking. My heart says otherwise. Something tells me she needs to know someone else is in her corner right now. *I can be that person.*

She sets her bag on the counter. "All right, but promise me you'll tell me everything when you get back."

Holding up my hand in Scout's honor, I say, "I promise."

Since I have my wallet and phone, I don't need to go back upstairs. "Text me the address?"

"I will." Natalie then adds, "Be gentle. She's strong, but her Achilles' heel is her vulnerable side."

I know. I found out the hard way, but I don't say it, feeling protective over the time I've had alone with Tatum. "You can trust me." I head for the door with the two of them in tow. Just before I reach it, my phone buzzes in my pocket.

"The address," Natalie says.

"If you hear from her again, convince her to stay." I walk out and down the stairs. It's faster to take a cab since one's already heading my way. I raise my arm, and when it zips across the lane to the curb, I look back at them. They're still standing there like worried parents. "I'll take care of her," I say and then get in the back of the taxi.

On the ride over, I debate if I should warn Tatum that I'm coming. If I do, she'll leave. I know it. I've also learned how she handles confrontation. She ditches the situation. A trait she inherited from her mother.

If I don't tell her, she may leave as soon as she sees me.

I'm willing to take my chances.

The ivy-covered restaurant has seating on the sidewalk, but I don't see Tatum. I stop at the hostess stand, and say, "I'm looking for a friend. I'm just going to cruise around real quick."

"Let me know if I can be of assistance," she replies with a smile that I'm used to receiving.

My parents gave me my good looks, and I'm just naturally charming. Amusing myself while I search the restaurant, I don't find her, but there's a large patio out back, so I make my way outside. As soon as I do, I see her under a flowering tree in the corner. *Seated alone.*

I'd love a chance to admire how beautiful she is in a deep pink dress with bows on top of her shoulders. Her hair is in a ponytail high on the back of her head, and her chin rests in her hand.

I keep moving, though, wanting to be the one she can lean on. As soon as her eyes spy me coming, she's stiffening her spine and clasping her hands on her lap under the table. I barely reach the vicinity before she's asking, "What are you doing?"

I take the napkin from the plate and whip it in the air,

freeing it from the shape of a fortune cookie, and sit down across from her. "I'm having lunch."

"Here?"

"You don't mind, do you?"

She looks around like I'm making a scene. *I'm not.* Just having lunch with a gorgeous woman on a Sunday afternoon in June.

Leaning closer, she whispers, "The check is on its way, Harrison." She tries to catch the waiter's attention by raising her hand, but when that fails, she adds, "I was already planning to leave."

"Change your plans and have lunch with me." My voice is even, my offer genuine.

We share an exchange, and then she asks, "How do you know I haven't eaten already?"

I glance at the clean plate in front of her and the silverware that shines on either side of the porcelain. She continues looking around for any last-ditch efforts, but when she can't think of any, she says, "Fine. I'll stay to keep you company, but don't drag this out. Just lunch, and then we go our separate ways. Okay?"

Grinning, I adjust the napkin across my leg and pick up the menu, settling in. "What do you recommend?"

"Harrison?"

My gaze slides over the top of the menu. "Yes?"

"*Okay?* No dragging this out."

"Fine. Long lunches that lead to lazy Sunday afternoons in bed, which then lead to dinner and a hot bath right after. Your body slick against mine, coming until—"

"I will get up right now."

I love getting under her skin, but I like her smile even more, which she's granting me regardless of the threat. I chuckle. "Okay."

"Good. As for the rest of that, it's not happening either, and the eggs Benedict is their specialty."

Lowering my menu, I ask, "Did you know eggs Benedict is named after a Wall Street broker who ordered the dish at the Waldorf Hotel in the late 1890s."

"There are conflicting stories regarding that." Her hand goes to her chest. "As a New Yorker—born and bred—I like the broker one the best."

"What was it like to grow up here? Having a park as your backyard and walking the streets to get to school? I've never really understood city life when it's more like a concrete jungle."

"That's because you have to spend time here to get to know it. There's magic found around every corner. You just have to look for it."

"Maybe you can show me."

"Maybe. I'm pretty busy these days." She looks away, studying every other person on this patio in avoidance of my eyes. But then she exhales heavily and meets my gaze.

I can't successfully hide my smile when I see hers first.

The server arrives and clears her empty mimosa glass. "Anything else?"

Ordering, I reply, "Two eggs Benedict, a pitcher of mimosas, and flat water for the table."

Her pen is still poised on the pad, but nothing was jotted down. She's looking at me when she asks, "Oh, I thought we were clearing this table?"

"Nope, we're staying and brunching together." I grin right at Tatum. "Right, Tate?"

"You know that annoys me—"

"Brunch ends at two," the server snaps at me.

Glancing at my watch, I reply, "More than an hour is plenty of time. Thank you."

Her straight hair cuts through the air when she turns to leave.

When we're left to our own devices, Tatum asks, "Did Natalie send you?"

"No. I volunteered for the job."

"And what job is that exactly?" She crosses her arms over her chest, reminding me a lot of Natalie by the action. "Operation rescue Tatum from the humiliation of being stood up by her mom? Save your breath, Decker. I got this handled."

I didn't expect her to let her guard down for me, especially after this morning, so her defensiveness doesn't come as a surprise. I do the only thing I hope will lower those walls for me again like they were this morning. "I owe you an apology."

Her eyes widen. It's nice to surprise her for once. "For?"

"For what I said this morning. You like to pretend stuff doesn't get to you, but we're all human. I can only assume you felt some anxiety about meeting your mom after what happened at the party, and I felt it was taken out on me. It stung, considering I thought we were having a good time together."

Her body language has changed. Not from the champagne or because I'm laying out a ton of wisdom. It's because I'm here. I'm listening. And, most importantly, I'm treating her kindly. She's receptive because she's trusting my authenticity. I care about her.

Tatum is so fucking frustrating, but there's something about her that I just can't let go of.

"I did take it out on you. Some habits are hard to break. It was easier to blame you than to admit I had hoped this time with my mom would be different." When her arms lower, so do her eyes. While she toys with her napkin, her shoulders roll in on themselves, her body caving into her pain. "She'll have a great excuse, one that will end an argument."

"Will that reason take away the hurt she's caused you, the pain of feeling abandoned?"

Her eyes dart to mine. "I haven't been abandoned, Harrison."

Reaching across the table, I hold my hand palm up for her. "You may believe you have to be strong all the time, but with me, you don't. I like you." I laugh to myself. "Prickly on the outside, soft on the inside. What's not to like?"

"I haven't been abandoned," she repeats, but it feels more for herself than to convince me. The drinks are served, and our glasses filled. When we're alone again, she says, "It's not the first time I've been stood up by one of my parents, but it doesn't sting any less."

Taking a long sip, she sets her half-empty champagne glass down, and adds, "I don't know how to make them understand how much it hurts when they don't show up."

"It's not your job to make them understand. It's their job to love you unconditionally. As for standing you up, I know I'm a poor substitute—"

"You're not." She finally rests her hand in mine, and our fingers wrap around each other's. "I don't know why you're here after how I treated you this morning, but I'm glad you came. It takes a strong man to show up like you did. So, I want to apologize to you because you're right. You did nothing wrong. I just let my insecurities get the best of me when you deserved better. I'm sorry."

Our food arrives, and after the server sprinkles pepper over our eggs, she's quick to walk away again. My stomach growls, but this conversation is too important to put off. "How many times have we started over?"

"More importantly, how many times will you give us another chance?"

I turn her hand over in mine, remembering kissing it this morning. "Well, as far as that goes, you've given me a chance or two. So, how about we stop taking chances and start giving each other the benefit of the doubt instead?"

Tapping her glass against mine, she says, "Here's to friends with benefits."

With a seriously ridiculous grin on my face, I laugh. "Now that's something I'm definitely drinking to. Cheers," I say.

Let the fun begin.

13

Tatum

HARRISON IS SO MUCH OF WHAT I REMEMBER OF HIM IN
Catalina.

Sweet.

Interesting.

Attentive.

Thoughtful.

And yes, flirty.

I think that's ingrained in him.

I've heard enough stories to know he's had his bad boy
ways, but I was never treated like a one-night stand despite
being exactly that.

He didn't have to show up today, but he did, and from
what Natalie said in the text, that backs what he told me. He
wanted to. He wanted to be here for me.

After the fight.

After the mean things I said in anger.

After treating him less than he deserved and kicking

him out of my apartment, he showed up in a big way for me. *As he said . . . steady, loyal, and reliable.*

He showed up when my mom didn't.

Swinging my purse beside me as we walk down the street, I ask, "Why'd you make me eat so much?" I'm teasing, of course. I tortured myself by stuffing my face full of food and champagne.

"You only have yourself to blame for that." He bumps into me playfully but keeps his hands tucked in his pockets. I kind of miss the little touches we've shared, the accidental and the purposeful ones over the years. "I guess I can take a little responsibility. If I had made pancakes this morning, you would have just drunk mimosas instead."

Keeping my eyes forward, I don't let the moment pass without saying what I need to get off my chest. "I would have done the same for you."

"What is that?"

"You think I'm stubborn to a fault, but I would have come to you if you were in my shoes."

He stops in the middle of the sidewalk like a tourist. "Is that what we're calling it? Stubborn?"

Shrugging, I reply, "Bitchy works too."

"Too far. I've never once thought about you that way."

When grumbling New Yorkers gripe when they have to move around us, I take him by the arm and pull him off to the side. "Did you think about me often?"

"More than I should for a woman who hated my existence." *Dare I tell him that I never hated him? That I'd simply hated that we never had a chance?*

Wrong place?

Wrong time?

If I'd only met him in the city . . . Well, I wouldn't have walked away so quickly.

His attention is stolen by the candy store window display. A proposal scene with a giant Ring Pop sitting in a swirl of cotton candy with the words "I Do" in colorful edible dots. He says, "It's June. Fitting display for a wedding month, but it's making me hungry."

"Hungry? We just stuffed ourselves."

"No, you stuffed yourself." As he rubs his stomach, the hem of his untucked shirt rides up. Not as much as I'd like but enough to have me wanting more. I know what's under it, and his body never disappoints. "It takes a lot of food to keep this body going."

"Only food as fuel?" Fine, I do my share of flirting with him too.

He grins, turning back to me. It's not surprise that lies in that wry grin, but I think satisfaction. Yep, he's winning. If making me happy is a victory for him, I'll let him take the lead.

But then he tugs his lower lip under his teeth, a lip bite that has my mouth hanging open. Who knew that would be the thing to drive my mind wild with fantasies?

Apparently, he did because he lifts my chin until my mouth closes again, and whispers, "Be careful, Devreux. You're drooling."

Tugging the door open, he enters the shop. And I'm still standing here like a damn fool in front of a giant Ring Pop proposal. Self-consciously, I wipe the sides of my mouth, just in case. *Oh, thank God.* All good. I open the door and join him inside the store.

With a handful of candy bags already in hand, he eyes the sea salt caramels when I walk up. "I didn't know you were such a . . ." I hold up the candy in front of my face.

"Sugar Daddy?" He snatches the lollipop from me. "Very

funny." He's laughing and drops the candy in one of his many bags.

"What can I say? It was lame, but the joke still landed."

"Get to shopping, Tate. We need more candy." He takes a pre-packed bag of the sea salt caramels and then cruises down the gummy aisle.

Since we're the only ones in the store beside the employees, I walk down the other small aisle and ask, "So what's with the candy, Decker? Secret sugar addiction? Part-time job providing candy to kindergarteners, or—" I gasp.

He moves a row of Junior Mint boxes, but let's be honest here. He didn't have to do that to be able to see me. "Or what?"

"Luring your prey with your sticky sweets."

"Damn, that escalated quickly."

"Granted, I'm the prey, and for the record, I love Twizzlers."

"A licorice girl," he says like it's a whole genre of women in and of itself. I'm not sure what to make of that response. He returns the boxes to the shelves, and adds, "I like candy, but I thought it would be nice to get Natalie some. Nick told me he's been running out at night to satisfy her sweet tooth."

Hearing him talk about my best friend with firsthand knowledge surprises me. Living there has its perks, I guess. But his action behind that knowledge surprises me more. "The pregnancy must have her craving all kinds of things she doesn't normally eat." I round the endcap and run right into him. Some of the candy falls to the ground, and we're both quick to kneel, bonking our heads together, which sends me backward to my ass.

A bag of Sugar Babies lands on my lap, and he says, "Fitting."

I'm not actually sure why, but it starts in my belly and overwhelms me until I burst out laughing. With his candy all over the place, he starts laughing too. Rubbing over the red mark on his forehead, he asks, "Why are we laughing?"

"I don't know," I say, giggling too hard to stop. "But it feels good." It does too, like a hard-earned day off.

The store clerk starts shoving the candy back in the bags like a maniac. "Are you okay?" A certain someone might be high on the sugar.

Harrison waits for me to answer, concern suddenly jading the blue of his eyes.

"I'm fine," I reply, holding my hands out. "Help me up?"

Surprisingly, the clerk takes one of my hands, but Harrison starts laughing again, and says, "I got her. Thanks." He takes my hands in his, his thumb gently rubbing over the top of mine. "Hold tight, ba—" He doesn't finish, but I wish he had. He hasn't called me baby that many times, but I remember every one of them. Usually, he says it in the heat of passion, except the first time and now the almost last one.

He pulls me to my feet, his hands holding tight to mine, the toe of our shoes touching. There's this moment between us—thick with tension, ripe with an imagination running away, a lightness from the laughter remaining—that feels so good.

Us against the world. It reminds me of what I have with Natalie. *And that is strange because I never thought I'd have anyone else in my life like her.*

Harrison isn't a knight riding onto my life's page to save the day.

No, he has his story to create. Resting his hand heavy on my head, he asks, "You okay?"

I swat him away. "I'll be fine. By that welt on your head,

it looks like you got the worst end of it." Then I reach up and rub my fingertips so lightly over the bruising skin.

"I never claimed to be a tough guy, but I didn't expect to be taken out by a five-foot-three Tasmanian devil dressed in pink while in a candy store. You match the store, by the way. Almost like you planned it . . . I'm onto you, Tate."

"Onto me? I'm innocent."

"Innocent? You called me a murderer for buying candy."

Shrugging, I laugh under my breath. "I watch a lot of true crime stories. What can I say?"

He starts collecting the candy into bags again but looks up at me with a grin. "You never cease to surprise me."

"What do I cease doing?"

"Apparently helping, but I'll let it slide."

I finish straightening the skirt of my dress and then bend to help him. He's already standing back up. "Oops. My bad."

"It's okay. That skirt's too short to be bending over in anyway."

My gaze darts down to my legs. "What are you talking about? It hits mid-thigh. The one I wore to the concert was shorter."

"That was too short, too." He starts for the front of the store like he didn't just judge me.

Following him, I say, "Good thing you're not my dad then."

"I'd be more worried being your boyfriend."

I stop between the giant lollipop stand and a large display of Necco Wafers. Does anyone even eat Neccos? I grab one package because now I'm curious what the hell they are. Walking up behind him, I tap him on the back with the roll of colorful wafers. "Ah. I see," I start when he turns around. "Worried because other guys would be looking at me?"

Snatching the Neccos from me, he adds it to the pile he's buying, and tells the clerk, "Add that to my order."

I lean my back against the counter, eyeing him. I let my smile carry on. "You know, Decker, you kind of sound like you might be jealous."

"Pfft. What or whom would I be jealous of?"

"That's what I can't figure out, but give me some time and I will."

He hands over his card to pay for the candy and then angles my way. "Listen, Devreux, I'm not jealous."

The funny thing is he doesn't sound mad, not even a little perturbed. Maybe a little defensive, but he's volleying the banter right back just fine. He takes the bag from the clerk, and we head toward the door, which he holds open for me.

Despite the eight million people in the city, as soon as it closes and we're alone, it feels private. Out on the sidewalk, he stops in front of the Ring Pop proposal, and as he looks around, he smiles again. "Why do you care if I get jealous?"

"Just wondering why you would. That's all."

I turn to lean, but he catches my arm. "You may have forgotten about how good we are together, but I haven't."

As we stand in front of the perfection of the confectionary display, our conversation hasn't taken a turn for the worst but traveled down a much more intriguing path. I hold my purse strap in my hand and shift on my heels. "What made you think of that?"

"I don't know," he replies, tapping the window. "Maybe it's the magic."

"What magic?"

"The magic you spoke of. You said magic can be found around any corner, but you have to be looking for it. Maybe we didn't. Maybe it found us."

Denying my heart beating rapidly in my chest is impossible. By how it feels inside, it's probably louder than the traffic. I turn to face the street, thinking it's best before I start letting crazy notions fill my head, like kissing him right here. I look down at my shoes, trying to get lost in the details instead of staring at the man next to me. "Maybe we should go."

"Yeah, maybe."

We start walking again, and I think changing the topic is a good idea. "What do you have planned for the rest of the day?"

"Thinking about seeing what you're up to."

Grabbing his shirt by the sleeve, I tug him down the street. "Come on. I'll let you tag along."

"First stop?"

"The lingerie store."

"Now you're talking my language."

14

Tatum

"THE FRENCH KNICKER IN WHITE, THE BLACK TEDDY, AND THE cheekies." He points at the table and then rubs his thumb over his bottom lip in contemplation. After putting enough thought into it to solve world hunger, he snaps his fingers and turns to me. "I think you need all four colors of the cheekies."

He actually was talking lingerie language.

Who knew that Harrison Decker was an aficionado when it came to lingerie and undergarments?

From the couch where I've been lounging for the last thirty minutes while he worked with the sales associate, I point at my chest. "Me?"

Seemingly confused, he replies, "Yes you. What do you think?"

"Oh, I didn't know you wanted my opinion on what lingerie I should buy for myself.

"Ha-ha." There is no chuckle to accompany the words. "I thought I was helping." He shoves his hands in his pockets.

It's a tic that Harrison has when he's trying to give room for other opinions. I'm a quick study when it comes to him.

Joining him at the counter, I eye the pieces he narrowed it down to. "Helping? You're a bull in a china shop." Picking up the turquoise cheekies, I discard them to the far side of the counter. I bring the silk thong back into the mix and then push the pile forward to be rung up. Leaning against the counter, I ask him, "Why do you have such a vested interest in what I'm wearing under my clothes anyway?"

He clears his throat and glances to the saleswoman. Bleached blond with her hair twisted back into a chignon. Messy modern, but still elegant. Later thirties, if I had to guess. Plunging neckline that reveals a hint of a lace garment underneath. Very slender. I mentally note that she doesn't have birthing hips, the term my grandmother once used when referring to how mine will come in handy one day.

I balk at that memory. Me and a baby. *That'd be crazy.*

Rubbing a hand over my rounded hip, I start to wonder if she's his type, the type of woman he dates in California?

Her eyes don't meet mine but go to him when the total is announced. "That will be eight hundred and thirty-seven dollars and twenty-three cents. Will that be cash or charge?"

Whipping my hand through the air, I make a whoosh sound as I hand the card over. I'd failed to notice his was already on the counter. Pulling it back across the slick surface, I inform him, "I'm buying my underwear."

He pushes the card forward again. "Okay, then I'll buy the teddy and the knickers."

"Why would you be buying me anything in this store, Harrison? Or any store for that matter?"

"Wishful thinking?"

"Are you asking if you're ever going to see these on me?"

"I'm hopeful." He is—his eyes, that grin that's tipping into a smirk, and the confidence that's always there in his body's frame.

"It's funny you say that when I didn't know where we stood after this morning. You got the worst of me." My gaze travels back to his black credit card just before she snatches it.

"On your card, sir?" she asks.

"I'm here, by the way. Standing right here and able to buy my own freaking overpriced underwear."

Jerking back as though I insulted her, she says, "I think I'll let you two work this out."

As soon as she walks away, I say, "You do realize she's hitting on you, right?" I shake my head in annoyance. "Like I'm not standing right here."

"The best revenge," he offers conspiratorially, "is to let me buy you these things like a good boyfriend. She'll be none the wiser to our plan."

"What plan is that? It's underwear. She'll probably think you're bankrolling an affair. And definitely have no respect for me."

"Why do you need her respect?"

Good question. "I don't need it," I lie. "I'm just saying—"

She returns, and I hush instantly like she might know we were talking about her. But then I say, "If you think paying for these things gives you automatic access to seeing them on me, you are—"

"The luckiest guy in Manhattan." He slips his hands on my waist and around to my lower back, and I let him. I also let him kiss my neck and then my cheek. Because he's not the only one who's lucky today . . .

Turning to the saleswoman, I say, "He's paying."

My eyes close, and the feel of his lips on my body again

has me giddy. *Every time he kisses me, I feel sexy. Wanted.* Yet not uncomfortable when he invades my space. That's different from other guys I've seen more seriously and casually. *Is he?*

Now that we've staked claim so publicly for her to witness, she's quick to speed this transaction along. At least she has the courtesy to hand *me* the bag.

As soon as we're back on the sidewalk, he takes my hand as we start walking again. "What are you doing?" I ask, pulling away from him. "She can't see us out here."

"Is that what you think, Tatum?" So smirky this Sunday. Just goes to show how far good looks and a bankroll will get you in life. He's confident, not to a fault but in a way that failure hasn't quite shaped. Even outside, I catch the sun worshipping at his feet. "You think what we did inside and holding hands out here was for her?"

"Well, sure, but . . ." I'm actually not sure what to say, so I look back at the store, wondering if I've misread the situation.

"No buts, but let me ask you."

I stare through the glass, but the saleswoman is nowhere to be found. "Wait a minute. Why do you get a but, but I don't?"

"You just got one." As the afternoon's carried on, Harrison's become decidedly more relaxed. Maybe champagne is his weakness.

Rolling my eyes, I slide my purse down to my elbow just so I can cross my arms over my chest. I never know how this will go with him, so it's best to be prepared, and by that, I mean brace myself for anything. "Let's move this along, shall we? What do you want to ask me?"

"What we did back there . . ." Looking down, he suddenly finds his shoes the most interesting thing around.

I should be offended since I wouldn't mind the honor, but him flipping from confident to coy in the matter of a few short back-and-forths is quite charming. Ugh. Fine, I find him the most fascinating thing around right now.

I can be honest with myself.

Lowering my arms to my sides, I take a step closer, and then another. I can appreciate how handsome he is even when I'm mad at him, but when I'm not so upset, he's definitely a temptation. "Yeah?"

"How'd that feel for you?" He closes the gap, keeping the question between us despite the other people passing by in a hurry. "My hands on you, my arms around your body, holding you close, and kissing you without a care about who sees us. How'd that feel, Tate?"

Hearing him call me that name hasn't bothered me since the morning I ran into him at Natalie's, sort of like the man himself. In fact, both have grown on me tremendously. "I . . ." Now I feel shy. I force my head up just so I can look into his eyes. "I liked it."

He nods, his smile genuine. "I did, too." He reaches for my hand again, but I meet him in the middle, and our hands clasp together.

I'm not sure if I like feeling this mushy inside over a guy or if I love it, though I'm leaning toward the latter at the moment. "Do you have plans for the rest of the day?" *Please say no.*

"Yes."

Disappointment deflates the hope that had been building in my chest. "Oh . . ."

"With you, Tate, if you don't mind me tagging along for the rest of your errands."

And *that* makes me happy.

My hold on him tightens, and I cling onto the hem of his

shirt with my other hand. "What if we skip all that to go back to mine and hang out?"

"Is that what the kids are calling it these days? Hanging out?"

Laughing, I shake my head. "I have no idea what the kids call it, but let's just see how the day rolls by." I really hope that includes rolling around in my bed. I don't know if I should be mad at myself for wanting him so much or thrilled that I get another chance. Either way, it beats sitting alone in my apartment.

His contentment is reflected in his expression. Not a care in the world lines that great face. "I really don't mind going with you. Where's the next stop?"

Eeks. "*Wellllll*, about that? I kind of don't have any errands."

"Just the lingerie shop today?" He tugs me into his big and deliciously strong arms. "I like your priorities."

Peering up at him, I confess, "My priorities were actually just to taunt you. I didn't need anything from that store."

The vibration from his chest is felt as soon as the sound reaches my ears. "Your taunts are actually tempting," he says, angling down to place a kiss just beneath my ear. The man knows how to tempt himself. "And teasing. Do you know how hard it—"

"No, tell me how hard it was?" I lick my lips and then bite them. I can feel how hard it's getting, inspiring me to get to this hanging out in a hurry.

Releasing my hand, he moves beside me and throws his arm over my shoulders. We start walking like we've walked arm in arm for years. It's disconcerting. *It's nice.* "I can't say I'm upset we're going to your place to 'hang out' after that comment. But I have to ask, how much farther?"

15

Tatum

TRYING TO RIDDLE THROUGH WHAT MY RELATIONSHIP WITH Harrison Decker is would take a genius. I don't have the time or interest. I just like the feel of his lips on mine and the way he holds me as if I'll disappear if he doesn't.

We didn't quite make it to the bedroom. Pinned to the hall wall, he forces his lips from mine, and then he drops to his knees, not so upset about me wearing a short skirt when it benefits him.

It flies up, and he ducks under, pressing his nose to the apex of my legs. I still with my palms to the wall behind me. Hot breath engulfs, and then the air is sucked right back in. "Fucking hell," he moans right before he cups me with his mouth and does it again.

My knees go weak, so I anchor a hand on the top of his head for extra support. His short nails gently scrape down my outer thighs as he takes the cotton thong down to my ankles.

I step out of one side then the other, and then rest back

again, closing my eyes and wondering if I'm going to survive his mouth on me. He takes no prisoners, and my vagina is next in line. Lord have mercy, I can't wait.

Anxious for more, I ask, "How are you doing down there?"

A finger is dragged through the split of my lips, and he leans forward to kiss. "So good."

The finger is replaced with his tongue, and the mercy I prayed for isn't granted. He thrusts like he's rushing against the clock, licking me with the flat of his tongue before returning to finish me. My leg is lifted over his shoulder, and the other is wedged against my other leg. He fucks me with his tongue and fingers, relentless in his pursuit to send over the edge without a chance to take a breath.

Holding on to his head with both hands, I feel the orgasm building, blooming, reaching the far edges of my body until I can't hold it inside. "Oh my God, Decker."

My body pulses, the weight on my leg giving way as the back of my head hits the wall behind me. I suck in a harsh breath before letting the sensations take over. Darkness fills the inside of my lids and then sparks of ecstasy light up my body like the Fourth of July.

It's quick, like I was, leaving my breath heavy in my chest but feeling so good. *How does he already know my body so well?* I pull my skirt off his head to reveal him resting his forehead against my lower belly. His breathing matches mine, his shoulders rising and falling as well. He looks up. "Did you call me Decker when you came?"

Laughter escapes me as he lowers my leg, steadying me. "I did."

He's chuckling as he straightens my skirt and holds me by the waist. "That's a first."

Fisting the front of his shirt, I pull him closer, kiss his

lips, and then whisper against them, "If you're not careful, I could get used to this hanging out business."

"As long as you're only hanging out with me, I'm good with it."

Veiled jealousy perhaps. At least I know I'm not alone in it.

I wrap my arms around his neck, holding him close. "Want to hang out in the bedroom so I can return the favor?"

"No. I'm good," he replies casually as though he doesn't want to be a bother.

News Flash: I'm happy to be hot and bothered if I'm with him.

Staring at him in astonishment and a little horniness I was hoping to satisfy, I ask, "What do you mean you're good?"

He cups my face and kisses me softly, my scent lightly coating his hands and mouth. "I mean, I'm good, baby. It gets me off to get you off."

"But—"

"No buts, remember?" Stroking my hair away from my face, he tucks it behind my ears. "Unless you insist. I won't deny your needs. Not ever."

I'm touched by his generosity and the sincerity in his tone, but then I say, "Yeah, I insist," because I need to feel him inside me again like last time. No walls or barriers —*physically or emotionally*—both of us in the raw, in this together.

He brings out something I never felt with anyone else, a craving to deepen the connection. I've never been this way, gone without a condom before, and now I'm hoping he didn't think to stop at the store.

I'm not above begging if that's what it takes. We've now climbed over that wall.

For me, there's no going back with him.

He sweeps me into his arms and walks into the bedroom. I can tell he's going to drag this out, probably to be romantic and stuff, which is sweet but not necessary for me.

Setting me on the bed with so much care that I'm afraid he thinks I'll break, he stands beside me and starts to undress. "You sure you're up for more?"

"I'm up for *so much more*," I say, running my hands over my chest.

I sit up and pull the ribbon holding the straps together on one shoulder, watching his reaction. His body gives him away, his erection growing in his pants.

He cups my face. *Damnit.* I don't want sweet.

I know how to spur him on because one thing I've learned is that Harrison Decker loves dirty talk. "Do you remember when you bent me over that counter in Catalina?"

"There's not one thing I don't remember about that night."

"I want you to do that to me again."

"With the mirror?"

"Yes." A wry grin appears on his face, so I add, "Yes, there's my bad, bad boy."

"Not a boy, babe."

Rubbing my hand over his cock, I reply, "Feels like all man to me." I pop the snap of his jeans and slide the zipper down. Peering up at him, I lick my lips and then ask, "May I? Just one taste?"

His shoulders straighten, so commanding, so sexy, and he replies, "No sampling the goods. You take it all, or you don't get any." He has a naughty mind to match mine. "What do you say?"

"Yes, and please."

"Fuck me," he growls, tugging his jeans down.

Why is it such a turn-on to role play with him?

I lie across the bed on my stomach and settle in just as he frees his dick. Bobbing in front of me, I take hold with one hand and then wrap my lips around the tip.

The feel of his fingers dig into the hair at the back of my head, encouraging me, but now that I'm in control, I intend to have some fun. I swirl my tongue around several times before allowing him to push past my lips. He's slow, calculated, letting me lead and cover the distance with my hand.

The sound of his moans mixed with mine, the struggle he has not to take control of my head, light touches accidentally push, causing me to gag, but only one time. He's a quick learner, too. I go deep and then tease back again until I find a rhythm that I can get lost in.

His body moves against my mouth, and his breathing becomes labored. It's not but a few minutes before steady turns erratic, and etiquette goes out the window. He's guiding me like a missile on a mission, and I take it, every bold inch of him like a hometown hero.

He pulls back suddenly and grabs me under the arms to pull me off the bed. As soon as I land on my feet, he says, "Get the fuck in there and be in position. You have until the count of ten."

A smack to my ass sends me in the right direction. I don't need to be told twice. I rush into the bathroom, my ass still tingling, and shove my crap to the far side of the counter. Bending over, I pull my skirt up and then brace myself on the cold marble.

I know for a fact that wasn't a solid ten seconds, but seeing Harrison enter the bathroom in the reflection of the mirror, his eyes locked on my backside, and smirking . . . my thighs rub together in anticipation.

He takes his time, hands on my upper ass and then sliding lower, two fingers running through my wetness and then rubbing it on his dick. Leaning over me, he kisses my back as he positions himself. "Did you think I'd come in your mouth when I could come in that sweet pussy of yours?"

Dear Lord, thank you for Harrison Decker.

He takes a hand full of my hair and pulls back until my chin is raised. Our eyes are locked in the mirror when he says, "Brace yourself."

I claw my fingers just as he takes me by the hips and slams into me. I hold my chin high, watching him as his face contorts. Lust. Greed. Gluttony. Pride. Most of the seven deadly sins are hammered into me. But if I search his blue irises, a hint of something softer appears when he looks at me. Like a rose, that same feeling continues to bloom inside me.

Closing my eyes, I try to block out the tenderness and focus on the other sensations I'm feeling. A quiver is felt and begins to spread outward. When I open my eyes, a fogged mirror hides part of him away from me. I reach forward and wipe it away, wanting to see every part of him claiming me.

"I'm so close, baby."

Baby. My heart flutters when I hear it.

I push up because I'm about to have another orgasm. Our stars collide, sending us both barreling over the edge from light to dark and sinking into the abyss of the beautiful aftermath.

My cheek rests on the stone, the cold feeling good against my heated cheek. I'm finally dragged back into reality when he says, "Was it as good as you remember?"

His hands rub over my shoulder, the sweetest Harrison

returned after a quick trip to the dark side. He helps me up, holding me upright until my balance returns.

Wrapping my arms around him, I rest against him, and say, "Better."

And that's why I made a pact with this man.

Because every time is better. And every time, I feel the utter joy and danger in being with a man who is such a self-less lover. *Because how do you pick yourself up from that once he leaves?*

16

Harrison

I'm a bag of bones craving another hit—*of her*.

It's more than attraction. Tatum's quickly becoming an addiction. She wanted to shower, but I asked her to stay. There's something earthy and sensual about giving our bodies to each other, losing control, and then lying in the aftermath of what we experienced together.

Leaning over, I kiss her back, both of her shoulder blades, and lick the space between and higher on her spine, leaving one last kiss on the back of her neck. Sweat and the salty air mixes, the taste an aphrodisiac. Our night has been more than I've ever had with anyone. I'm not even sure how we fit so much life into the last eight hours, but they're the hours I'll still be reminiscing about on my deathbed.

I drag my finger lightly over her skin, glistening in the moonlight, and then leave one more kiss because I'm not sure if I've kissed that spot already. "What if I want to call you?"

Tatum opens her eyes, a smile appearing. "Why would you want to do that?"

I can't figure her out. The women I've had sex with always want more of my time, not less. Do I suck in bed?

Nah. That can't be it.

The curtains billow in the breeze coming off the ocean, the sound of the waves heard through the open door to the balcony. Somewhere far off, music drifts through the air, though it barely reaches our ears. It's another layer to set the scene, making memories that will stick with me.

It was funny—maybe quirky is a better word—when she had me agreeing to a pact. Now, there's an unsettling in my gut that I'm not sure how to deal with. I slide down next to her, lying on my back, and turn to face her. "You might be the strangest girl I've ever met. You don't want me to call or text. We skipped the foreplay and got right to the sex."

"That's a rhyme."

"Oh no, you don't. That's cute, but I'm not letting you dodge this."

"You're cute," she says, tapping my nose, trying to detour this conversation. I've noticed she has a knack for avoiding things she doesn't want to talk about.

I tuck hair behind her ear. "I want to get to know you, Tate, but you make it hard." I shouldn't have phrased it that way—a perfect setup for jokes—but I try to keep us on topic. "Did I do something to upset you or—?"

"No." The answer is unhurried but to the point. "I've never had anyone question sex without strings."

"Maybe they didn't want more than that."

Her grin slips away as a strong breeze blows over us.

"What do you want me to say, Harrison, tell me and I'll say it," she says, her voice losing strength.

What is going on inside her head? What's happened that I'm reaping the repercussions?

"I don't want you to speak for me, to make me feel better. I want to hear what you want, what you need."

She wiggles, her hand sliding down my bicep. "Is this a roundabout way to tell me that you want to have sex again?" That's what it is with her—*only physical*.

Catching her hand just before it disappears under the sheet, I bring it between us and then kiss each fingertip and then her palm. "You have me right here wanting to learn everything about you, and you're still not going to let me in, are you?"

"You're not tired?" she asks. Closing her eyes, she blocks me out of delving deeper. I guess I got my answer. It doesn't take long for her breathing to steady and sleep to take her from me.

I stay up, hoping the sunrise comes before our goodbyes. Maybe the new day can shed some light on what I can't see lying here. We don't have that kind of time.

My dad was right. Nothing worth my time was built on hopes and dreams. It takes action to make things happen. I don't have a minute to spare to get the answers I need from her. With less than an hour before she needs to leave, I wake her up with kisses along her cheekbone and running my fingers through her long hair. "Tatum?" I whisper.

Her eyes slowly open and then close, her breath uneven as she tries again, stirring awake. "What time is it?"

"Four thirty."

She groans, her eyes still closed. "I have to get up, but I don't want to. I like it here much better."

"I like you here much better too. What about a later flight?"

She gasps as she bolts up. "Natalie." Jumping out of bed, she grabs a shirt, *mine to be exact*, and slips it on before rushing into the main part of the two-bedroom suite.

"What are you doing?" I call from bed.

I hear what sounds like her and Natalie talking in hushed voices and the door closing. "I'm sorry," Tatum says.

Indiscernible whispering follows, and then her friend asks, "He's still here?"

"Shh," Tatum says. "Yes."

After more whispering, I hear her friend say, "Don't be late."

"I won't."

Tatum returns to the room, closing the door quietly behind her. "I just remembered that I had the hotel keys. She's been locked out all night."

"Shit. She couldn't get one from the front desk?"

Moving into the bathroom, she flips the light switch on. Peeking back out, she says, "She said she tried, but I was carrying her wallet yesterday, so she didn't have ID." A mischievous grin sneaks onto her face. "Guess where she's been all night?"

"Where?" I hold the covers open for her, and she slips right in next to me as if she doesn't have a flight to catch. We lie next to each other with her tucked against my side.

"In your room with Nick."

Score one for my best friend. If anyone needed to get laid, it was him. Maybe he can learn to relax again. "That's interesting," I reply, trying not to sound like an asshole full of pride for my friend.

"I hope Natalie got laid."

"Really?"

She nods. "She's been on what she calls a love embargo for quite a while. This trip has been good for her to break back out of her shell. And Nick seemed like just the guy to help her."

"Not to brag, but he's a good guy, too. Stressed, but who isn't these days?"

"I'm not."

The response throws me a second. It's too late to get into how she's living a life so carefree when I have other motives in mind to get more time with her. "Nick is gold. She's lucky if—"

"I don't want to talk about them. We have so little time left. Do you mind?"

Holding her closer, I ask, "Why would I mind?"

The tips of her fingers graze over the skin on the outside of my eyes before her hand lowers to my chest. "One day, you're going to have smile lines. It's not fair."

"It's not fair that I'll have wrinkles? I'm pretty sure all of us will if we age naturally."

"No, I mean, you'll be even more devastatingly handsome than you are right now."

I kiss her forehead and then fall back to my pillow again. "You know, the pact isn't legally binding. It's just us, two parties, who can make or break it."

She pecks my lips, but there's not enough time to deepen it before she's getting out of bed. "Let's not mess this up by trying to make it something it's not. We'll just cause each other a lot of heartache, so why go through the trouble?"

"But what if—"

"I need to get ready. Will you stay until I need to leave?"

And just like that, she shut down all options but the one I've been trying to get around this whole time—a goodbye.

"I'll stay," I reply, swallowing down the scraps she's leaving me along with my pride. My heart lodges in my throat, and when the door closes, I close my eyes, hoping to wake up in a different state of mind.

A kiss wakes me up, and then another. "I'm leaving," she whispers.

When I open my eyes, the lamp on the dresser is on. It's not bright, but there's enough light to see she's fully dressed. She's stunning—the image of her before me will compete with remembering her at the peak of orgasm, sharing a laugh on the yacht as the sun sets, and feeding me grapes and then savoring it on my lips. Who am I kidding? I'll remember everything about her, even this goodbye.

She walks to the door in silence.

I pull the covers off, not caring that I'm naked, and get up to help her with the luggage. It's a good guise to actually be near her again.

Just as she yanks the handle from the top of the case, she kicks the bottom to get it angled. "Don't get up. You can stay and sleep."

"I want to." I go to her and hold her head to look at her as if I'll never see something of this magnitude again. It's not just her beauty, though. The soul that she carries in the amber of her brown eyes is magnificent like buried gold "I need to say something—"

"Please don't." The pain heard in her voice causes an ache in my heart. Her gaze falls from mine as her hands take hold of my arms.

I hate that my heart beats loud in my ears, and panic fills my chest. I'm losing her, and I'm just not ready yet. "What if I don't agree?"

"You already did." Her eyes finally return to mine. She throws her arms around me, holding me so tight that I think she might be panicking over this goodbye as well. She rests her head on my chest, her heart also beating just as fast.

I hold her, dipping my head against the top of hers and closing my eyes, savoring and memorizing everything I can.

She slips away too soon. I catch the subtle swipe from the side of her eyes, the jagged breath she takes, and how she forces that chin in the air, collecting herself back together again. "Go to bed. Get some sleep. That's what I'd be doing if I could stay." Playfully shoving me away, she says, "Go. You have hours until it's time to check out. Enjoy the bed."

"I'd enjoy the bed a lot more with you in it."

"Me too, but I need to go."

The space between us grows as I give her what she wants again. Climbing back into bed, I'm tired, but if this is the only way to end us on a good note, I'll do it. With the door pushing against her back and her suitcase handle poised in her hand, she looks into the living room of the hotel suite. I hear her friend ask, "Ready?"

"One minute."

She runs over and kisses me once more—lips pressed to mine like it's the last she'll ever get. I cup her face and hold her there, giving her one that will make her regret ever leaving.

Pulling back, she dips her forehead to mine and takes a breath as though it pains her. Then she returns to the door.

When she looks back at me, I ask, "Has anyone ever broken through that fortress?"

The slightest shake of her head follows, and then she says, "No one's ever made the effort."

I tuck my hands behind my head, sure as the day is new that I would be that man. "I always did love a good challenge."

Her head tilts as a smile graces her face, reaching all the way to her eyes and shining happiness right into the irises. "I give you all the outs in the world, and you're making it your life's mission?"

"No, I'm making you my mission." I wink at her.

She laughs, but I can see the color in her cheeks deepening. "There's nothing wrong with a good ending, Harrison, and we got one of the best."

"You wait and see, Tatum. This isn't over. This is just our beginning."

17

Tatum

New York - Four and a half years later . . .

I RETURN to the scene of the first passion-filled crime to get my panties off the floor, but they're not there. I look further into the living room and behind me toward my bedroom just in case they got kicked somewhere. There's no sign of them anywhere. I even check the spare room I currently use as my purse and shoe closet.

Not in there either. "Have you seen my underwear, Harrison? I can't find them anywhere."

"Check my jeans," he calls from the bedroom.

Walking into the bedroom, I ask, "Why would they be in your jeans?"

"I was going to keep them."

"Why?" I stop at the end of the bed. "As a souvenir? To add to your sordid panty collection you have back in California?"

Looking the way he does, I'd be easily lured if he offered me candy or anything for that matter. Hell, he doesn't even have to entice me. I'm a willing volunteer. He grumbles, "Why do I feel like this is leading me back to the candy murderer accusation?"

"I didn't accuse you of using candy to lure innocent victims into your murdering lair. Nor am I accusing you of sewing panties together to make a girlfriend."

His eyebrows are raised in shock like this stuff doesn't happen, and he says, "Your dirty mind may be a complete fucking turn-on, but damn, you get dark."

"I didn't come up with this stuff. I listened to a podcast that was that exact thing."

"You might want to lay off the true crime for a while."

"You're probably right. I can't even look at a banana anymore without thinking a milkman is going to shove it in my tailpipe and kill me with it."

His brows knit together, and he stares at me like *I'm* the milkman. "Do milkmen even exist anymore? And are we talking cars or human tailpipes?"

"They exist in the Midwest. Remind me never to go there. As for the tailpipe, you don't want to know."

"Yes, Tatum, you're much safer in New York City," he replies sarcastically and then has the nerve to laugh it off. He only knows what he hears on the TV. Stereotypes and I'm sure just the bad stuff. My city is my second love. I can't imagine living anywhere else.

But that does beg the question: *What is my first love?*

That remains to be seen. I've been reserving that spot for when it's revealed to me.

I'm starting to sound like Natalie's sister-in-law, Juni, or her mother-in-law, Cookie. Even Natalie dabbles in destiny. She claims that's what brought her and Nick together.

"What's wrong?" he asks. Snapping out of my thoughts, I didn't realize I'd been staring at Harrison the entire time.

I bend down and discover my thong tucked into the pocket of his jeans. "Nothing. Just a lot on my mind."

"Anything you want to talk about?"

Holding it by the hip band, I teasingly reply, "We might need to discuss this panty problem you have," and then swing it around the tip of my finger. "If you really want them, you can have them."

He's chuckling. "You make it sound so pervy that I can't even enjoy it now."

I don't even know what he's talking about, but I didn't mean to out his fetish. "Before I enable this habit, how many pairs have you stolen?"

Resting back, he tucks his hands behind his head, amused. "None. Yours were the only ones, and I know you won't believe me, but I just tucked them in my pocket so they wouldn't get dirty on the floor."

As thoughtful as that is, I cross my arms over my chest and study him with narrowed eyes. It's not hard to do as the guy is drop-dead gorgeous. I'll play it up anyway. "Suspicious."

"I can imagine since you're into all that stuff."

"I was going to add, but believable." I bend down and tuck them back in his pocket. I didn't actually care if he was stealing them. I just wanted in on one of his dirty little secrets. "Your honesty kind of took the fun out of it."

"You are so kinky, Devreux. Now get your ass in this bed, and let's binge-watch a show."

The covers are lifted for me when I approach. I climb under and snuggle against his side, resting my hand on his abdomen. "Binge-watching a show together is next level, right after hanging out."

"Is that so?" He bends his neck to the side to look into my eyes. "I'm ready. Are you?"

When his arm tightens around me, holding me so close that I may never want to leave this cocoon, I reply, "So ready."

At some point . . . I'm guessing three hours into our bingeing, the food arrives. Harrison springs from the bed to answer the door while I starfish on the mattress. It feels much too big and lonely without him in it.

A buzz on the nightstand has me rolling to my stomach and reaching for my phone, but then I pause when I realize it's his phone. It would be rude and violate his privacy to read his text messages, but the fool doesn't have a password on it. A fingerprint isn't even required to unlock it, so what's a person to do?

I lift on my elbows and spy the name—*Natalie Christiansen*—on the screen. Why is my best friend texting the guy I'm having intimate relations with?

No time like the present to find out and satisfy my curiosity.

Taking the phone in hand, I swipe to open the message and read: *Is everything okay? We didn't hear from you, and I'm worried.*

Why would she be worried?

Maybe because he hasn't come back from his mission to save me. I type: *Having a great time. Tatum is amazing.*

I put a smiley face and then erase it, thinking Harrison wouldn't use that. He probably uses frogs and the death face in his texts.

A return text from her arrives: *Really?*

Really, Natalie? My fingers fly across the screen: *Really. She's incredible. Great in bed, funny, an excellent cook. I couldn't dream of meeting a woman so complex and intelligent. I'm so grateful to have her in my life.*

My phone buzzes this time, but it's a call. I snatch it and roll onto my back. "Hello?" I answer as innocently as I can.

"Nice try, but what'd you do with the body?"

"Wow, no faith."

"Plenty of faith. I absolutely believe you'd get away with murder."

"I don't know if I should be proud or insulted."

She replies, "Proud." Her laughter echoes, and then she starts to tell Nick what we said.

"*Helloooooo*, I'm still here, Nat."

Harrison saunters in, holding two plates on top of a pizza box. *A welcome distraction.* Setting it down at the end of the mattress, he says, "Dinner is served." He goes into the bathroom and returns with a towel that he neatly places under the box.

He's a keeper.

He took care of me, and now he's taking care of my duvet. *God, that's something Nick would do for Nat.* He just keeps surprising me.

"Who are you talking to?" he asks.

"Natalie."

In my ear, Natalie says, "Ask him to report in."

"She said to report in." I laugh because this is so ridiculous.

"Tell her you're all good and taken care of." He winks, and I melt a little on the inside.

"He's taken good care of me, so no need to worry," I speak into the phone. "Our food's here, so I'm going to let you go. Oh and no need to worry. Harrison is safe with me here.

"Tatum," she replies, giggling. "Oh my God. Have the best time tonight."

We have already. "Thanks. We will. Now go have fun with your hubs, and we'll talk tomorrow at the office."

"Every detail, Tate. I mean it."

"Block off the morning. We have so much to talk about. Good night."

"Night."

He hands me a plate with two slices of pepperoni on it and then sits back in bed again. I ask, "She made you promise her details?"

"Yeah."

"She's living vicariously these days. The baby adds to her fear of missing out."

His eyes are directed at the TV screen. He hasn't started the show, but he's checked the volume and coloring. "Eh, we should all be so lucky to have what they do and a baby on the way to boot."

"There will be no booting of the baby on my watch."

Turning to me, he chews his bite, but I can see questions populating in his eyes. Just as I take a big bite, he asks, "So you're warming to the idea of being a godparent?"

"I am. I don't want to think about the tragedy that would place this child in our home, but I'm kind of excited to play such an important role in their life. How do you feel?"

"I feel the same." His fingertips run along the veins of my forearm. "I like knowing I'm in it with you as well."

"Yeah, I agree. It's not so overwhelming when you split the duties."

When I lean over to give him a kiss, my hip pushes the play button, and the show comes back on. We've talked enough about it to know where we stand. I feel good, even better being in the trenches with him. Their child will never lack love or support. I'll be there for every event and celebration in their life.

We binge, both food and the show, and then fall asleep wrapped in each other's arms.

Pain permeates my muscles, a soreness developed from a great workout or sex with Harrison. It's the latter, and I'll take it over and over again. But it sends me to the bathroom, slinking over to the medicine cabinet to search for pain relievers.

Naturally, I have sex with a machine of a man and think there will be no repercussions afterward. Not complaining. My hoo-ha may be exhausted, but I feel more relaxed than I have in a long time.

I've been busy, and there's been a lot of pressure coming from my current clients. The release was needed, and Harrison did a stellar job—three times to be precise. I pop two pain relievers and take a sip of water from the bottle I left on the nightstand before climbing back into bed.

His presence gives me comfort—his body warm and protective. I lie down and focus on him instead of the ache between my legs. My lids grow heavy, and it doesn't take long until I'm falling asleep again.

Unfortunately, this time, like earlier, I don't wake up to the smell of bacon or a hot-ass chef cooking me breakfast. I do have the pleasure of watching him shower, though, and that is pornographic.

I open the door to give him a kiss, and he tries to pull me in. "Join me. I'll make it worth your while."

"Mmm. You are so much trouble for me."

His lopsided grin stirs inner desires. No, I must stay focused. "I wish I could, but I don't want to get my hair wet because it will take too long to dry. I'll just take a quick shower after you."

He soaps his body, spending a little extra time on those incredible abs of his. I'm not sure how many crunches he does to define those, but it's a session I need to sit in on soon. "You sure?"

"Barely," I sigh longingly. "But today is the first day of the rest of my life. I have a plan in place that I am ready to put into action, so I need to get to the office."

"Sounds exciting. Hope to hear more about it when you have time."

"Really?"

"If it's something you're passionate about, why wouldn't I?"

It might have been in that moment that I see him differently. I see the handsome face and great body, know he could charm a gambler out of all of his money without wagering a bet, and has a sweet side that not many are privy too. But right then, I can feel in my bones that he's going to be a part, even a major part, of my life for years to come . . . Maybe forever.

An overwhelming emotion surges through me, and I'm quick to say, "Thank you." I shut the shower door and try to gain control of whatever this is I feel inside. It's good, light, filled with joy, but a lot . . . too much to figure out when standing in a steamy bathroom with him naked.

So distracting to my goals.

He makes me want to climb into that shower with him and enjoy the pleasure of our bodies connecting for hours. I must resist.

The best way is to start getting ready for the day with my normal routine. Just a little out of order until I can take a shower. I brush my teeth and wash my face. Smother my face in moisturizer and then pin my hair up on top of my head.

When he moves into the bedroom, I hop in the shower. This time, he opens the door. "I need to go. I have a showing this morning and need to get dressed." He leans in and kisses me. "Can I see you tonight?"

"I want that."

"I'll text you later, and we can make plans."

"Sounds good. Have a great day." He risks it all and leans in to kiss me again—deeper with intention—getting his face wet just to be there for me. He pulls back, licking his lips as if he'll taste more of me that way.

That man is smashing down my barriers, and I don't think I have a say in the matter. My heart is softening to this, whatever this is, and for the first time in my life, I kind of like it.

When he's gone, and I step out of the shower, I dry off and then pull my clothes out and lay them on the bed. With Harrison still on my mind, I open a drawer and grab my birth control packet from the bin where I keep it. He's distracting to more than my goals. I enjoy thinking about him and how nice it's been the past few days.

I return to the bed to get dressed and then retrieve a glass of water to take my pill. Feeling good and ready to tackle the day, I pop a pill from the package. Being too rough, it goes flying across the counter until it bounces to a stop.

It's while reaching for it that the silver foil packet catches my eyes. I've not thought about this in a few days. Sure, it's a routine I've had for years, but something in my gut has me counting the remaining pills.

Thirteen . . . is that right? I take it like clockwork, so I know I'm good to go.

But am I right?

I come in here and pop the pill from the packet. The pills corresponding to the last few days have been popped. So that is correct. The only question is if I took them. Going crazy trying to figure out this mystery, I start ticking through the days to remind myself.

Thursday - I took the pill with a bottle of water prior to meeting Natalie at her house. That was the same day she told me she's having a baby.

Friday - I took it before I went to the gym and ran into Elijah.

Saturday- I woke up and took it with a Diet Coke I had on my nightstand from the night before.

Sunday - I took the pill before brunch. . . *Wait. Did I?*

What happened on Sunday? Instead of days, I navigate through the events of that morning.

Harrison cooking breakfast.

The fight we had.

Running late for brunch.

Put the pill in the case in my bag to take when I got there —timing wise, that worked best.

I waited and had a mimosa . . . or a few.

Being stood up.

No, that can't be right.

Staring down at the pill in my hand, I feel my stomach tense. My gaze rises, and I'm met with a ghost-white reflection. I run to check the bag I was carrying that day. Pulling the pink purse from the shelf, I open the clasp and unzip the pocket to find the tiny pill case.

I remove the case with such precision that I don't hear a thing until I shake it. The rattle of a pill is as loud as an earthquake to my ears. Damnit.

Now I remember, I didn't take the pill on Sunday

because I was too distracted by Harrison and my mother. I return to the bathroom and pop it in my mouth along with the other to cover for the missed dose, chug some water, and then swallow them down. Relief is felt in fixing that mistake.

With all the troubles I've had lately, at least I'm not pregnant.

18

Harrison

"THIS IS ONE OF THE MOST COVETED UNITS IN THE BUILDING, and from my research, the apartment is a steal." I stand back near the kitchen island and let Lara, Kaz's wife, take it in.

She walks the length of the wall of windows, stops to look out at the view, and then turns to me to ask, "Why are they selling then?"

"Legal troubles. He needs to liquidate fast."

She turns her attention back to the view of Central Park. "Ah. Hence the steal, but it needs to feel right."

"There are numerous units available in this price range. You can walk away and find another in the next building. It all depends on what you're looking for."

Glancing at me over her shoulder, she says, "I like this building because it feels like a family could live here. Kaz and I had modern design in our last home, but my tastes are changing. Instead of white and minimal, I want warm and inviting, kid-friendly."

I don't dare ask if she's pregnant. I made that mistake

once at a bar in my early twenties. I was two sheets to the wind and congratulated her. She wasn't, and I was punched by her boyfriend.

With Lara's arm lithely placed over her stomach, she strolls the main room and then ends up in the kitchen. "I'm hoping we can start a family soon. The tour and the hours . . . It's been hard to find the right time."

"I can imagine." My phone vibrates in my pocket, but I made a rule when I started out in this business that the client in front of me deserves my complete attention. Especially when dealing with multimillion-dollar homes and the potential for hundreds of thousands in commission.

"Do you want kids one day, Harrison?" She's not crossing any lines with me. I'm an open book, and I've known her for a few years. "Someday. Like you and Kaz. The right time. The right place to settle into."

Her eyebrow arches, and she adds, "The right woman."

I chuckle. "Definitely with the right woman." Tatum comes to mind, but that's jumping ten spaces ahead. I move to the stove. "Top-of-the-line appliances are included and brand new."

"That's nice," she says under a soft laugh that tells me she's onto my distraction. "Kaz loves when I cook."

"Eating on the road must get old."

"For him, the bedroom is most important. He sleeps for weeks after the tour. I'll need complete blackout curtain or shades, preferably automatic, though that's something I can have installed after the purchase. I really don't want a renovation. I do that all day long for my job. I don't mind minor changes, but I'd rather be able to just move in." She snaps her fingers as something occurs to her. "We definitely need a tub to ice down his muscles. A rock star's life is never as glamorous as people assume."

"It has a freestanding tub. As for the bedroom, if you don't like this one, I have another place I can show you that might work better."

She follows me down the hall. "You mean you weren't going to anyway?"

I wait outside the door to allow her to feel the space when she enters. "Listening to Kaz, this place was about what you wanted." She's smiling when she turns back. "But hearing your priorities, it's about what's best for him."

"That's marriage, if you're one of the lucky ones."

We see two other apartments—one she loves and one she thinks he'll love. I'll leave that for them to decide. As soon as I drop her off at the hotel where she's staying, I pull my phone from the inside pocket of my jacket and check my messages in the back of the SUV.

That's strange . . .

Tatum—missed calls (2)

Tatum—1 text message. I tap to open her chat box.

Seeing the round box with her initials has me realizing that I've missed an opportunity—TD. Touchdown. Just thinking about scoring with her yesterday, getting her off in the hall, and then her returning the favor has me wearing a ridiculously big grin. *Fuck me, that mouth and body are magical.*

I could veer off the main path, getting lost in those memories, but when I read the messages, concern tugs inside.

First message: *Where are you? I need to talk.*

What would she need to talk about that can't wait until tonight when we made plans to see each other? Since hours have passed, I decide to call. Listening to the ring, I start to wonder if she might be one of those people who never answers their phone. Based on her master avoidance skills, I'm sure of it. "This box is full," the AI voice says.

"Figures."

Looking out the window, I don't even know where I am in the city to be able to tell her when I can meet her or where. I text anyway: *Just got out of an appointment. Is everything okay?*

I wait and watch for three dots to roll across the screen, hoping they do, but nothing comes. Should I detour the car to her apartment building? Or should I keep heading back to Nick and Natalie's?

Natalie.

She'll know what's going on. Just as I pull up her number, we hit a pothole, causing me to glance up. I recognize some of the landmarks, so maybe it's best I just ask about Tatum when I get back.

The vehicle pulls up to the curb, depositing me at Nick's. A weird feeling twists in my stomach as I rush up the stairs. Tatum and I haven't been texting up to this point. It's been the bane of our relationship, or should I say the lack of texts, actually. So it's surprising to see this one, but the missed calls are even more strange to receive. The smallest bit of hope grows with every step I take that maybe Tatum will be here, and I can ask her instead.

I'm hit with the smell of something delicious as soon as I walk in. "Hello?"

"Hey, Harrison," Natalie calls from the back of the house. When I reach the kitchen, she's cutting carrots.

I'm tempted to hit her with fifty questions, but I have to play this carefully. The last thing I'd want to hear is that Natalie told Tatum I was acting possessive and psycho. "What are you cooking?"

"Chicken noodle soup." She looks up with a self-deprecating grin. "I think it's called nesting actually. I can't seem to want to do anything other than get the house ready for this baby."

"That's understandable." Pulling a barstool out, I sit. I'm hoping she won't notice my bouncing knee. I'm not foolish enough to believe it will stop until I hear from Tate.

Leaning against the other side of the island, she asks, "How was your day?"

"I think it went well. Lara has two great choices. She only has to decide what's most important right now. The rest she tends to fix and personalize. I was gone longer than expected, though. Have you heard from Tatum today?" *Worst transition ever.*

She starts to laugh, stirring the pot, and I wonder if it's just the soup by how she glances at me out of the corners of her eyes. "She was meeting with a client today. I haven't gotten an update all day." Setting the spoon down, she continues, "Some clients like to be babied and decide every detail instead of letting us do our job, especially with so much money involved. Others don't want to think about a thing and let us handle it all. She's working with the former, so I've not heard anything from her. It seems you two are finally getting along."

"A lot of years and troubles have flowed under our bridge, but . . ." I chuckle, smiling ear to ear. "Yeah, we're getting along."

I understand her curiosity in how Tatum and I made amends. I also get that Tatum's her best friend and most likely tells her everything.

"Yesterday was good?" she asks.

"It was a great day." I shrug, feeling a little gun-shy to reveal too much. "Things between us are evolving. Yesterday helped."

"I'm happy to hear that, Harrison. For both of you." She looks around as if she's checking for eavesdroppers, and then says, "Tatum's birthday is in two weeks."

And there's the gut punch. "She didn't tell me." *And I hadn't asked.* It's obvious we still have ground to cover if we are going to move forward.

"She usually loves making a big deal out of it and celebrating all month long. But this year, she's been silent, so I'm not sure what's going on. Maybe the situation with her mom, but I'd love to surprise her and do something to show we care."

"So you want to have a party?"

"Yes, and I'm hoping you can help keep her off the scent."

"I'll do whatever you need." *What do you buy the woman who not only has everything but can buy anything she wants? On top of that, she's a professional gift-buyer. I'm so screwed.*

"I was thinking it could be the week of her birthday, but on Tuesday night, instead of Thursday when she'll expect it. I know a Tuesday is a weird night for a party, but she doesn't have anything scheduled as of right now. I think it's the only way to pull this off. What do you think?"

"Sounds like a good plan. You said it's that Thursday?"

I try to ignore the all-knowing grin. I just need the details. Not the side of sass.

"It sure is," she says.

Good to know. Good to know.

While she goes over this elaborate scheme that she apparently just whipped up off the top of her head, I look at my phone, wondering why I haven't heard back from Tatum.

"Harrison?"

I look up. "Yeah?"

"Did you hear anything I said?"

I look to the left, trying to recall, but all I get is, "Two weeks Tuesday."

She starts cackling. "Oh my God, you're smitten with Tatum." Adjusting a knob on the stove, she then passes by and pats me on the way to the stairs. "That is the cutest thing ever."

"Don't say anything to her, okay? She's skittish."

"Boy, don't I know it." Climbing a few steps, she turns back to add, "Your secret is safe with me. Will you still help me with the plan?"

"Anything you need."

"I'll text you the details. If you're hungry, there's food in the fridge, and the soup will be done in an hour." She starts walking again. "I want to get the mural sketched so I can move onto painting. There's so much left to do and only seven months to do it. I'll be back down in a few minutes to check on the soup."

"Thanks, Natalie."

"My pleasure."

I can't sit here wondering what Tatum needed to talk to me about, so I decide to try to find her. I'll start with her apartment.

19

Harrison

I CAN'T GET PAST HER DOORMAN.

After pleading my case, he threatened to call the police. At least I know she's safe in this building.

Standing outside on the sidewalk to avoid getting a criminal record in New York City, I call her. Again, there's no answer. "Fuck."

Going a different route, I call Natalie. "Hello?" She answers like she didn't see my name pop up.

"Natalie, it's Harrison."

A soft laugh is heard. "I know. Does anybody not have caller ID?"

"Nope. Hey, I'm still looking for Tatum. I went by her apartment, but she's not around. Do you think she's at the office?"

"I can find out. Hold on." The line goes quiet as I stand here waiting, trying to recall if she ever told me where in the city the office is located.

I shift, thinking I should grab a cab because I'm either

heading to STJ's offices or heading back to Natalie's. I walk to the curb, but when I hear, "Harrison?" I stop in the middle of the sidewalk.

"It's me."

"She's at the office. I just confirmed on the security camera. It's after hours, so no one answered, and I didn't want to call her because it would ruin the surprise."

"I'm not trying to surprise her. I'm trying to find her."

"Same thing," she says. If pep in her step could be heard in a voice, she just nailed it. "I'll text you the office code to get in. It will be so romantic."

Holding my finger up like she can see it, I reply, "I think that's making this bigger than it is."

"She'll love it."

"Natalie?"

"Yes?"

She sounds too happy to burst her bubble. I shake my head, but I'm smiling. It's good to have Tatum's best friend's support. "Don't forget to text me the code. Oh, and the address."

"Doing it now. Good luck!"

"Thanks. I'm going to need it." With my toes hanging over the curb, I throw my arm into the air to get a taxi.

SoHo isn't far on a map. Throw in some major traffic and that's an hour I'll never get back. I have no idea if she's still at work, but I'm going to give this my best shot. Just not empty-handed.

I turn in circles searching for a flower shop, or gift store, or anything, but most appear to be closed. I'm left with two options—coffee shop or a hot dog stand. Since the line is twenty people deep at the coffee shop, I rush to the stand, knowing this is fucking stupid but do it anyway. "Two hot dogs, please."

Five minutes later, the elevator opens on the floor, and I walk toward the glass front door. After punching in the code, I gain entrance and start slowly scoping out the place. Pink walls, floral designs, and white desks. It's very feminine, and I can see Natalie's and Tatum's tastes represented —high fashion mixed with low-key cool and pretty.

The lights are off, but as the sun sets outside, it's easy to spy one light coming from an office down the corridor. But the last thing I want to do is scare her, so I try to figure out how I let her know I'm here.

"Decker?"

I whip around to see Tatum standing with a stack of gifts in her arms. "Hey. Hi. I got your messages. Well, there were no messages per se, but missed calls. Anyway, I'd show you, but my hands are full of wieners." *Fucking hell, why'd I say that?*

Her gaze volleys back and forth between my hands. A grin wiggles across her lips, and then splits as she starts to laugh. "Do you need some alone time with your wieners?"

"Fuck, I sound like an idiot. I brought you a hot dog, but I'm not even sure if you eat them."

She comes closer and signals toward the office where the light is streaming. "Come on." There's no sign of distress or urgency. Her body language is relaxed despite holding the gifts. I'm starting to think I was reading too much into a few missed calls.

I follow her into the office and look around. Although there is one, there's no need for a name placard next to the door. This room has Tatum written all over it. The walls are painted in bold black and white stripes, her desk is white as well as the console and shelves behind her to break up the pattern. Accents of pink dot the space from bookends to pillows on the deep green velvet couch. Windows expand from one end to the other corner. "That's a helluva view."

She sets the boxes down on a table in front of the couch and looks out like she's just noticing it for the first time. With her hands on her hips, she replies, "For a people watcher like myself, it's terribly distracting."

"I bet. Hot dog?" I offer her my wiener and then laugh inwardly because yes, I'm a prepubescent boy all of a sudden.

Her bottom lip drops on one side as she stares at the offering. Damn, I almost take the rejection personally.

Then she takes it and says, "I haven't had a street dog since I was fourteen. I threw up for five blocks trying to get home after getting food poisoning. You can imagine what a delight I was for Natalie. Barely teenagers. Trying to be cool. And her best friend puking all over the sidewalk every thirty feet." She sits on the couch, leaving room for me unlike how she sleeps, hogging the middle. "I was lucky it came out that way. Here goes nothing . . ." She takes a big bite.

I'm not sure if I have the stomach for it now. "You don't have to eat it. The flower shop was closed."

She chews, but a smile shines in the shape of her eyes. "You were going to get me flowers?" I nod, but then she says, "The dog is much more original. Way to stand out."

I set my hot dog down on the table, and ask, "You called me?"

"Yeah, Um . . . I had a . . . moment today." She follows me and sets her dog down, too. "Earlier. Much earlier," she replies, waving me off.

"I'm glad you reached out to me. Do you want to talk about it?"

"Not really. It was silly. Nothing was actually wrong in the end. I think I just . . . hm. Did you know we've never texted? Well, you did a little while ago. I was going to text back when I knew what to say."

I'm not sure what to make of her right now. There's a frenzied pace to her words, and she bit off more than she could chew quickly, almost like she was wanting to end the conversation. "And you don't know?"

She blinks a few times but doesn't lose eye contact. I appreciate that. "I'm not sure it's worth talking about anymore."

As if she crossed that T, she appears finished with that line of questioning. That has me changing tactics. "How was your day?"

"Busy. I have a client that I can't seem to please. He insists on meeting after meeting about the most trivial stuff. Like those boxes." *And she's off like nothing ever happened.* "He wanted to see the gift-wrapping options and how we can mix it up for him. Our wrapping is custom-made to fit the occasion, but he wants me to whip something together just to show him the bow. It's ridiculous. His wife won't care about the box once she sees what's inside."

"What's inside?"

She rolls her eyes. "Don't even get me started. That's a whole other list, and he can't decide. So basically, I'm showing him boxes for a gift that might not even fit inside. He told me that I'm doing too good of a job, and I made this difficult for him. He wants to meet soon to discuss everything over lunch again. I'm exhausted. He only eats pasta with me because his wife doesn't allow him to eat it."

"Is he hitting on you?"

"*Of course, he is.* I see right through it. But when he's spending six figures on an anniversary present, I'm supposed to be available."

"No, you're supposed to find the perfect gift. That doesn't

include you." I shouldn't have snapped, but I fucking hate men who prey on women. It's different if they ask you to, which has happened to me before. It just wasn't my brand of kink.

She jerks her head back. It's subtle, but I see the change in her demeanor. A beguiling smile, that look in her eyes that tells me I've lit a fire inside, and her hand rubs over my knee. "Oh my, Mr. Decker, do I detect a note of jealousy?"

"Is that a turn-on for you?"

Stilling, she keeps her eyes locked on mine as she seems to digest the question. "You're a turn-on for me." She leans forward to kiss me. I won't turn her down. Fuck, I want her just as much. I always want to know what's going on inside her head. Rejection won't win me points, so I kiss her. The feel of her lips pressed to mine makes it hard to stand on some made-up principle.

I stop, though. I hate myself for doing it, but it has to be done. "I want to take you to dinner, or we can order in if you're not up for it. I just want more time with you. I like hearing about your day and your thoughts on wrapping paper. I like seeing where you work and . . ." I run a hand through my hair, looking down. When I look back up at her, her eyes are set on mine, but there's a softness at the corners.

She asks, "And?" The anticipation is thread through the simple request.

"And I get why he'd want more time than he should get with you." The fucker better not try anything. "Given the chance, Tate, I'd spend every minute with you, too, if I had my way."

"Have your way with me then, and let's go back to my place." Taking hold of my hands, she urges me forward. "We can order food and hang out in bed, watch TV, and you know, just be together. Only the two of us."

"You sure that's what you want?"

She gets up and settles on my lap, wrapping her arms around me. "I do, Harrison. It sounds like the best date ever." My head is kissed and then my temple.

I'm not sure I can take credit, but the woman who is used to getting anything she wants doesn't want much with me . . . *wait*, that came out wrong. She's content with me. *That's better.*

With my arms around her middle, I hold her on my lap and look at her. "I think so too. You ready to head out, or do you need to wrap some things up first?"

"I'm ready. I was working late to avoid going home alone. My head will wander to a billion places that I don't want to go if left to its own devices."

She's starting to open up without having to use ploys or tactics. That's progress, and I'll take it. "You sure you don't want to talk about anything?"

"Not yet." Her arms tighten around me, and we kiss again. "Is that okay?"

Rubbing her hip, I nod. "Of course. Whenever you're ready, I'll be here." I want to push to get answers, but pushing Tatum will only push her away.

She hops off my lap, her skirt clinging to her curves, her high heels solid in her stance. The woman is skilled standing in those all day. She moves around her desk and takes care of a few things before asking, "Ready?"

I stand and join her at the door. When she closes it, I take her hand, and we walk through the empty office together. At the elevator, she asks, "How'd you get in?"

Wrapping my arm around her shoulders, I reply, "Natalie."

A small smile appears, and she looks up at me. "She's hoping we get together."

"And here I thought we already had." The door slides open, and we step into the empty elevator. "We once made a pact not to."

"Since we're making this up as we go, let's start with breaking our own rule." I caress her face and then kiss her because I need to. Because . . . I fucking missed her today.

20

Tatum

ALERT THE PRESS!

Letting Harrison into my world has been surprisingly easy. *Shocking, I know.*

He has me feeling hopeful. Despite not knowing what comes next, about the pregnancy, or even what we're going to binge-watch, I don't mind the unknown so much when I'm with him.

Simply because he's here.

He's shown up.

Literally. Well, four or so years later, but I feel like I'm seeing what he meant now. As if he knew to wait until now. As if he was waiting until I was ready to welcome him into my heart. My life.

"You wait and see, Tatum. This isn't over. This is just our beginning."

I can still hear him making that promise—so sure of himself. That promise he made back in Catalina was kept. He did that. *For me.* He says what he means and stands by it.

Other than Natalie, Harrison Decker is the only person to make me believe he'll be there for me. No matter what. Maybe that's why I'm not so stressed.

It's been a long time since I've felt this much for someone. He's given so much of himself to me that I'm not sure if he's received the same from me in return.

These haven't been baby steps. They've been millimeters I've been taking. That time is over. I'm ready to take a leap with him.

I turn my head abruptly to the man beside me in bed when a bulb goes off inside my head, shining light on how I treat him. I think he's right. I have been holding the past sins and pains from every other guy I dated against you, for my parents not being around, and the loneliness I've felt from being left behind. I lightly caress his cheek. I made a mistake missing out on great he is all the years.

The slumbering sounds of the sleeping giant next to me have me clicking off the TV and snuggling to his side. Even without waking up, his arm tightens around me, subconsciously making the effort he mimics when he's awake. It's too soon for me to dive into my emotions all the way, but I'm feeling buoyant. I giggle, amusing myself.

Checking the time, I see it's after midnight. Not late compared to my partying days, but maybe those days are behind me. More nights in bingeing shows, *and Harrison*, is much more entertaining. I close my eyes, relishing the feel of my future beside me.

My night is restless, and I toss and turn, memories from Catalina coming back from years ago . . .

Catalina - Four and a half years ago . . .

Moving quietly around the room, I toss the rest of my belongings into my suitcase and lock it, careful not to wake him. I could walk out of here. It's been fun, a good time spent with him, but flings are meant to stay at the scene, not trail people back to their real lives.

My instinct is to run and not prolong the inevitable. But my heart keeps intervening and keeping my feet where they are. Relationships require responsibility, and that's just not something I'm into. Why would I give up my freedom to stay home all the time?

Harrison seems like the kind of guy who likes to go out, so maybe that wouldn't be an issue. Him living on the West Coast is, though. I don't know one couple who has survived a long-distance relationship. My mom even gave up her own goals to travel with my dad to support him.

Yeah, I'm not interested in dating someone I can't go to bed with each night or have to get off by hooking up over video conferencing. The cards are stacked against us, and my gut tells me to run.

It's what I do best—avoid putting myself in situations that are doomed to fail. *Avoid giving my heart to someone for them to just leave me, too.* Not. Doing. That.

He sleeps so peacefully that I go closer just to admire him once more. *Is he worth trying for, though? Was he disappointed with the pact because he considered us worth more than one night?* With the light from the bathroom shining a path to the bed, I give him a kiss on the head and then bend to press my lips to his one last time.

My heart is racing, and my mind is in conflict. I grab the pad of paper and pen with the hotel logo from the nightstand and scribble my number quickly on it. Folding it in half and then in half again, I move to his shirt and tuck it in the front pocket.

I may have made a rash decision with the pact, but I've given him a way out. I don't know if he'll take it, but I need to believe that what is meant to happen will in the end.

New York - Four and a half years later . . .

"I don't understand?"

We had four great days. I was starting to get used to having Harrison around. And then California called, and he was right back on a plane. I miss his kisses all over my body and seeing his sleepy face in the morning. Although I like that we're now texting, I prefer the old-fashioned way of communicating with him—face-to-face.

Five days apart from each other and we've resorted to him miming a fork and bringing it his mouth over live video. He says, "It's food that's served to you."

I start to laugh. Fine. I'm busted. I still find him not only amusing, but quite endearing in his efforts to entertain me. "I know what dinner is, Harrison, but I'm lost on the date part."

"*Ohhh.* That's easy. It's when someone, aka the date, comes to your building and picks you up to take you out for food, drinks, sex, whatever you want."

I roll my eyes, and then start laughing. "You're incorrigible, you know that?"

"I actually do know that. One of my nannies used to call me irredeemable to my face and then would tell my mother what a delightful child I was."

Huh? "Cute story . . . *I guess.*" Holding my finger up, I add, "You're also frustrating."

"Again, not the first one to call me that. But you mean it

in an utterly adorable way, right? Not like this mean nanny I had at five used to call me?"

Staring at him, I say, "Yeah, totally. How many nannies did you go through?"

He lies in bed, exposing those manly hairs on his chest—maintained, but still enough for me to run my fingers over. He woke up just to spend time with me. I'm glad he did. It just makes my heart ache a little to know this might be it for the day.

With a chuckle, he replies, "A few, but who's counting?"

"Your mom most likely." I giggle. Wiping the mascara wand on the bottle, I say, "I just don't understand why we can't order in when you get back? I like being home with you and the last option you mentioned." Leaning forward, I open my mouth as I put on mascara like I'm performing surgery—meticulous to coating each lash individually.

"The sex? You like the sex, Tate. That's good to hear because I can't wait to be with you again."

"I just miss spending time with you."

"That's music to my ears, but we've gone from zero to sixty in a matter of two weeks at best. I'm not complaining, but I feel like I've failed you in some ways."

"You haven't."

"Let me take you out on a date." I hold up the phone to see his face and smile when I do. He's lying on his side, appearing ready to fall asleep again.

Can I really deny him something he wants so badly? "If it means that much to you—"

"It does."

"Okay," I reply, kissing the screen and wishing it was really him. I move back into the bedroom to retrieve my shoes. "What should I wear?"

"Something that makes you feel pretty."

"How about something that you think is pretty on me?" I waggle my eyebrows at the phone.

"No. I think you're gorgeous with nothing on or dressed for a party and every way in between. So wear what makes you feel your best because you're beautiful to me."

Swooning was something I thought only happened in fairy tales, the movies, or romance novels but never to me. Yet here I am, about to fall backward on the mattress needing a moment to recover from his charm. "You make it hard to go to work."

"You make it hard."

"Only a couple of times last night," I say, giving him a wink.

Holding the phone to his mouth, he kisses me. I hope we always start our day together, whether he's here or there.

We could, whispers a voice in the back of my head.

This could be my life.

All I have to do is not screw it up.

He asks, "How's six thirty tomorrow night?"

Just take it.

"That works." I can tell he's tired. New York being three hours ahead gives me the advantage. "I think you're wonderful."

"Oh yeah?" He licks his lips, and it's seriously distracting. "What happened to incorrigible and frustrating?"

"I think I was seeing everything through the wrong lens."

"And now you're not?"

"No. I see clearly."

He lands a peck on the phone, and says, "Good." Though he could have said about time as easily. "I'll see you tomorrow, Tate. Have a great day."

"I'll see you then. I can't wait."

Giving in to the good things in life isn't so difficult, after all. I can find happiness. It just took finding the right person to make me see what's right in front of me.

The next day

"Look, Mr. Daly. As I appreciate the compliments regarding my job, we will need to keep our relationship professional and focused on your anniversary gift for Mrs. Daly, or we'll need to part ways. How would you like to proceed?"

I shouldn't have given him an option. I could have walked away when his hand landed on mine. Natalie would have backed me. Doesn't matter how big a client he is.

But taking a breath, I know I have done everything that I should by not only calling him out on reprehensible behavior but also giving him a second chance not to be an asshole.

He slides his hand back to his side of the table, his gaze going to the printout in front of him, next to the scraped clean plate of pasta. "I think Mrs. Daly will like the ring."

I smile. "Excellent choice. Your card will be charged, and I'll make sure it's on the yacht by noon on the day of your anniversary. I've already handled the catering per your requests, so I think we're all set. Do you have any questions?"

"How is a pretty girl like you still single?"

Standing up, I grab my purse, sliding it down to the nook of my elbow. I pick up my pad and pen and tuck them into my bag. Resting my hand on the table, I lean forward, and say, "Because most men can't handle my bite."

I walk away from the table, not shaking like I would have done two years ago. My voice didn't tremble. I walk out of the restaurant feeling proud, proud of the career I've built, and that I stood up for myself.

Outside, I take a deep breath, letting the warm summer air wash over me. But then I get going because I don't want to sweat.

When I get back to the office, I give Natalie a play-by-play, but when she has to leave early for an appointment, I get back to work. I used to have to network to get new clients. Now I just have to check my email.

After ordering the ring for Mrs. Daly, I hang up with the jeweler and check my phone just in case I've missed anything. I notice the little monthly star highlighting my menstrual app. That's odd. I could have sworn my period isn't due for another day or two.

I double-click it to clear it and start going through the extensive list of emails. If I don't, I'll never get out of here, and I don't want to be late, not tonight.

Renee comes in, and asks, "Working late?"

Late? I glance at my phone. "Oh shit." I jump up, scrambling to toss everything in my bag. "I am late."

"For?"

"A date."

"A date?" she asks, her interest piqued as she leans against the door. "Do tell . . ."

I glance up, but I'm not looking to spill the beans. She says, "Wow, he must be special to make you smile like that. *My, my*, Tatum."

I giggle, letting it out like a little schoolgirl. "He is." I grab my phone and toss it in my bag just as I reach her. "He's special, all right." I pass her, and as she trails me toward the elevators, I add, "Don't tell anyone. I don't want to ruin it."

"My lips are sealed."

After we part ways, I hurry. I know that app is probably

unreliable, or I forgot to enter something correctly, but I had wanted to stop at a pharmacy to grab a pregnancy test to put that niggling in my stomach to rest. I'm undecided if I actually need one, but feel I should have one handy if I get worried again or . . . just in case. It's good to have one or two on hand. If I catch a cab, by the time I get home, I'll have just enough time to change clothes.

I'm kicking my shoes off as soon as I enter the apartment, my bag dropped by the door. My dress is unzipped in the back by the time I reach the bedroom and I'm naked when I'm standing in front of my lingerie drawer. I pull the teddy Harrison bought me and slip it on. A little black dress over it may not be original, but it's a classic for a reason.

T-minus ten minutes.

I have a date, and with a man I thought I hated. Life sure does throw some curveballs. I squeal with giddiness, running into the bathroom, but my stomach clenches, causing me to stop. Resting my hand on the doorframe, I pause as the taste of bile coats my throat.

I rush to the toilet and lift the lid. The thought of throwing up messes with my head, and I'm not sure if that's making me sick or . . . *Surely not . . .*

Paranoia sets in, ready to ruin my happiness.

I'm not pregnant. *Don't be ridiculous, Tatum.*

I pad through the apartment back to the front door to pull my phone from my bag and check my period app again. That icon a shining star as if that can make up for the monthly pain women have to endure. I scroll down the page, and yesterday's date is highlighted as the first day of my period.

That can't be.

With the phone in hand, I run to find the calendar I keep in the kitchen. I track the dates by the foods I eat each day, so I don't have to wonder why I'm suddenly five pounds heavier. I flip to last month and then compare on the app.

My breath stops hard in my chest just as a text pops onto the screen.

Harrison: *I got here early because I can't wait to see you. No hurry, but I'm parked out front in the black car when you're ready.*

My heart slides into my throat like a lump I can't swallow down.

I've met the sweetest man I've ever known and now . . . well, I don't know what now. I need to take a test and put this worry of the unknown behind me.

The unknown. I sigh.

My old familiar enemy. I'm never allowed too much happiness.

I was embracing the unknown not long ago, as long as I was in it with him.

Holding tight to the good memories, I finish getting dressed and then head downstairs in a slight daze.

The doorman opens the door, and there he is—*the best sight in the world.* I could cry if I let my emotions continue to get the better of me. I won't, though. Seeing him in a dark suit and tie against the backdrop of a white shirt, Harrison is the most handsome man I've ever seen. His dark blond hair layered on top hangs just over his forehead. It's shorter than when I met him, but still so California that I can't help but want to run my fingers through it. He even looks tanner. I guess it's from all that surfing he said he did.

"You're breathtaking," he says, coming toward me with a bouquet of sad-looking bent and broken orange poppies, actually sounding out of breath. *Oh, my sweet man.*

He hands them to me and then kisses me on the cheek. He's also a wise man to know not to mess up a woman's lipstick unless she wants you to. But it's been a week. I want him to.

Throwing my arms around him, we embrace like we mean it. "I missed you so much," I say.

"I missed you more than you'll ever know." With my head tucked against him, I close my eyes and savor his words and the feel of him again. He kisses the top of my head, and when I finally look up, he says, "Hi," like we're not standing in the middle of New York City, but alone in the apartment just the two of us.

"Hi." Screw it. I mess up my lipstick and kiss him. "Thank you. These are beautiful."

"They're poppies. I carried them on the flight. They don't last long once cut."

And my knees weaken from the sweetness. Holding the bouquet to my nose, I say, "They're perfect. My doorman can deliver them to the apartment." We drop them off and then head for the car. When I dip to get inside the car, the corner store catches my eyes, and I step back out again. Standing against him, I place my hands on his chest. "Do you mind if I pop into the store real fast?"

He glances behind him and then turns back. "I can run and get it for you."

"No," I reply, moving around him. Walking backward, I encourage him into the car. "I'll be quick."

"I'll be here." His smile could knock a woman on her ass if she's not careful. If I weren't on a mission, I'd be running into his arms and jumping that hunk of a man.

Not wanting to keep him waiting. I grab a two-pack of tests, avoiding the cashier's eyes. After I pay, I rip the box open and dispose of it and then tuck the tests safely inside my clutch to hide. No sense in ruining our reunion by worrying him.

21

Tatum

SILVERWARE CLANGS.

Crystal glasses chime in celebratory toasts.

Dinner plates are delivered full and then swiftly cleared after dinner.

Voices fill the space, but they're all indistinguishable in hushed tones. Just white noise in the chaotic restaurant.

Except one.

One breaks through my thoughts.

"Tate?"

My gaze returns to my dinner date, the dashing Mr. Decker. "Yeah?"

"You seem lost in thought. What's on your mind?"

"Nothing."

"Your mind is blank?" He smiles, so it's easy to pick up on his joke despite the steadiness of his tone.

My cheeks heat, slightly embarrassed by my mental absence, and I laugh lightly. "No. I was just people watching."

Reaching across the table, he covers my hand with his. This is the hand I want to hold, longer than tonight and tomorrow. Hoping . . . I don't know what to hope for. He says, "I like to Tatum watch myself, but that's a personal preference."

Fuzzy thoughts on what I want or am doing, what will change if I'm pregnant and what will stay the same. I look at my untouched wine, a glass I ordered for cover, and then reach for my water glass instead.

"Yeah . . ." I take two big gulps, emptying it. *Again.*

"What's going on?" He slides his full glass of water toward me without a second thought.

"Tatum watching. I get it. I like to watch you—shower, sleep, watching TV. I really like watching you cook."

He sets his fork down and takes a heavy breath before asking, "What's happening here? Did I do something wrong?"

"No." I push my barely touched grilled tilapia away, knowing the few bites of that and the asparagus are all I can stomach. "It's not you." I turn my hand over, fingers wrapped around, and our palms pressed together.

"Then what is it? You don't like the food or the restaurant?"

"I love this restaurant. You got everything right tonight, from the flowers to the food to that suit. If I haven't told you, you look very handsome tonight."

The side of his lips rises, and though it's not a smirk, his smile's gone rogue. He's too attractive wearing his heart on his sleeve like he's doing now. If I didn't know him, I'd expect arrogance or even some braggy tales from the past.

I clearly misjudged him.

"Then what's wrong?" he asks.

"Just stuff on my mind." I don't want the attention on me. I hate it sometimes despite my reputation.

"Please talk to me."

How can I not share but still expect him to be open with me?

I can't.

I made a pact with myself the night before he left to treat him how he treats me, so I take a breath and open my mouth. "I stood up to Mr. Daly today after he touched my hand inappropriately. I've not been feeling my best today, and nobody's said a word about my birthday this week when Natalie and I have usually been planning it for a month. Also, I have no idea where in the world my parents are because I haven't heard from them since Natalie's anniversary party. The last few weeks I had with you were the best I've had in years because of a man I spent years hating." I sag in my chair, exhausted. "Then it felt like we shifted back to square one when you left for almost a week. But worst of all, the tilapia had no flavor."

"I'm sorry about your birthday. I wonder if she's been a bit distracted with her pregnancy, and the awesome suggestions her brilliant sidekick has suggested for STJ?"

I smile, because he could be right. She has had a lot on her mind. Tossing all manners aside, I rest my elbow on the table and my chin in my hand. "Honestly, my birthday has been the last thing on my mind. Call it age or maturity or too much other stuff to worry about, but I'm not upset about not having plans yet. Everything just seemed off while you were gone. I was busy as usual, but I don't know."

A server refills the water glasses and then leaves. "I'm flattered to hear I was missed, but I don't want you sad." Harrison asks, "Did I catch that you're not feeling well or just a bad day?"

Sitting up, I had hoped to blend that in with the rest a

little better and wished he hadn't heard it at all. "My stomach is just a little off. That's all. I don't think I made a good choice for dinner with that going on."

"We should leave. Rumor has it that Natalie has been on a soup making quest. Chicken noodle last week, Nick said he was stuffed on tomato basil and vegetable while I was gone. I heard Italian wedding soup is on the stove today. Seriously, she makes enough for an army. Nick can eat but not all that. We can head over there. I know she'd love to see you, and the soup might settle your stomach."

Smiling, he knows just how to make me feel better, and I'm discovering that it doesn't always lie with Natalie. Don't get me wrong, I love her. But maybe there's more room inside this jaded heart of mine. "Soup sounds good. I'll text her."

"Let me."

He texts her when he sends his card to pay the bill and then grins while staring at his phone. "She said she'll have two bowls ready."

"But you ate your dinner. Are you still hungry?"

"I can always eat." He signs the check and then comes around to offer me a hand. "Ready?"

"So ready."

On the car ride over, he gets a text. "Whoa!"

"What is it?"

He grins in disbelief and runs his hand over his head. "I just got a shot at landing the townhome next door to Nick and Natalie."

"The listing?" I ask in disbelief myself. "It's completely remodeled, prime location, and the best neighbors ever."

"Yeah. It's amazing. Nick told me the owners are well-connected in this city. If I land them, that will open the door for so many opportunities."

"Natalie, Nick, Andrew, even Jackson are all great connections."

"They've sent me names for potential clients. I have a lot of meetings set up for next week."

Dusting my nails across my chest, I act coy, and say, "Not to brag, but I'm not so shabby myself in this town."

When I drop my hand between us, he's quick to hold it. "Know someone in the market?"

"Natalie told me I should buy it." When his mouth drops open, I raise my hand. "Don't get too excited. I can't afford that place on my own."

"Fuck, Tate, you had my mind wandering."

"You don't have to wonder. Money's not taboo to me. Money is just money. My family has a lot of it—my parents and grandparents, aunts and uncles. They're loaded. If you really want the juicy gossip, I don't have to work. I just like to. But none of this is news. You can read it online." I pause, sitting back, and then add, "I don't just like to work. It actually makes me feel like I have a purpose." I see him taking it in when it dawns on me that this is news to him. "You didn't google me?"

"No. Guess I should have. I would have tracked you down sooner."

"Because I'm rich?"

His brows pull together. "No, Tatum. Because I liked you."

My fingers tighten together with his, and my heart pounds to a new beat, one that I'm sure is the drum his marches to as well. My mind starts wandering into his holdings. Maybe I shouldn't be nosy, but I suddenly feel it's something we can just put out there and be done. Neither of us needs each other's money anyway. "I heard you have money to burn."

He scoffs and then starts chuckling. "I would never burn money, but if I wanted to start a fire, I wouldn't miss what's needed to make a bonfire."

"Family money?"

"Some funds and I've done well over the past six years in real estate."

I like that he's made his way, even in the family business. "Just curious."

Angling toward me, he asks, "They said I could stop by to see it if I'm there before nine."

"If you're asking, I think it's a good opportunity like you said. You can establish yourself in the neighborhood." *And then maybe he'll have a reason to stay.*

"But the soup?"

"The soup can wait. I'm feeling better."

"Do you want to come with me?"

I grin. "Bet your bottom dollar."

He punches in a code that was sent to him, and the moment we walk into the brownstone, I regret it. It's the most beautiful home—light and airy, creamy-white walls, wide-planked beige wood floors off the marble flooring at the entry. I grab the sleeve of his jacket. "Harrison?"

Covering my hand with his, he looks at me. "Yeah?" he asks, keeping his voice low like we're trespassing.

"How much?"

I feel his body vibrate with laughter as I visually get lost in the stunning kitchen.

"I'm thinking between twelve and fifteen million. I'd have to see the comps. Fully renovated, it could go higher," he replies. "You like what you see?"

"It feels like a home, a sanctuary in the middle of the city." I turn to him and ask, "How many square feet and bedrooms?"

He stops and stands in front of me. "Are you seriously interested?"

"I can't afford it but just humor me."

"Okay." He opens his phone to read the spec sheet. "Four floors like Nick and Natalie's. This one has an elevator. Looks like a closet. Five bedrooms. Five and a half bathrooms. An office on the top floor. A den in the basement along with a gym. Twenty-five hundred square feet out back."

I'm still stuck on how the sunlight sends rays across the living room floor. Heaven.

"Want to hear more?" he asks.

"No," I reply, my heart already too invested in something I can't afford. "I'm good."

"Hello?"

We both turn around to the sound of a woman's voice. Harrison says, "Hi, I'm Harrison Decker. I was sent the code to tour the property."

With purpose, she comes toward us with her hand held out. "Yes, of course. I'm Dolores. I live here. It's so nice to meet you. Natalie raves about you." She shakes his hand firmly by the looks of it and then turns to me with one hand on her pregnant belly.

"That's great to hear. Nick is my oldest friend." Harrison looks at me, and adds, "This is Tatum Devreux. She's—"

"Hi, I'm a client of his."

Her smile is as welcoming as her home. "Oh," she says, looking back at him. "That's impressive."

"I didn't expect you to be here," Harrison says.

"Yes, I'm running late to meet my husband and kids for dinner. I'll get out of your way so you can tour the home."

I say, "Thank you for letting me see it."

"I'm happy you're here." Holding up her finger, she asks, "Are you of the Devreux Shipping family?"

"Yes."

Her hands clasp together over her baby belly, and she nods, appearing pleased. "That's so interesting. Very well. Carry on. And I look forward to hearing from you tomorrow, Harrison."

"You definitely will."

Her heels clack across the marble floors in the front of the house, and I imagine that being mine. The sounds of home.

Leaning down, he whispers, "You didn't have to say that."

"I'm only telling the truth. I have a regular jeweler, evening dress seamstress, dry cleaner, butcher, and bakery. It's about time I had a personal real estate agent."

"I'm going to be personally thanking you later. How's that for service?"

"Ten out of five stars every time."

When we finish the tour, and I'm officially in love with the house but out of my league financially, we go next door. He opens the door and has me enter first. "Why is it dark in here when they're home and expecting us?"

"Not sure, but the soup smells good."

"I smell the candle Natalie always burns but not food." He shuts the door, and I call, "Natalie?"

Turning back to Harrison, I ask, "Are you sure they knew we were coming over?"

He laughs, taking my hand. "Of course. They probably just went upstairs for something since we detoured next door."

"Maybe. It just feels off."

"It's fine." He starts to lead me down the hall. "I live here when I'm not at yours, so we're not doing anything wrong."

Spotting the half bath, I escape. "I need to use the restroom." Before I shut the door, I say, "I'll just be a few minutes. Start without me."

"Start what without you?"

"Soup. You said you're hungry. Soup it up. I'll join you shortly."

He stands there staring at me like something's wrong but then sighs. "*Okaaay.*"

I shut the door and immediately pull out both pregnancy tests. Reading the package of one, I rip the other and tug out the plastic stick. When I've read down to the fine print, I open the other and then do the deed, peeing on both.

I wasn't nervous before, distracted by so much other stuff from the restaurant to the house next door, but standing here two minutes of the three is pure torture.

"Are you okay, Tate?"

"Good," I say with a locked door between us. "I'll be out soon."

I look at my phone, wishing it showed seconds on the screen. Pacing the tiny room, I'm going to wear a circle into the floor. I check the time again, too nervous to check the tests.

When three minutes have finally passed, I brace my hands on the sink counter, take a deep breath, and look in the mirror. "It will be okay. Either way." When the pep talk doesn't seem to calm my shaking hands, I swallow hard and just look down.

Blinking, I find my vision is blurry. I squeeze my eyes closed and try again. This time it clears, but my legs feel numb as though they're going to give out from under me.

Two tests. Two lines on each.

I plop down on the toilet and grab the wrapper from the trash can. Reading the directions again, I mentally check off each step and then study the results before comparing them to my tests.

Pregnant.

Pregnant. . .

I start to sweat and need air. Grabbing the tests, I swing open the door and rush out and right into Harrison's arms. "What's wrong?"

Waving the sticks around like a crazy person, I reply, "I'm pregnant."

"Surprise!"

22

Harrison

"Oh shit."

The room falls silent as I watch Tatum's expression fall with it. The sound of the sticks bouncing across the floor grabs everyone's attention. Turning toward the living room, I see the crowd is silently staring. Natalie's front and center with her hand over her mouth.

When Tatum tries to breathe, it comes out rapid and uneven. Still holding her, her body gets heavier, so I tighten my grip and then start moving her toward the bathroom. I'm not sure if she's going to faint or not, but I need to get her out from under the wide-eyed glare of the others.

Rushing forward, Natalie picks up the sticks and squeezes in behind me before the door is shut. I set Tatum on the lid of the toilet and crouch down in front of her, not sure how to tamp down my panic. "You're pregnant?"

Her eyes are glassy, her cheeks flaming red. Her tears break the barrier of her lower lids and roll down. "I'm pregnant." Looking at Natalie, she asks, "Who are those people?"

"It's a surprise party."

Tatum drops her head into her hands, and her mortification is seared into her face before it's hidden from view. "Oh my God. Everyone knows now." She looks back up, and her anger takes over. "A surprise party for who?"

"You," Natalie replies, half-heartedly. "I'm so sorry. We were trying to surprise you, and I thought it would cheer you up. Harrison was in charge of getting you here."

A hard glare hits me, and Tatum says, "You knew? You knew, and you let me make a fool of myself." When she stands up, we all shift around the small space to give her room. Poking me in the chest, she says, "You knew, and you let me announce to the world that I'm pregnant?"

"How was I supposed to know you were in here taking a pregnancy test? I thought you just had irritable bowel syndrome from the fish."

"What fish?" Natalie asks.

"Langley's on 10th," I reply.

"I love that place. The tilapia is chef's kiss," she says.

Tatum crosses her arms over her chest and looks away as though she can't stand the mere sight of me. "It was off, okay? It was tasteless." Indignant in her stance, she has her chin raised to the ceiling, even refusing to make eye contact with her friend.

I recognize the signs of her walls going up.

By how Natalie moves closer, she does, too. "Tate, you're pregnant." Taking her wrists from their crossed position, Natalie holds her hands. Her smile is kind, and her eyes are full of some understanding I'm not privy to. "Look at me."

Envy courses through me when Tatum follows through with the request. I don't know if she'd do the same for me. Tatum asks, "What?"

"You're pregnant," Natalie repeats, sounding it out even slower this time as if Tatum needs to let it sink in.

Maybe she does. *I do.*

Maybe she's in shock. *I am.*

When Tatum turns to me instead of Natalie, she says, "I'm pregnant." Her tone is hard to read, but I'm sure she's feeling a million different emotions like me. Even though she's said it a few times now, I'm still lost to how I'm supposed to feel and find myself waiting for her to give me some indication. "Harrison?"

"Yeah," I say, numb at the moment.

She comes to me, wrapping her arms around my middle and resting her cheek on my chest. "Are you all right?"

Natalie moves to the door. "I'll leave you two to talk."

When the door closes behind her, I lean against it thinking I might need the support. "Harrison?" she asks, her voice quieter than a whisper.

I look down into her soulful browns, the tears not so prevalent now. She caresses my face, and I close my eyes, leaning into it. "I need a sec."

"Me too, but I didn't get it."

When I open my eyes, I see the smallest of smiles before she hugs me again. I hold her, embracing her and keeping her as close as I can. "I'm sure that was shocking to experience, especially alone."

"I chose to be alone. I wish I hadn't."

"I'm sorry."

"For what?" she asks, resting her chin on my chest and looking up.

"The surprise and not warning you."

"If you would've warned me, it would have ruined the surprise." She laughs humorlessly and then leans against me, this time facing the mirror. "I guess we were both surprised."

"Tatum," I say, shifting to the side to put space between us. Not to push her away but I need room to think. "I don't know what to say or ask. I'm confused. You're on the pill."

"I am. I missed a day but made up for it the next. I just . . ." She sits back down on the toilet again. "I don't have an explanation, Harrison." Picking up one of the sticks, she stares at it a minute before breaking down in tears.

Quick to kneel before her, I bring her to my shoulder, holding her and letting her comfort me. "It will be okay, Tate. I promise it will be."

It takes another minute before she swipes toilet paper to wipe under her eyes and looks up. I hate that her makeup is messed up, knowing that will only add to her upset.

"There's a house full of people out there waiting to see me, and I'm a mess—my face and my emotions," she says.

"We don't have to stay. We'll go. Everyone out there will understand."

"They'll understand because I just announced to everyone that I'm pregnant. Oh God." She drops her head into her hands again. Speaking through her fingers, she says, "I can never leave this bathroom again. Just have my mail forwarded. Do you think I can get food delivery in here?"

As much as I like that her sense of humor is intact, I worry that she's not fully processing what's happening. "If Natalie is the delivery person." Taking her hands away from her face, I then ask, "Did you know at dinner? Is that what was on your mind?"

"No. If I had, I wouldn't have announced my pregnancy to a room full of people." Her arm flies out. "I don't even know who's out there. Please tell me not my parents."

"I don't know." I take her spot on the toilet, needing to get my thoughts on this situation together. When I scrub my hands over my face, I feel her standing against me.

She takes one of my hands and opens it to expose the palm. Her lips press to the skin, the kiss unhurried, her lips lingering. I watch her kneeling before me with her eyes closed, taking in everything about me, and notice how our roles have changed.

When she looks up, she asks, "Are you okay?"

"You're pregnant, and you're asking me if I'm okay?"

"Yes." Worry weaves through her eyes as she stares into mine.

How can she even think of me at this time? I caress her cheek, seeing the change in her happening before my eyes. "I'll be okay. How about you?"

"A little numb. A little okay."

It's not what I expected from her. This news is . . . well, not what I thought I'd hear for years. "What do you want to do?"

"I'm thinking I need to face my demons and join the party. They already know, so maybe I should join the party and have a laugh with them."

"Laugh?" I ask before realizing who they really are to her. "Maybe so. They're your friends who care most about your well-being."

A beat doesn't pass before she picks up on what I said. "Friends, not family?"

"I don't know, Tatum. I didn't put the party together." Angling toward the door, I add, "I can go do reconnaissance."

Nodding, she adds, "And can you ask Natalie to bring some of her makeup?"

"Sure." I open the door and look out. Natalie is leaning

against the wall with a clear bin in her hands. I still close the door behind me, needing to talk to Natalie alone for a minute. "Are her parents here?"

"No," she whispers. "I got a card, though."

Hrm. I'm not sure how she's going to feel about that. Yes, she's embarrassed over the pregnancy announcement, but I'd like to know what their excuse is for missing her birthday? That seems like a lot to deal with at this moment, though. "She wants makeup."

Holding up the small bin, she grins—not full of happiness like it should be on this occasion but sympathy instead. "I got her covered."

I see Nick across the way. He's sitting like a nervous soon-to-be dad in a waiting room.

"Is she sure she wants to have this party? Everyone will understand if she wants to leave," Natalie asks.

"I don't know. Whatever she wants is probably best."

I exhale when my chest gets tight. Rubbing over the knot with my fist, I take another breath.

"Are you okay, Harrison?"

"Me? I'm fine." I hate that she felt the need to even ask. That makes me wonder what clues she picked up on. I move out of her way. "I'm going to talk to Nick while Tatum gets ready."

Before I slip across the entry into the other room, I feel her hand on my back. When I turn, she says, "It's all right not to know how to feel. It's a surprise for both of you."

My throat feels thick when I swallow, and my mind is muddled. I nod, but I'm not sure why. I just know I need fresh air. When I head for the front door, Nick says, "What are you drinking?"

I could be good and order a bottle of water or even a soda. But I know damn well that I need something stronger.

"My usual." When I step onto the stoop, it feels like a lot of night has passed though it's still young. I sit on the top step and look down at the sidewalk, trying to wrap my head around the facts of what just happened.

Tatum's pregnant.

I'm going to be a dad. Or maybe she chooses something else . . . That's a discussion for another day, or at least, not in the middle of her surprise birthday party. I pull out my phone and flip to a few photos taken before I left California. It was an impromptu going away dinner with just my family.

It didn't matter that I reminded them I'll be flying back and forth. My sister took the lead and organized for all of us to get together. A photo of my niece and baby sister smiling like goofballs fills the screen. A lot has happened since Catalina, and I need to figure out how best to handle this.

"Harry, I need your help?" my sister says. It sounds like she's crying though, which isn't like her.

"Are you okay?" I ask, already knowing the answer.

I try to shake the memory of that night . . . and let what's happening right in front of me guide my reaction.

This is about the woman I'm dating being pregnant with mine. We may have been doing it like rabbits, but none of this makes sense. The door opens behind me, and I'm quick to shove my phone back in my pocket. "Was that Madison?" Nick asks, closing the door.

"And Harlow."

He knows why I was looking. They'd be the first people I'd think of after Tatum in this situation. Handing me a glass of whiskey, he sits on the other side of the landing, leaning against the concrete balusters. I take several sips noticing the soda is on the lighter side. I don't mind and take another. "So Tatum's pregnant." We might as well just get it out there.

A slow exhale then has him replying, "So I heard."

"Everyone did." I roll my eyes. If I embarrassed easily, this would be the time. Fortunately, I don't. "I think I would have preferred being told in private first."

"Sorry you had to hear it that way. It won't change things, but there are not that many people. Natalie kept the list on the smaller side. A few left, thinking it best to call it a night like Jackson and his date, a few co-workers of theirs. Look, Harrison, a lot can happen—"

"A lot has happened." My confusion wrinkles my brow. I'm not stupid. We may have been doing it like rabbits but none of this makes sense. I say, "We've been driving this relationship at warp speed like we wouldn't get a second chance."

"This is your second chance. You're in it."

Looking down at the glass in my hand, I nod. "Second chance." I glance over at him. "I'm not sure what Tatum will do . . . I just . . ." I take a long pull from the glass and rub my hand over my head as I swallow the liquor. "What do we do?"

"I'm no expert. I'm just some old married guy, but take it day by day, hour by hour if you need to. This isn't about anyone but the two of you."

"I don't know if she'll keep the baby or . . ." I empty the glass. Maybe I shouldn't have had a drink when Tatum doesn't have the luxury of numbing her thoughts the same way, but I'm considering another. "My heart is fucked up over this. I don't want to be put in the position—"

"Minute by minute if that's what it takes, brother." He stands, taking a sip of his drink before looking up at the night sky. "I think we should shut down the party."

"It's not my call."

We go back inside to find Tatum holding a glass of water in one hand and a steak fry in the other while talking to

Andrew and Juni. Natalie is bustling around with the remaining guests mingling, the conversations and laughter overshadowing the music playing in the background.

By looking at the scene, no one acts as though anything happened out of the ordinary. I'm struck by the casual mask everyone's wearing as if they didn't just find out Tatum's pregnant at the same time I did.

Tatum looks back and sees me. A gentle smile graces her lips before she sets her drink down and comes over, her hand resting against my chest. She looks up, her cheeks slightly pink from the cry she had earlier. "Are you okay?"

Nick squeezes my shoulder as he walks through to the other room.

I cover Tatum's hand, wrapping my fingers around hers, and then slowly nod. "I'm . . . confused."

"So am I."

Wanting to reassure her, I force a smile. "Surprise. It's your birthday party."

Her expression softens. "You listened to me gripe about that and didn't say a word. You're very good at keeping secrets, Mr. Decker."

"So are you." I don't intend it as a jab, and nothing in my tone would say otherwise.

That doesn't stop the slight cringing I see around her eyes and mouth. "I think we need to talk, and this," she says, glancing back over her shoulder at the other guests, "this isn't the place."

"If you want to stay, we can."

"I feel like a rain check might be in order. They'll understand." She pulls away to leave, but I keep holding her hand. It's not that I only like the feel of it in mine. I need this connection. *I need her.*

Turning back, she gives me a smile. "It's okay, Harrison."

I'm not sure when the roles we played reversed, but I feel better as if we're in this together.

I release her hand, but when she walks away, my gut twists, still unsettled.

23

Harrison

How is she so calm when I'm freaking the fuck out inside?

And I'm the one who had the whiskey. She's thriving off water alone.

Tatum's lying in a lukewarm bath covered in suds, and I'm researching getting pregnant while taking birth control pills. Sure, I always knew it wasn't 100%, but what the fuck? I still trusted it.

As tempting as it is to pour myself a drink, I need to get her fed properly. Natalie sent the entire pot of soup back with us, and it's just hot enough to serve. I find the bowls and ladle the soup inside. I can't find a tray to carry it on, so I load up my hands and tuck the crackers under my arm. When I turn around, she's standing there. Her straight hair hangs over her robe-clad shoulders. A makeup-free face brings attention to her bright eyes that are filled with amusement. She giggles. "Need a hand?"

I must look like an idiot trying to juggle everything.

"Maybe more." I set everything down on the island when she comes into the kitchen.

"You did all of this for me?"

"I can't take credit for the soup. I'm just the reheater."

Running her finger along the island, she stops it beside me, and then she slips her arms around me. "But you reheated it for me. I don't even know where you got the crackers."

"Whoever does your shopping thought it was a necessary staple. Who does your shopping for you?"

"A company we found through STJ. Two sons wanted to take the burden of grocery shopping off their mom for a year when she was going through chemo. They didn't live in New York, so they contacted us for help. We found a great startup for just that thing. It was nice to do something that can make a real impact on someone's life. We didn't charge them because it allowed us to open a division that focuses fully on helping those in need."

I've not been privy to this side of the business or of Tatum. There's an excitement in her eyes as she speaks, yet until now, I knew nothing about it. "I haven't heard about this, not from Nick or Natalie."

A self-deprecating expression fills in the features of her pretty face. "Feels like we're bragging so it's not something we really advertise. It's through word of mouth. We're not looking for pats on the back."

"How does it work?"

"Through the submission process. We have someone in the office who narrows it down to five and then presents them to the company, and everyone has a vote that counts. Sometimes it's one, sometimes two a month." She pulls her hair over her shoulder, the silky strands instantly returning to where they came from. "Anyway, I work with that company who grocery shops for people who don't have time, mobility, or interest." Raising her hand, she adds, "I fall into the last category. No shocker. They stock the staples, and then you give them your likes, etcetera."

There are a million businesses who can shop for you, but that this one has the charitable angle definitely makes it more interesting. I'll have to watch for investment opportunities. That aside, she has me wondering if New Yorkers even have grocery stores like the ones back home. "Have you ever grocery shopped?"

She's quick to answer. "I'm sure I have. There's a fruit stand down the street, and the shops for the other things are just past that."

"I'm talking about a large grocery store where everything's all in one place?"

"I'm not sure I have." She shrugs indifferently, taking a cracker from the wrapper. "Does it matter?"

"No. Not in the scheme of things, but what about the baby?"

She starts choking with cracker crumbs stuck to her lips as she grabs for the water. Chugging some down, she clears her throat and then shoots me a dirty look. "What about the baby?"

Wow, that's a trigger. I need to avoid those landmines in the future, if possible. "Are you okay?"

"I'm fine." She clears her throat once more and takes another drink. "What did you mean what about the baby?"

It was a dig. I know it, and she knows it. Now the baby knows I'm an asshole. I can't help wondering how Tatum's going to manage this. "I know you can take care of yourself, but this is bigger than you or me."

Offense widens her eyes and has her jerking away from me. "Excuse me? I don't like what you're insinuating."

Insinuating . . . What the fuck am I doing? "Fuck. I didn't mean you're irresponsible or anything."

Moving to the other side of the island, she says, "That's not sorry."

"I'm sorry." I don't have an ego that keeps me from apologizing when I'm in the wrong, and on night one, I'm in the fucking wrong. Lesson learned.

She crosses her arms over her chest, looking at me like she doesn't know me at all. "What's wrong with you?"

I'm coming to realize that I can't stay silent on this topic. "I need to talk about this. I thought we'd come home to do that."

"Home. This is my home, not yours. Yours is in Los Angeles. I don't know if you live in an apartment or a house, near the beach, or above Sunset. I don't know any of that."

"But you could. I want to take you there. I want to introduce you to my family."

"The family that shuffled you off on a bunch of nannies?"

The low blow hits its intended destination—below the belt. I'm not saying it's not owed, but I'm starting to see some of the old Tatum returning. And that won't bode well for me.

I stare at her, cautious like I'm trapped in a cage with a pacing tiger. Is it going to eat me alive or let me live? One thing I won't accept is a dig toward my family, at least not from anyone else. "I joke about the nannies. The stories are true, but I find them funny. If you want to know the real reason I had so many, it's because my mom was working at the time. Four kids is a lot to handle with a full-time job. My dad wasn't the kid-rearing type. Still isn't." The happiness in her eyes escaped as soon as I screwed up and opened my mouth. But the fire that now resides inside means this isn't going to be resolved with an apology.

There are lines we don't cross, and my family is mine. "The sacrifices fell on my mom's plate. Instead of putting us in a daycare, she hired nannies to keep us home. They would take us to our sports and make our meals instead of having to eat from a drive-thru. So if you want to punch me with what a handful I was, go right ahead, but be careful when you get too close to dragging my mom into this."

Tatum doesn't seem to understand that when I speak of my family, she's now a part of it, a member I'm willing to do anything to protect.

The breath she sucks in is harsh and not taken easily. Her hands release the edge of the island, and she takes a step back. "I'm not sure what just happened, but I don't want this."

"This or us, Tate?"

"Are they one and the same?" There's no spite in her tone, and the fire is starting to simmer. The question still stings, though, and I have a feeling I'm witnessing her pattern. Push me away to save herself the pain from another day. At least I know what she thinks of me.

"I know my answer, but what is yours?" I ask.

"This isn't a tit for tat, Harrison. I'm not mad. I'm learning. Natalie once told me that she and Nick had to learn how to fight. They had to understand where the other came from instinctually. I'm trying to fight my own habits and give you the benefit of the doubt." She exhales in a huff and then sighs, coming back around the island.

Holding the hem of my shirt, she adds, "I'm trying for you."

I see it in her eyes, the sincerity shaping her expression,

and the way she holds my shirt like she's trying to hold on to me.

"It's going to take more than an argument about nannies and grocery stores to scare me away."

A soft smile hangs on her face. "I had teachers during the day when I was little and a nanny who was also the housekeeper. She still works for my parents, maintaining the Manhattan property. So I get it. We come from similar backgrounds even though things were different."

"I don't want the same thing I had. I don't want nannies raising our kids. During the day, fine because we have to work, but at night, I want to be there for them."

"Our." Not a question, but just something to chew on. Taking a step back again, she turns away and then walks to the windows. "I guess this is all leading to the conversation I didn't want to have." Shadowed in the darkest part of the room, she looks back. I can still see the look of uncertainty in her eyes. "I was waiting to have everything confirmed at the doctor's office, and you're already making plans for more."

"False positives are rare."

"They happen, though, just like someone getting pregnant while on the pill. We're the exception. It makes me nervous about finding out if we are when it comes to this as well." Her hand sits on her middle like she might feel something.

"You should eat," I say, the heaviness releasing from my chest.

Returning to the kitchen, she takes the spoon and sips the soup to challenge me. Setting the spoon down again, she says, "We should talk about what happens next." I don't know what to say. I want her to lead. I need her to. Not because I can't, but I don't want to plant hope where none is allowed to grow.

She reaches over and takes my hand in hers, studying it. Running the tip of her finger over the veins on top of my hand, and then with her gaze cast down, she says, "I can tell you're nervous." When those browns meet my blues, they're filled with warmth, and comfort is found inside. "Maybe even scared. Is that what you're feeling, Harrison?"

I can only bring myself to give the minutest of nods, but it's enough to encourage her to wrap her arms around me, and confess, "I'm scared, too."

Something real we share has me engulfing her in my arms and kissing the top of her head. "I don't want to fight with you. I just . . ." I know better than to say the words sitting on the tip of my tongue. Words that would put a stake in the game, and if she chose otherwise, would leave me devastated. It might already be too late for that anyway. We've only dated for a few weeks, but it took years to get to this stage, and I don't want to lose her before we have a chance for more.

She tilts her head up. "You just what?"

I swallow those words down, choosing different ones based on what's best for her. "No matter what happens, I'm not leaving you."

Her gulp is loud enough to hear, and tears sparkle in her eyes. "Will you go with me to the doctor's appointment tomorrow?"

This is big. *Huge.* Her trust in me was revealed in the form of an invitation. Any other time, she would have asked Natalie.

This time, she asked me.

24

Harrison

"HARRY, I NEED YOUR HELP," MY SISTER SAYS. IT SOUNDS LIKE she's crying, though, which isn't like her.

"Are you okay?" I ask, already knowing the answer. Sobs fill the line. "Madison?"

"The hospital. I need you."

The freeway under my tires is too loud to catch everything over my Bluetooth. "Madison, where are you? You're at the hospital? Cedars?"

There's a long pause that has me panicking more than I am already. "Yes, Harry. Hurry . . ."

"I'm on my way, Maddie."

The phone goes dead, and I call my eldest brother, glad Nick caught a ride with Cookie. "Dawson?" I say as soon as the connection is made, trying not to drive like a demon on a mission, though I am.

"Hey, are you back in town?" His tone is too casual for an emergency. I don't want to break the news to my entire family, but she called me first, so the job falls on my shoulders.

"Madison just called me. She's headed to the hospital."

"Why? What happened?"

I change lanes to pass this fucking slow car driving in the fast lane. "We didn't get that far, but I'd assume it's for the baby."

"Cedars?"

"Yes. I just got off the ferry. I'm going straight there."

"Why are you the first to tell me if you're just getting into LA?" Dawson is the most competitive of my brothers, if you take me out of the equation.

"I don't know. Call Mom and Dad. I'm calling Jameson."

"Okay. Hey, Harrison?"

I lay on my horn when some idiot cuts me off. "What?"

"Don't speed. You getting in an accident won't help the situation."

"Point taken."

Following the Decker phone tree protocol, my younger brother, Jameson, doesn't answer. He might be sleeping in since it's Sunday. I leave him a message and then try to call Madison back, but she doesn't answer.

Dread settles into my bones.

We've been through hell the past few months, my sister most of all, only to have that fucker turn his back on her when she needed him most. While my parents sat in disbelief and disappointment, she had three brothers who not only could take care of the situation with him but would rally around her.

My mom worried about Madison only being nineteen and that a baby would derail her daughter's dream of being an entertainment lawyer. I get it. At the time, Maddie was enrolled in college and a straight-A student.

I worried she wouldn't live to see twenty.

Why'd she pick a bad boy? I mean, I know why girls fall for them, but a weed dealer who dabbled in nighttime street racing for bets probably doesn't share the same long-term goals as my sister.

As predicted, he was out of the picture as soon as she told him. Things got worse for him when he tossed a few bills in her face and told her to handle it. She decided she would have the baby on her own.

I run into the ER and head for the nurses' station. "Harrison?"

Turning to the side, my mom runs into my arms. I used to be the one rushing into hers. "What happened?"

"Dodson came around and wanted to talk to Maddie. I knew it was a bad idea."

The name of that loser gets me angry. I almost killed him the first time he laid a hand on Madison. If my brother Dawson hadn't been there . . . I probably wouldn't be standing here.

I don't know what he tells her, but I do know my sister. She's not weak like the prey he treats her. I highly doubt anything comes with a please when he tells her how it's going down.

My mom takes me to the corner of the waiting room and whispers, "I don't have the details from Madison. All I heard from the nurse is that she was in a car accident and can't tell me more."

"Fuck," I exhale, looking toward the nurses' station.

"I'm glad you're home," she says, hugging me.

Hugging her back, I ask, "Where's Dad?"

"Santa Barbara. It will take him hours to get here." Annoyance colors her tone.

Mat walks in and looks around. Seeing us, he heads our way. "If you tell me that fucker had anything to do with this . . ."

"Please put your energy into Maddie's recovery." My mom goes quiet, and then adds, "And this sweet baby she's carrying." Tears roll down her cheeks, and she sniffles. "I can't handle thinking about that horrible man. He won't leave her alone."

"Mrs. Decker?" We turn to see a doctor standing nearby looking for my mom.

"I'm here," she says, rushing toward him. *"How is my daughter?"*

Mat and I stand behind her like two bodyguards flanking her, and my gut twists with concern.

"Madison's doing well, but we're concerned about the baby."

Present Day

Sitting in waiting rooms is the worst. Doesn't matter if nothing's wrong, the fear still creeps in, implanting the what-ifs.

I toss the magazine from 2017 back on the pile and decide pacing will serve me better.

A corner door opens, and a nurse stands there staring at a chart. When she looks up, she calls, "Mr. Devreux."

Tatum's got a good sense of humor this morning. I hope she can keep it after whatever news we're given. The name doesn't bother me. Today, it attaches me to her as more than just the guy who knocked her up. "That's me."

I walk toward her and follow her down the hall. I'm shown to a room to wait by myself. Before I have time to read all about the Heimlich from the poster, a knock draws my attention, and then the door opens. Tatum smiles the second she sees me and hurries into my open arms.

She says, "We're pregnant."

My arms don't leave her, and I don't look down. I stay still in the moment, closing my eyes and releasing a breath that feels long-held.

Gentle sobs rock her body as she clings to me. I can't decipher between sadness or happiness from the sound, but I steal a second to savor those two words. I'm not sure what's going to happen between us, but at this moment, we're united as one.

When she releases me, she grabs a tissue from the box

on the counter. Wiping under her eyes, she looks at me. "What do you think, Harrison? I need to know what you're thinking."

Yesterday, I had determined she needed to lead. Today, she needs me. "Have you made a decision you haven't shared with me?" I ask cautiously.

She plops down on the hard, plastic chair and shakes her head. "I don't think I should keep anything from you. This baby is yours as well as mine, but it's growing inside me, so I appreciate you asking." Her eyes find the anatomical makeup poster of a pregnant woman. Although I think parts of this scare her, I'm not sure what she'll decide.

Getting up again, she comes to me and leans her head on my chest. "It wasn't real yesterday. It was shock factor and reaction. I was trying my best not to believe it because what if those tests were wrong."

I realize we all process things differently, even on different timelines. When I was freaking out last night, she was waiting to have confirmation. I'm not sure that either is right or wrong, but I know that I did a disservice to her last night. What will I do this time?

Looking up at me, she continues, "I'm going to have this baby."

I reach out for the wall beside me, needing the support. I'm not sure what I expected, but that doesn't seem to be it. But I can wholeheartedly attest that's the answer I was hoping for.

It's strange how life comes at you. It wasn't but a few weeks ago that she hated me. I couldn't even get Tatum to make eye contact. If she did, it was full of a rage I couldn't extinguish. Time has given me a second chance. Life has changed for her and for me. I can only hope for the better for both of us.

I've stood too quiet because she asks, "What do you want to do?"

We don't have any details worked out. There's not one plan in place. How could there be? All of this is unexpected, but the direction of our lives has changed, and I'll change with it. *I am nothing like* him. Unlike Madison, Tate will not be left to raise this baby alone. "I want this baby, Tate."

Again, she embraces me, not waiting, not seeking my permission, just full-on hugs me. It's not something I'm used to in general with girlfriends. But like I've always known, Tatum is special.

"What happens now?" she asks.

"Not sure. There's a lot to think about and plan. But now that we know—"

"And half of Manhattan because of the surprise party last night."

I give her that, tipping my head. "I think we take a few days to just enjoy this. You want this baby. I want this baby. There's a lot to celebrate with this new life."

The nurse comes in and says, "Okay, you're all ready to go, Ms. Devreux. We've set your next appointment." She hands her an appointment card. "And we look forward to seeing you then. Congratulations to you both."

"Thanks," I say, letting the news sink in.

We hold hands as we leave. I'm not Mr. Devreux, and she's not Mrs. Decker, but we're together, happy, and bringing a new life into the world. It might not be a perfect bow to some, but life feels pretty damn grand to me right now.

Just as we push through the exit doors, I ask, "Hungry?"

"Starving. I'm craving French toast. Want to go get breakfast? I know a great diner up ahead."

I'm pretty sure cravings don't start this early. I also never expected to hear Tatum request diner food since she's more the Michelin-starred restaurant type. I'm happy to oblige her every whim if it means spending time with her and enjoying this next stage together.

As we walked down the street, I ask, "When can we tell our families?"

She stops and pulls her phone from her bag. Reading a text message on the screen, she then holds it so I can see it. Her parents will be in Manhattan for one night.

This Friday.

The night after *her birthday.*

"I guess on my birthday. No time like the present to tell your parents you're pregnant," she replies.

Remembering how her mom acted at the anniversary party, I say, "Well, this should be interesting."

25

Harrison

"I was worried about being a godparent, and now look at me?"

"Am I looking at the pint of ice cream in your hand or the fried chicken on your lap?" *Ow*—the whack to the bicep came fast. She may be pregnant, but she can still deliver a wallop.

She's been pregnant for just over a hot minute and is adapting quick to her new life. I think she figured out the perks—me willing and ready to satiate her cravings—real fast.

Lying on the couch, Tatum laughs, gut-giggling, from it. The woman is delirious . . . *with power*. She doesn't have to worry, though. I'm more than willing to feed her cravings, hunger or sexually, anytime she wants.

When she catches her breath, she says, "I meant because the thought of being a godparent scared me, and now I'm going to be a mom." She's quick to move the food to the coffee table before turning to me on the other side of the couch. "Oh wow. I'm going to be a mom, Decker." Only a second passes before she adds, "You're going to be a dad."

Dad . . .

I think of my dad.

And Corbin Christiansen—*Nick's dad.*

Those are the dads I know. Different in a lot of ways and similar in others. I don't really feel old enough to be called Dad. Imagining a kid calling me that brings a smile to my face, though. I've loved being an uncle—*the favorite uncle*— to Harlow. But what I have realized is that I've secretly wanted to be a dad for years but packed away that dream since I didn't have the woman I wanted to be tied to for the rest of my life.

I relocated the dream of having a family of my own into my heart. *Not sure why.*

Tatum and I can both admit that pure physical attraction brought us together. The sex is outstanding. *Still is.*

Truthfully, though, Tatum never indicated one way or the other that we'd one day be friends. Lovers came unexpectedly. *It was as though my heart's been waiting for her to catch up.* She may be covered in crumbs with a hint of chocolate stuck to the side of her mouth. Yep, that's my woman right there, but that's also the mother of my baby, and I couldn't be happier.

Taking her hand, I rub my thumb over her soft skin. "It's funny because I think we skipped a few steps, but I'm not beholden to some old-fashioned notion. We may have just had our first date, but I think we're past that now. Tatum, will you be my girlfriend?"

"Why'd you have to go and do that, Harrison?" Her foot nudges my leg.

I take her by the ankles and stretch them across my lap, then rub her feet. "What did I go and do exactly?"

"You're being sweet and romantic. It makes me question if you're just doing that because I'm pregnant."

"I kind of thought I *was* romantic before."

"You were. *You are.*" She leans forward, grabbing hold of my forearm, and says, "I want us to be together because we want to, not because we feel we have to. I don't know what's going to happen in the future. I don't know how this works at all. I just know I want a life full of love, not the sadness I've felt in the past few years."

"I want that for you, too. I want you to feel the freedom you did when we first met."

"I was living back then without a care in the world. Or at least the cares that I had overcome." Flopping back, she throws her arms above her head to rest on the arm of the couch. It's hard to find the humor in her laughter, though, and that sadness she speaks of is the thing I've had trouble reading. She nailed it. "Poor guy. You didn't know what you were getting yourself into."

"What changed over the years?"

"Me. Everything." Her gaze shifts to the TV, though it's currently off. "I'm the same person, but I've grown and have more responsibilities."

"Let's get back to that sadness." I reach as far as I can to cover the divide between us. I touch under her chin, and ask, "Why are you so sad, pretty girl?"

It's good she doesn't rush her response. Her eyes are fixed on mine like she might find the answer. "Meeting twenty-two-year-old vacation Tatum is not the same person you're meeting at twenty-seven, tomorrow." She winks. "I'm not going to prematurely age myself." This time the giggle is soft but genuine. "This is real life, my life, and I've come to realize everyone eventually leaves me behind."

"Behind what? I'm not trying to be a smart-ass, but what

are others keeping you from that you can't find or do your-self?" When she doesn't say anything, I start getting some of this shit off my chest. "You're amazing—happy, sad, mad as all fuck, sexy, natural, and dressed up. Every version of you is worth loving. For yourself. You don't have to wait around for something that might be all you think it's cracked up to be. You can create it. You can create the life you want to live, Tatum. Don't let the world get you down. Don't let others determine your happiness."

"You sound like a life coach."

"I've been known to motivate . . ." It's the perfect setup for a wink, but this isn't about being cocky, patting myself on the back, or foreplay to bide time before dinner. This is about making sure Tatum finds what makes her happy. Not for me and not for the baby even though a kid needs to see that behavior modeled. This is about her.

I continue, "This is about creating the life you need instead of searching for it in others." She hasn't really let me into her life to see this, but from what I've observed over the years, I think she's placed that expectation on others like her parents, boyfriends, or Natalie. That's not saying she's weak, but that she's lacked the contentment within herself to know she *can* take the lead in her own life.

She swings her feet to the floor and sits up. Staring at the food on the coffee table, she says, "Now I feel bad for indulging."

"I didn't say that to make you feel bad. I eat In-N-Out as soon as I land in LA."

"I know what you mean. I just think I probably should have gone into work today."

"Don't you have your meeting with Dolores soon?"

Checking my watch, I have a few minutes before I need to leave. "I need to go, change clothes—"

"You should bring some clothes over here since you're always having to go back to Natalie's."

Now I'm the one staring. That's what I call a turnabout. Warp speed indeed. "Are you sure?" I know how absurd it sounds that I'm asking to keep a few shirts over here when my baby already moved in.

She nods with a smirk. "I'm sure." Getting up off the couch, she adds, "Lounge time is over. We have money to earn to support this kid. Mama's gotta go earn some bacon. And you have a new listing to get." Strutting into the other room, I watch that fine ass as she shakes it for me.

Just before she rounds the corner, she stops and whips around. Spreading her body lengthwise against the corner, she raises a leg and arm to look sexy. Does she not realize she doesn't have to try with me? She purrs. "Or, if you have a few minutes, I could show you my birthmark."

"Oh yeah? Where might that be?" I'm already heading straight toward her.

"Nowhere that the sunshine can reach."

Fuck me, the vixen. I'll lose a listing before I miss out on discovering a new territory to conquer on her body. Grabbing my hands, she tugs me into the bedroom and has her way with me.

~

"My apologies. Traffic is awful."

Dolores opens the door wider to allow me entrance. "You're not coming from next door?"

"I had an appointment in Tribeca, something I had to handle."

She walks into the heart of the home. "Hope everything's okay."

I shut the door and follow her. "Yes, it's perfect."

And I'm completely satisfied.

When she sits on the couch, I choose the seat across the limestone and brass coffee table, and she says, "Harrison, I'm going to be up front with you. I've dealt with playboys and hotshots who have tried to get this listing. That's not what I'm looking for."

I'm not liking the sound of this or the way she's staring at me like I'm just another hotshot in New York City. My California pride is offended.

"I adore Natalie and Nick. Andrew Christiansen, who lives two doors down, manages my portfolio, and I've raised money for The Jacobs Garden, Juni's passion project. Every last one of them has spoken highly of you," she continues.

"That's nice to hear." I lean forward, resting my forearms on my legs and keeping my hands clasped together. "Is there a but coming?"

"But," she starts, not a trace of a smile, much less one that says I got this listing. "That was your girlfriend, not a client. Natalie told me about trying to talk her friend into buying the house, the same one you're dating. I would also assume she's the same person who left makeup on the fold of your collar."

Makeup?

Shit.

Because of the fun Tatum and I had, I didn't have time to change clothes. I wore this suit not only last night but also this morning to the doctors and lounging at Tatum's apartment.

I look down at the rug, tracing the lines of the design. I don't like to lie. Some agents will say anything to get the listing and do anything to close a deal, even if it means tricking a client or an interested buyer. I won't lower my morals to sell a property. "I'm dating her. That was actually our first date." When she doesn't say anything but sits back as if she's ready to hear the story, I confess everything. "I was in charge of bringing her to a party that Natalie was throwing for her. It was a surprise party for her birthday. But then I got this chance, and she told me to take it. We detoured here before going to the party next door."

We sit in a silent standoff for what feels like minutes. Rationally, I know it's only seconds, but the heat is getting to me under the collar, tempting me to tug it to get more air.

Dolores's features have a hard line to them, but they soften, and she says, "Thank you, Harrison, for confirming I can trust you." She smiles, and I take a deep, relieved breath. "I'm giving you the listing because I know you're not only trying to make a name for yourself in the city but you also come highly regarded by your friends. And I like Natalie. I also like to help others when I can, and I think this listing will give you a nice reference when you sell it over listing for seventeen million." *Oh thank God.*

I was going eighteen, but seventeen gives me flexibility.

She adds, "The only condition is that I don't want you to lie to me. If you can agree to those terms, you've got yourself a listing."

Standing, I hold out my hand. "I won't lie to you, Dolores. And I truly appreciate your trust in me. I do agree to your terms, and thank you. Very much. You won't regret this, I promise."

"I like hungry agents. They work harder than the established ones. Get me over this listing, Harrison, and I'll introduce you to everyone in this city." She stands and shakes my hand.

"You've got yourself a deal."

When I reach the sidewalk and the door closes behind

me, I fist pump and punch the air. "Yes. Yes. Fucking yes!" I turn around and jump out of the way of an older lady in her speeding electric chair. "Sorry." That doesn't temper my excitement.

I run up the stairs to tell Nick and Natalie, finding them on the back patio playing backgammon. "I got the listing," I say, pulling out a chair next to Natalie.

"You did?" she asks, a big smile on her face. "Dolores can be tough, but I knew she'd love you."

Reaching over, she rubs her fingers on my collar. "Is that makeup?"

"Apparently. I need fresh clothes. I can't believe I had to meet her wearing this."

"Why did you?" Nick asks, moving his pip. "You could have changed clothes first. Your stuff is upstairs." His eyes peek up at his wife, and there's a mischievous look in them. "Sorry, babe."

She huffs. "This baby has scrambled my brain. I never used to lose, and now it's all I do." She's still not showing, but there's a fullness to her face that wasn't there before. It looks good on her, and has me imagining those small changes on Tatum.

Angling toward me, she asks, "Can we talk about Tatum and the pregnancy?"

"Sure, I could use the outside perspective."

The game is forgotten as her attention redirects to me. "I'm happy for you both. I'm just a little shocked. Or a lot, honestly. It's a big change from us having to referee the space if you both occupied it to you guys having a baby together. It makes me nervous."

"I hear what you're saying, and there's not a thought in there that I haven't shared. But I want this baby."

"What about Tatum?" she asks as if that's even a question.

"I want the full package, which includes her. I care about her, Nat. I get where you're coming from. Tatum and I don't make sense on the surface or from our history. But when we're together, we do. We click."

Nick takes a drink of his beer and then says, "We don't want either one of you to get hurt, but Natalie and I also know we can't butt in or protect you. We just have to air the initial concerns, which you've now addressed."

Natalie gently rests her hand on my arm. "You know I adore you, Harrison, but I worry where that leaves us if something goes wrong."

I wasn't expecting to have this conversation, but there's a lot of things I didn't expect to happen when I came to New York, mainly to fall for Tatum all over again. Fall? My stomach tightens because I may not have said anything to her or have to answer to my friends, but I can't lie to myself.

My relationship might appear to be only a few weeks old, but we were something special back in Catalina. I knew that then, which is how I was so sure she'd be in my life again. We've had some obstacles in our way, but the road ahead has been cleared, and I'm not taking any shortcuts when it comes to her.

"Your allegiance lies with Tatum. I understand that, and I'd never come between the two of you, but maybe we're supposed to work out. Maybe this baby is a sign that we're tied together in this universe," I say.

"You sound like my mom," Nick says under a chuckle.

"Cookie might understand what's going on better than I can, but I know what I feel and what I see."

Although Natalie's hand had already returned to the table in front of her, her attention and the joy in her eyes shine on me. "I can't ask for anything more than someone who loves her through the good and the bad. Do you love Tatum?"

And there it is. All I have to do is tell the truth, but I should tell the woman I love first. "I hope you understand that I need to talk to Tatum before I talk to you guys."

"We do, man," Nick adds. "Go change clothes. You look like shit. And then I suspect you won't be joining us for soup?"

More? I start laughing. "Not tonight, but what's on the menu?"

With her arms in front of her already explaining, Natalie replies, "French onion. I got the best gruyere at the market today for the topping."

I scoot my chair out. "Sounds good." Gripping the back of it, I debate how I'm supposed to say this without getting Natalie excited and Nick rolling his eyes at me, ready to say I told you so. Ah, fuck it. They're my best friends. If I can't share my happiness with them, who can I? My family, but that's the next step. "I'm going to take some of my clothes over to Tatum's, so I might not be around as much in the next few days."

Their reactions are predictable, sans the I told you so, but that's what makes them so great. They voice their concerns up front, but when all is said and done, they support Tatum and me. "Oh, and we're having the baby. I didn't know if you thought we might not, so yeah, I'm going to be a daddy."

"Harrison," Natalie says, getting up quickly. She hugs me, and I think I feel her body rattle with a soft sob.

"Are you crying?"

"I'm just so happy for you, and I get to have a baby at the same time as my best friend. This is such a beautiful day."

Nick comes around and pats me on the back before pulling his wife to his chest. "C'mere, babe." To me, he shakes my hand. "Congratulations. Look at us all grown up and becoming dads."

"Didn't see that coming."

"The best things in life aren't the ones we plan. They're the ones that happen naturally," he says.

Nick could be talking about his own relationship or mine. *Maybe both. Definitely both.*

Whatever the grand plan was for me, I'm glad Tatum and this baby are a part of my destiny.

26

Tatum

"Don't be nervous."

His voice is soothing, despite me being too anxious to say anything.

Holding my hand on top of his leg, Harrison says, "Look at me, Tate."

I look at the handsome man next to me in the cab and nod, too anxious to say anything. His hold tightens, giving me security, and he kisses me on the cheek. "It doesn't matter what they say or don't say. All that matters is what's right here in this car. You. Me. And this baby."

"I can't drink." Panic rises inside. "I shouldn't admit it, but I need a glass of wine or something when I'm around them."

"The French drink wine when—"

"I'm not French, and I'm not drinking. I understand it's a coping method." Taking a deep breath, I exhale, seeing the restaurant up ahead. "I'll just have to get by with . . . I don't know. Water and you. That's enough."

He chuckles. "Glad I can be of service. But for real, you say the word, and we'll leave."

"Thank you." I do feel calmer though I won't truly feel better until this dinner is over. I can usually handle dinner with my parents, especially on my birthday, knowing I'll get something fabulous or a blank check. But this dinner is different. Not only am I introducing my boyfriend to them but I'm also telling them I'm pregnant.

Sure, I could wait on the latter, but why? My friends know, so it's only right that my parents do before Page Six does.

We walk into the restaurant, and we're directed to the bar to wait. "What do you want to drink, baby?"

Baby . . . I remember the first time he called me that and how for that time I was with him, I felt like his. Now hearing it in public like it's a fact, I find peace because he's truly shown me how much he cares. It may seem like a little thing, but it's more than I've ever let anyone else in. "Perrier with lemon, please."

I remain standing awkwardly off to the side near a column as he works his way between two couples to order the drinks at the bar. It wasn't that long ago that I was jealous of him talking to those women after The Resistance concert. Rubbing my baby, I relish in the comfort that spreads. Now, here I am about to be the mother of his child.

This is quite the plot twist.

He returns, handing me a drink. "This place is packed. Do we need a reservation?"

"My parents got one. The name Devreux carries weight in certain circles."

He sips his drink, indifferent. None of that seems to impress him. It's something I appreciate.

"Harrison?"

We both turn toward the sound of a woman calling his name. My instinct tells me to mark him, grab onto him, to do something to stake my claim. But that's not something I need to lower myself to do. I hold the cold glass a little tighter when I see a blonde with legs hanging out of a very short skirt. It's a skirt I would totally wear, which makes her more annoying.

Peeking over at Harrison, I'm thinking he's caught in some fight or flight mode the way he's eyeing the exit but knows he's stuck with me.

She throws herself at him, at my baby daddy, hugging him as though she owns . . . or has had sex with him. I'm tempted to step away to give them privacy. Not really. It's the jealousy I'm trying to walk away from, but that's inside me, so yeah. Fun times.

Oohing over him, she says, "You look so good."

"I did not expect to see you, Talon."

Talon? I flip my hair over my shoulder and raise my chin. She asks, "Why didn't I call you back?"

"I guess because I never called," he says and then smoothly takes a gulp of his drink. Yep, he's all mine, ladies, and I can't be more proud. "I thought you got married?"

"I was supposed to. Got to the altar when he presented a prenup, so I called it off."

She shrugs like it is no big deal. "If he doesn't trust me, we have nothing."

"Agreed."

Patting his chest, she laughs, but it's fake as fuck. "So I was thinking we should give it another go."

He reaches for my hand, but since I had kind of slinked away, he has to bend to get it. "This is my girlfriend. She's having my baby. God, I can't wait."

I need alcohol for this. Hitting him with a glare for dragging me into this, I do what a good girlfriend would and face her with a smile. "Yep, we're having a baby together. I mean, the sex is fantastic, so go me. I don't need him for the money though, but I'm glad he's loaded." Poking her with my elbow, I continue, "Loaded. *Wink. Wink. Nudge. Nudge.* If you know what I mean. This baby didn't happen magically."

"I'm gonna go," she says, scrunching her nose and looking at me like I'm a lunatic.

Whatever gets the job done is what I always say. Not sure what worked, but something in there got her to leave him alone. I take a long sip of my bubbly water, looking at him innocently. When I swallow, I then say, "She sure left in a hurry."

"Wonder why?" His sarcasm drips as his arm comes around me, and he kisses my head.

"I didn't get a name in that introduction, just that I'm your girlfriend and your baby mama."

"I'm sorry. I didn't think it mattered since I have no intention of ever seeing her again. Her name is Talon. She's a flight attendant."

"And you've had sex with her?"

A cocked eyebrow highlights his wide eyes. "Is that something you really want to know?"

"I already know, or you would have denied it. Since you didn't, I guess I got my answer."

We're close to fighting over this, and that's not something I want to do tonight or ever when other women are involved. We're together, or we're not. There's not going to be an in-between. But I was privy to him handling that situation, and I can't reason myself into being mad.

I take his hand and hold it proudly. I'm just about to tell him how I really feel, not about that woman, but about him, those three words that I haven't said to any man I've dated.

He drags his phone from his pocket, and when he checks it, he says, "Table's ready."

Probably best . . .

After going to the hostess stand, we're led through the restaurant to a quieter corner. To my surprise, my parents are already seated. There have been birthdays where they have been late . . . or just not shown up. I release Harrison's hand to greet both of them with a hug. Then turn. "This is Harrison Decker, my boyfriend. Harrison, Camille and Laurence Devreux."

A round of greetings is followed by us sitting down at the table and placing our drink orders. I order another sparkling water, and Harrison orders the same. A little squeeze of my leg under the table follows. Before he pulls away, I grab it, holding it like a security blanket.

"No vodka or wine?" my mom asks.

"No, I have an early meeting tomorrow, and I want to get up to work out." That's too much information. Rambling is always a dead giveaway to a lie. It doesn't have to be a lie, though. I could work out. I need to.

My dad says, "Happy Birthday. Has it been a nice day?"

"I had a lovely day yesterday. The office celebrated. Harrison and I decided to celebrate with you since we were seeing you guys today."

"I'm not a guy, Tatum," my mom says, hot on my heels about the slang. Her attention turns to Harrison. "Weren't you at the Christiansen's anniversary party?"

Harrison answers confidently, "Yes, I was there. Nick and I grew up together. We weren't introduced unfortunately, so it's nice to finally meet you."

My mom leans forward, her eyes studying him. "You and Tatum were not together at the dinner, from what I remember. But you did go running after her."

Glancing at me, Harrison smiles, self-assured and ready to slay the dragon. "I didn't run after her. I was checking on her well-being." He gave her more than that rude question deserved.

"You are the other godparent." A little laugh escapes her.

"I am."

My dad jumps in the fray. "You've been dating him since then?"

"Officially," Harrison replies. "But I've wanted to be with your daughter from the moment we met."

"And when was that?" my mom asks.

I say, "Almost five years ago. We met in Catalina at the same time as Nick and Natalie."

"The baby news is wonderful. They are such a lovely couple. Don't you think?"

I say, "Of course, we think so, Mom. They're our best friends."

The drinks are delivered, and everybody takes a sip at the same time, like returning to your corner in the middle of a boxing match. I'll refresh and then get pumped up for the next round.

My dad delivers the next punch. "A new relationship and a birthday. A lot of pressure comes with that, Harrison. What did you get Tatum for her birthday? She has very expensive tastes." *Oh he did not just go there.*

Leaning forward, Harrison replies, "Well, sir, I haven't given her the present yet. I was waiting until we got back to the apartment."

I could worry about the small details like him telling my parents he's coming home with me. But tonight, I have bigger fish to fry. We've gotten over one hump with that meeting my new boyfriend. I'm thinking we should wait until after the main course to tell them about the baby. I wish Harrison and I had discussed when to drop the bomb-shell before we got here.

My parents seem to be in top form—aloof, quick with the judgments, and ready to take advantage of any short-coming that presents itself. Basically, just like my childhood.

We order our food, and the conversation veers toward lighter topics, ones more suitable for their moods, like their travels and what they're planning for the holidays still six months away.

An envelope slides across the table during dessert. I don't need to open it to know what it is, but I do, putting on the show for them, like a blank check will ever make up for my lost childhood. "Thank you. I appreciate it."

"What do you think you're buying with it?" my mom asks.

"I'm not sure. Something special." *Maybe, this birthday's gift will go toward my baby.* Right now, I don't want to tell them. I don't want to gift them with this beautiful news.

But my nerves are starting to get the better of me again. *I don't even think I can eat dessert.* I look at Harrison for assurance and find it in the depth of his blue eyes.

I fold the check and put it in my clutch before I find Harrison's hand under the table again. This is the moment. The one when I tell my parents they're about to become grandparents.

"Mom? Dad? Harrison and I would like to tell you something important."

My mom is onto us, her eyes looking back and forth between us like she's watching Wimbledon. "Why build it up? Just say it."

One more glance is exchanged with my one ally at the table before I say, "I'm pregnant."

Boom.

Just like that.

I'm in. I drop the bomb. And then I sit there and wait for World War III to begin.

Except it doesn't.

There wasn't any noise before I confessed my secret, but now it's dead quiet in this corner of the restaurant. The waiter even stops by, but as soon as he opens his mouth, he closes it and rushes away again.

My mom asks, "This is a joke, right? The godparent thing was too much, so you having your own baby at this point in your life is not a good idea. Please tell me you're trying to get a rise out of us like you did when you were a teen."

I can't say I was hoping for the best. I was expecting the worst. And she beat those expectations. "You're a horrible person."

"Tatum," my dad snaps at me.

"You both are. I don't know why you had me."

"Because of the inheritance," my mom replies like that is normal.

Harrison is standing and pulling out my chair. "We're done here."

I don't remember breathing or not breathing. I only remember the look in their eyes as we got up and decided to leave them behind. I also remember how the world got quiet that night, my thoughts screaming in my head.

Harrison was holding my hand but already held my heart. And that night he proved it. On the sidewalk, I tugged him to a stop. When he turned back, unsure why I did that, he asks, "What's going on?"

"I love you."

27

Harrison

I HAD PLANS.

Romantic plans.

Plans that included us dancing in the living room, romancing her on her birthday, and then telling her how I feel about Tatum. But after that . . . after her parents just told her that she was born so they could receive a fucking inheritance, I'm livid. *How can parents do that to their own flesh and blood? On her fucking birthday, no less.*

Standing on a sidewalk in the middle of Manhattan wasn't my plan for romancing my girl, but my brave beauty —who loves me—needs to know this truth. "I love you, Tatum."

She never appeared to second-guess what she confessed, and neither do I.

Nodding, she asks, "You do?"

"Call me crazy, but I've fallen completely in love with you." Raising her hand to my mouth, I kiss it. "You drive me nutty sometimes, and I find you so hard to read at other times. But we have something special, a connection that time and distance never broke. Can't break." Pulling her into my arms, I say, "I love you, Tatum. All of you."

Her smile cracks open, and her arms tighten around me. "I love you, too. So much."

I catch her rolling her eyes, though. "What is it?"

"I have nothing to complain about other than water under the bridge that you never texted or called, even when you had a way to get my number."

"Yeah," I say, sighing, "I fucked up, but I'm willing to do the time to make it up to you." Swaying her hips back and forth, I ask, "What are you going to do for me for making the same mistake?" I waggle my eyebrows so easily pleased.

Her laughter is so good to hear. I know her parents' disgusting attitude and comment will settle in, but I don't see regret in her eyes. Yet. *She's much stronger than I am.*

"How about we get home so I can show you how I plan to make up for that mistake? I might even need to make up for it several times over."

"It's your birthday, but I'm getting the presents. I like how you celebrate, Devreux."

"Just you wait, Decker. I'm about to show you how sorry I am for letting this happiness slip away back then." Tugging me toward the curb, she's quick to grab a cab that just dropped off another couple. I duck in right behind her.

The lights from the stores that we pass flash through the cab of the car. It's not late, and it's Friday, but from what I can tell of New York, every night of the week is like this. Busy. Alive. We're not too far from the apartment, so it doesn't take long to get back.

By the time we reach the elevator, our lips are locked. The doors open, and I'm shoved against the wall in a kiss so hard that I might just have to take her right here in the hallway. We barely get her door open before our clothes start coming off.

My shirt at the entrance.

Shoes in the living room.

Her dress doesn't make it to the bedroom.

My socks and pants aren't on by the time we reach the bed.

Both of us are naked and climbing on the bed like we haven't been fed in weeks. There's been no mention of her family since we left, and I'm not going to bring it up. I'm just happy I'm the one she trusts enough to be with.

I never know what to expect when I am with Tatum. She may want to be in control, or she may want me to lead the way. It may be rough or romantic. The one thing I do know is that it's always amazing.

Our lips pull apart, and she says, "No need to worry about birth control."

"Guess not." Hovering over her, I sink into her sweet heat, watching her eyes as I push inside.

She takes a breath and then opens her legs even more as I begin to thrust. "Can you keep your eyes open and on me? I want you to try, okay, baby?" Besides how she looks at me when she sees me first thing in the morning, this is my new favorite. Just as I ask, her eyes stay locked on mine.

We've been through so much, but this makes the ache go away. We make love and fuck, but it's not until I lower my hand between us and rub that bud that she's sent over. I keep pushing and then pulling back, hoping to send her over into that beautiful abyss.

I keep thrusting until I hear her say, "I love you," in the heat of passion and then, "Harrison." Her body tenses, and then her release hits hard. I trail right behind her, falling deeper in love, in lust, and everything in between with this woman.

Lying together right after, I've barely caught my breath, but ask, "Can I give you my present now?"

As if she just got a shot of energy, she laughs. "I'm not going to say no."

I reach into the nightstand and pull out a box. "It's not a ring," I preface the gift, hoping to stave off any disappointment.

She laughs. "Okay. It's not a ring. *Noted*."

Setting the box down on her chest, I kiss each perfect tit and then her nipples before saying, "Okay, you can open it."

Giddy, she takes it, and asks, "What is it?"

Feeling it's more of a rhetorical question, I don't feel the need to explain before she's even seen it.

Laughter rips through her. "Did you actually buy this New Yorker a silver necklace in the shape of California?"

"I did," I say with all the pride I can muster, which isn't much since I just gave her everything I had of me.

"Put it on me, surfer boy." Lifting her hair up, she turns enough for me to clasp the necklace together.

"There you go."

Dragging the state charm back and forth along the chain, she says, "I love it more than I would have thought."

I return to kissing her tits and the space between. Looking up, I say, "That's actually not the gift. I mean, I bought it for you, but what I really wanted to do is take you home with me."

"Home?"

"Yeah, I can introduce you to my family, take you to my house, which I think you're really going to like, and anywhere you want to go or shop or see. I'll even do one of those cheesy Hollywood tours with you if you want. The whole weekend is on me, and I'll be your personal guide to LA." I kiss her again and say, "Happy Birthday, baby."

When she tenses and crosses her arms over her chest, I look up, questioning with my eyes. She looks toward the closed curtains, staring at nothing while I keep staring at her.

The smile is long gone, and her lips aren't deviating from that tight lip line striped across her face. Nothing about her current state is the Tatum I know, much less the one I just made love to. I push up and sit next to her, leaning against the headboard, and ask, "What's wrong?"

"You keep saying home."

"Yeah, LA," I say. Her eyes drift to the ceiling above me. That's closer. Progress, but her body is unchanging. "I know hopping from one city to another may not be that exciting, but there's great people-watching and—"

"I don't care about other people. I just want to be alone with you. Here. *Home.*"

I'm not sure what she's talking about, but her anger is growing, and from the way she's holding herself, she's digging her heels in for a fight. "Why do you keep saying that?"

I'm hit with a hard glare. "Because you're not catching the subtlety. I think I need to spell it out."

"You don't. I get it. You don't like the gift. It's fine, Tatum. Let's not make a big thing. It's your birthday, and you got a blank check. Life is great, right?"

I'm not as clever as I think I am. She can read between the lines just as well as I can read her subtlety. She sits up, her jaw slack in disbelief. "I thought so until you had to ruin it." *I ruined it?*

She flips the covers off and storms to the bathroom. I hear the lock click into place, but nothing else—not the tub or the shower. She needs to cool off, and I need to cool down.

I get out of bed, pull on my pants, and walk into the living room. Pacing the length of the windows a few times, I find my irritation still scratches under my skin. She once said that she wants to learn how to fight. It's a skill we could both use because right now we only know how to make things worse.

Do I go to her, or do I wait for her to come to me?

I didn't know I did anything wrong by wanting to show her my hometown and meet my family. My parents, my brothers and Madison, will not be anything but welcoming toward Tate. Harlow will love her clothes. And they won't see her as a fucking dollar sign.

Seems even sex can't knock my anger at her parents away. Tatum's asked me about whether I live in a house or an apartment, so I thought she would find it interesting to see my place. Meet the people I love most in the world. *But why the anger?*

Nick called us oil and water.

I used to believe that until Tatum lowered her walls and let me into her world. And then I realized whether it's oil or water, we're the same underneath. We mix just fine. It's the outside world that seems set on destroying us.

She's convinced only one can win. If so, will it be California or New York?

Maybe it's both or the one I never saw coming. Or fucking Connecticut like Dolores and her family, for all I know. I don't know anything, it seems, when it comes to us, except that we'll make up. So I stay, sitting down on the couch and wondering if this is where I'm sleeping tonight, aka the doghouse.

"I think dating is good," she says from the corner of the

hall. I find her in the dark, arms still crossed, and dressed in her robe. I listen. "We need more of those."

"I thought that's what we were doing?"

"Yeah, we were jumping ahead too."

She's not wrong. I say, "I thought you'd like the trip. You don't have to go."

"I think I should. I want to see that part of your life." It's not lost on me that she hasn't come closer. "Can we go this weekend?"

So now we're going to ramrod this weekend to get it over with? I don't have any other places to show to Lara this weekend, and no other showings either, so I reply, "Sure, I can be ready in the morning. You?"

Her armor finally lowers, and she takes small steps closer. Handling her delicately works wonders. I'm not tricking her into anything. I'm reminding her that she's safe with me. She sits next to me, close with our knees touching but not our bodies. "Same, except I have one request."

I'm not exactly waving a white flag of surrender, so it might be a bit early to listen to her list of conditions. Squeezing my eyes closed and pinching the bridge of my nose, I hope to ward off the headache I can feel coming on. Then I look up, and ask, "What is it?"

"I want you to put in an offer for me."

This is the turn I didn't see ahead. "On a property?"

"I want the brownstone next to Natalie."

"It's seventeen million dollars, Tate, and Dolores told me she won't accept anything that's not over that price."

"Then write an offer for eighteen."

My eyes narrow as I stare through my confusion. "What are you doing?"

"I'm buying a home. Neutral territory. A place where we both can exist equally."

"I don't want to only exist with you. I want to be with you —completely—whatever that means." I rest my hand on her leg, finding comfort selfishly in the small connection.

"I want to go to Los Angeles with you this weekend, but . . ." She pulls a folded piece of paper from her pocket. Holding open the blank birthday check, she says, "I want that house. Can you make it happen?"

28

Harrison

"Laws schmaws."

Tatum waves it off like I'm talking nonsense. "I'm not looking to spend time in jail for breaking real estate laws in place for a reason. It's fine. I have someone who can represent you, but at this stage, since you're dead-set on submitting eighteen, all they have to do is submit the paperwork."

I waited for most of the flight to bring up the fact that I can't represent the seller and the buyer because I already told her what the buyer wants. I wasn't prepared to have that conversation and her throwing out eight figures like it's nothing isn't something I'm used to.

Representing both of them is legal if I'm careful with my words. After that, Tatum would have been my first choice to represent. But I blew it by bringing up the client's wish and setting a precedent. With any other buyer, I would have been squeezing them for nineteen or twenty.

She napped half the flight and then watched a show before she was awake enough to discuss the house and offer.

"If I submit an offer, are you going to counter?" she asks.

"Maybe. I have to see what the clients want to do. As soon as we get back to my place, I'll call her."

"Your place." She leans her head against the headrest and rolls it to face me. "Tell me about it."

"I have a house on the Bird Streets."

"I don't know what that means."

"The Bird Streets is a highly sought-after section of homes above the Sunset Strip named after birds like Nightingale and Thrasher. You had me pegged for being stereotypical from the beginning. Guess I didn't disappoint."

She reaches for my hand and holds it. And if I'm not mistaken, I spot remorse laced into her features. "I'm sorry for saying that. I don't think you're stereotypical at all. If I did, I wouldn't be with you." She licks her lips and then adds, "I actually think you're very special, a treasure I've found somehow out of all the trash I've dated."

I lean over and kiss her. "I love you."

Kissing me again, she runs her fingers along my jaw, holding me there, and she whispers, "I love you, too."

~ Tatum ~

The seat belt sign comes on, and the attendant announces our arrival at LAX.

I've been to Los Angeles a lot over the years for shopping, vacations, visiting friends, and invitations to celebrity events. When I think of Hollywood, I think of mansions. That's not what I get with Harrison's house.

I get a home that a family could live in. Modern only in clean lines, the natural wood elements in the shelves and the tables keep it grounded and earthy in nature. The leather chairs and the plush couch have an elevated but old-Hollywood vibe to them. It's the art that stands out.

Standing in front of the fireplace after a tour, I stare up at the modern art that's bold in the use of orange and blues with a hint of red in the background. Art gives insight into someone's life. Considering not only is Harrison a real estate agent but that he pursued me well after he had a right to give up, the art fits the man.

It's the view that steals the limelight, though. "You can see all of Los Angeles and more from here." I look over my shoulder. "It's stunning. Open, like you. You know, if we're comparing that kind of thing, my view down the avenue is much tighter." I shrug. "Fitting with how closed off I can be."

He comes around me, slipping his arms around my middle. "I don't see it that way. You're not closed off to me. And you have an incredible view for New York City."

"True."

Kissing my neck, he says, "I'm going to contact Robert, the agent who will work with you on the deal, and then call Dolores."

"I wanted you to get the commission."

"Don't worry about me. I have a good deal going with Robert because I explained the situation. But ultimately, I feel better bringing him in to keep things on the up and up." He starts down the hall but comes back standing at the head of it and asks, "Are you sure about this? It's a lot of money, money you said you didn't have. If this is revenge, it might backfire, and where will that leave you?"

"They don't care about the money. They probably won't blink an eye."

Just because I've never spent more than half a million at one time before doesn't mean I couldn't." With a hand resting on my stomach protectively, I say, "I want that house." I now get why Natalie already touches her stomach though there's no pooch. *But there will be. For both of us.* Surreal. And now, I want to buy a house.

That house has so many benefits from Natalie being next door to Juni on the other side of her, the backyard, the neighborhood, and the location in the city. Most of all, it felt like a place I could call home with my baby. *With Harrison.* And if all I am to my parents is an inheritance check, then that's what I'll spend their check on too.

It stings. It still stings, what she said. *And my father didn't defend.* How quickly, without any hesitation whatsoever, my mom said I was born to satisfy . . . *sate* their love of money. I've received no text or call since last night to right that wrong either. I thought I also had their respect. I may have lived easily because of their money, but I still got a college degree, and I'm putting that to good use. What Nat and I do at STJ does good for many. *And not just those who can afford us.*

Harrison heads down the hall, adding, adding, "My mom said she stocked the fridge. Make yourself at home, eat something. There are drinks in there as well. I'll be back shortly."

I get a bottle of water from the neatly arranged ones in the pantry and then grab a bag of sour cream & onion chips because I'm pregnant and want them, and those are the excuses I'm using to justify the snack food addiction I've recently developed.

Meandering down the hall, I can hear him in the office. I return to the bedroom he showed me on the tour. I like that I get a whiff of his scent in the air. The room has the same killer view as the living room and even a door that leads to the large, shared balcony.

I eat my chips out there, staring as far as the eyes can see, and start to wonder if I could live out here permanently. This is where he's based. This is where he intends to return to. It's already set up and waiting for the family to be here.

I finish the snack and crumple the bag in my hand. This isn't a life I'm familiar with, but I don't think I can discount it if he plans to live here. Can I live in this foreign city? Do I want to?

All the reasons I love Dolores's house aren't replicated here other than it's a nice home to live with a family. There's a backyard, and the location seems great, but our friends, *his friend*, is even in Manhattan. Well, Nat is more sister than friend if I'm honest. *I can introduce you to my family, take you to my house, which I think you're really going to like . . .*

His family is here.

A row of surfboards lines the far end of the deck, and it makes me realize I'm taking away all the things he loves best by hoping he stays in the city.

Are we too different to make this work?

The last thing I want is to make him sacrifice a life that he not only created but built. That life is here. I'm staring right at it and everything he loves, the stuff he talks about, what he wants.

Feeling a little dizzy, I grab onto the rail to steady myself. I close my eyes and let it wash through me before it passes. It's the early flight and the airport crowds . . . I'm probably just tired. I should lie down.

I return back inside and take another sip of water before I toss my trash in the bathroom and climb onto his huge bed. The house is big enough to have some distance between the rooms, but occasionally, I hear Harrison laugh or say something loudly like he's talking to an old acquaintance.

Whether I had him representing me or how it turned out with me working with another agent, I'm glad I could play a part in helping him establish himself. If I want him to stay in New York, that's what I'm going to have to do.

"TATUM?"

My eyes open to the sound of a female voice calling my name. I blink rapidly a few times, but I can't wrangle my thoughts together. What am I looking at? Where am I? Sitting up, I look around the room, realizing I'm at Harrison's house. Where is he, and why is there an unfamiliar woman calling my name?

"Hello?" I call back, trying to shake the sleepiness. This baby is taking it out of me already, and we haven't even officially met.

Going to the door, I notice the office is wide open down the hall. I peek out. "Hello?"

"Hello?" she calls right back and then appears from the other end of the hall to where I'm standing. She's an older woman with light blond hair, gentle waves framing her face that only touches her shoulders. When she sees me, she smiles, and unlike the voice, there is a familiarity in that. "Hi, I'm Harrison's mom, Nora."

"Oh, hi," I reply awkwardly, unsure of how I look after my nap. I touch my hair and fidget with my clothes. "I was napping."

Her smile never wavers. "I'm sorry for waking you. Harrison got called to an appointment. Clients he's been working with for a while want to submit an offer."

"Ah." Do I move? Do I walk toward her? She seems nice enough, but I don't know what to think since she's not exactly my favorite person based on how she pawned him off when he was growing up.

I should move. I come down the hall, and she retreats into the kitchen, leaning on the counter, looking very much at home. I say, "Can I help you with something, or are you waiting for him to return?"

"No," she says, shaking her head and laughing. "I'm here for you. He didn't know how long it would take and didn't want to leave you stranded. I can drive you somewhere or take you shopping. Do you need anything?"

The back of my legs hit the couch, and I casually lean against the arm of it. "I'll be fine right here."

Coming around, she goes to open the large accordion-style back door. "I didn't mean to make this awkward. Maybe some fresh air will help clear it, and we can sit outside and get to know each other." She stops as if another idea has entered her head. "Or I could go?" She starts for the barstool and grabs her purse. "That's probably best. We can talk when Harrison brings you over for dinner."

Now I feel bad, and that makes this encounter not only awkward but a bit irritating. "You can stay. I just need a minute to get my bearings and to freshen up."

With her purse straps on her shoulder, she asks, "Are you sure?"

"Please stay."

She lowers her purse, and says, "All right."

After verifying I don't have makeup or drool running down my face after the nap, I join her outside on the deck. She stands and asks, "Would you like to sit up or by the pool?"

Hey. Hey. She's talking my language. I love a pool, but I'm confused. "What pool?"

"The one on the lower deck," she replies like I know what she's referring to.

I walk past where she's sitting and look over the railing.

Oh my God! That. Is. Amazing.

Ten or more feet below where I stand, another deck juts out from the side of the cliff with a rectangle pool built into it. I turn back to her, grinning like a loon. "I didn't know it was there."

"Yes." She nods, and adds, "It's nice for when he has kids one day as well. The gate can be locked up here so no littles can get down there."

Kids? Littles? Harrison has already put safety plans in place for the future. My hand goes instinctively to my belly as I look over at the pool again. "Smart," I reply, the word barely fitting around the lump in my throat.

She comes to stand beside me. "I brought strawberry lemonade since it's warm out today." She offers me one with hers in the other.

"Thank you." I take it and sip.

Leaning her arms on the railing, she stares ahead at the whole of Los Angeles, and says, "I was trying to remember how long it's been since I met one of Harrison's girlfriends."

"Have there been that many?"

She laughs and looks my way. "Many. I hope you don't mind me being honest."

"I prefer honesty."

"But there haven't been many I've met. None actually. I already knew his prom date since she grew up down the street, but other than that, I couldn't remember one that I've met. And here you are."

She shares the same blue eyes as Harrison. I know most of my kids . . . *kids?* When did this become a plural thing? A sharp exhale gets me back on track with my thoughts.

Genetically, my kids should carry my brown-eyed gene. But for a short moment, it's fun to imagine them with blue eyes like their daddy.

"Here I am."

"Harrison not only wanted me to meet you but wanted to make sure you're taken care of while he's gone. His sister would call him smitten."

"Smitten." I roll the word over my tongue as it brings a smile to my face. "I'm smitten too." But it's the smile on her face that tells me everything I need to know. *She's happy for him. She's happy that her son is smitten. With me.* Huh. I like that. I like her.

We eventually sit down and chat about me, growing up in New York, my family—I leave a lot out—and then share more about my work.

She's so lovely and kind, relaxed in that California laid-back way I always hear about. I can't get the woman before to fit what I had heard regarding the nannies. Especially after she spoke so fondly of her kids and raising them.

"Do you want to have children, Tatum?"

The question isn't out of left field. We've been talking about family for an hour now. But it's not something I've ever been asked other than maybe Natalie at some point in our lives. The other issue is how do I handle this, considering I'm pregnant with not only her son's child but her second grandkid. I won't lie about this baby.

It's a pact I made myself the moment the doctor confirmed I was pregnant. I've hidden enough of myself over the years. I won't drag a baby into that web.

This is about new beginnings for me, my child, and Harrison. This is about finding happiness right here in the middle of the chaos.

"I do want children. I'm not sure how many, but I do."

"Harrison always talked about having kids."

I laugh, and the release feels good. I'm surprisingly comfortable with her. "He'll make a great father."

"He'll be a better example than the one he had." She reaches over from her Adirondack chair to tap my arm, a lot like we're in this together. I like that. "Bill learned in time, but some habits die hard. He's a very driven man. We once lost everything. That changed him." She laughs to herself. "He used to have a bear of an ego. He's a good man but struggles with being in touch with his emotional side sometimes. He's getting better."

I'm not sure what to say, so I offer her an ear and listen. She goes on to say, "He still believes in tough love, so that's what he models."

She takes sips of her lemonade and then falls silent. She has a way of sharing so much of her emotion in her words. I say, "I'm sorry to hear of your struggles. Do you mind sharing what happened?"

"Not at all. I wear that story like a badge of honor. The market crashed and the housing market flipped on itself. He had a million listings, but there were no buyers. Everyone was too scared to spend the money. We had four kids, and we were about to lose everything, so we went to my parents, who paid our mortgage, our bills, and for the nannies we needed to keep our lives in order. My parents were very proud old money. They wouldn't allow us to look like there were any struggles. Appearances were everything." She angles toward me. "We owed my parents so much money, but then I got a listing and sold a house, and then another, and then another. For the first time in my life, I was the breadwinner. I was able to get the clients and find the buyers he couldn't. It took five years, but I turned everything around for us."

"I thought he ran the company?"

"He does. I was a real estate mogul at the time, but my top job was being a mom, and I missed it. So we transitioned the business back into his care, and I started to stay home again." She laughs as if she's in on an inside joke. "If you listen to Harrison, he had thirty nannies in two years. He also has a vivid imagination. It's not that he lies about it. It's that . . ." Her smile wanes. "I think he just missed me. Sweet boy."

My heart aches for him. And for the first time, I can see that she missed her kids too. *She missed time with her kids.* Whereas my mom probably missed where she *wasn't* rather than time with me. "He still is sweet. How many did he have over those five years?"

"Three. He did his best to scare them off, but they stuck around because they adored him even though he was a little hellion."

"I can see that."

When I see her chest rise and fall slowly, her smile remains. "Harrison has said such beautiful things about you, Tatum."

"He's always quick to tell me I'm pretty."

She's nodding. "That's sweet, but he never once mentioned your beauty."

"Oh."

"He told me how creative you are in your job, and that you're ambitious, and there's no stopping you when you set your mind to something." Kindness fills the lines in her face as she continues, "He talks about your sense of style and that you own a room the moment you walk into it. He knows I love home design, so he spoke of your apartment capturing such warmth that he prefers to stay there over Nick's."

She goes on to say he loves my sense of humor and smile, but the one thing she doesn't mention is him talking about my looks. I don't know what to think about that. Although, honestly, I'm more than amazed at how much she knows about me. *He's talked about me to his mother.* She knows of the things Harrison loves about me. *I'm floored.*

"Hey."

We both turn back to see Harrison standing in the opening of the living room. "Hi," I say, pushing up to greet him.

Nora stands, and they hug each other. She says, "It's so good to see you."

"You saw me last week, Mom."

"You'll never understand until you have kids of your own."

The eyes I missed staring into find mine, and he smiles, opening his arm and pulling me to his side. We kiss, and he says, "My mom didn't share all my dirty secrets, did she?"

"Your secrets are safe." Pointing at him, I add, "Except the nannies. I thought you were running a halfway house of errant nannies. Nope, just a kids' exaggerated memory."

"Really?" He turns to his mom for confirmation.

She shrugs. "There were three, Harry."

I've never heard him called that, but it's cute to hear his nickname and to see him in his element. Maybe I judged this place too harshly and out of fear instead of for the home he's created and the family he has here.

"I could have sworn there were more. Guess I need to stop telling that story."

His mom walks inside. "Probably best. I'm going to get home, but I'll see you two tomorrow night?" She swings her purse straps onto her shoulder again.

"I look forward to it and meeting the family," I say.

Escaping Harrison's side, I go to her and give her a hug. Her embrace matches her personality—warm and inviting. "It was so nice to meet you and spend that time together."

"I agree. You were a lovely highlight of my day."

When she leaves, Harrison's staring at me like he doesn't recognize me. "What?" I ask, throwing my arms out and letting them fall to my sides again.

"Nothing."

"It's something, so just say it."

He comes to me and brings me into his arms again. With a kiss to my forehead, he whispers, "California sure does look good on you."

29

Harrison

I SHOULDN'T HAVE BROUGHT HER HERE.

In a house buried in The Hills at an Oscar-winners property, some D-grade producer has been chatting Tatum up while I've been stuck discussing a house in Brentwood coming on the market soon and needing an agent. There are strings attached. There always are. These attachments come in the form of the owner wanting to seal the deal with sex in the jacuzzi while her husband watches.

No fucking thanks.

I don't have to play nice. My portfolio speaks for itself. "You either hire the best or you go find some fucker down in the OC wanting to make a splash here in LA. Literally speaking. You have my secretary's number."

Cutting through the crowd, I have my eyes set on my girl, excited that it's me she'll be leaving with. Leaving is the goal, too. These Hollywood parties don't hold the same thrill that they used to.

Since getting out of LA, I've had my eyes opened. Maybe

that's all it took for me to see the bigger picture of what my life could be.

Tatum's confidence exudes in New York, so I'm not sure why she's shrinking under the Hollywood lights. Only a few more feet until I reach her, but I'm jerked to the side and under a bellowing greeting, an ex squeals when she sees me. "Harrison Decker, where the fuck have you been?" She jumps me—literally—a crab claw-like hold around me and she hugs me tight.

Trying to peel her off me is a feat unto itself. Gemma Maze, former model turned serious actress, hails from the UK, and accepted the Golden Globe last year for her performance as a pig in mud in some psychological thriller. I didn't see it, not ever wanting to see her again, in real life or on the big screen. She loves her drugs. *Some things never change . . .*

I put her on her feet again and quickly glance to find Tatum. Hoping she would have missed this scene, that hope is shredded under the glare she's giving me. I push through the crowd to reach her. "I didn't—"

"I know, but I don't like it here."

"Let's leave then." I take her hand and start for the door. The scene is familiar to most who are here. I look like her bodyguard trying to get her out from the hoard of fans and paparazzi spotlight. I'll play that role for her if it gets her safely out of here.

When valet pulls my M2 around, we get in so I can get us the fuck out. It's a few streets covered before I ask, "Are you okay?"

"I'm fine," she snaps, staring out her window.

Yikes. Not fine at all. "I didn't know she'd be there."

"You dated Gemma Maze? I don't know how I feel about that, Decker. I thought you had better taste than that."

Reaching over, I try to lighten her mood. "My taste improved with age."

"It sure as shit did." The edge to her tone could slice through any tension if the tension was rolling off of her to begin with.

"I'm sorry for bringing you here. You like to party, and you always seem up for a good time. So, I thought—"

"That wasn't a good time. That was me watching you get lady-handled by cougars and coke heads." She cracks her window and inhales a deep breath. I stop at a stop sign and look over when she turns toward me. "I can't drink and I'm pregnant. I feel bloated and I'm not even showing yet. What's it going to be like when I'm nine months pregnant?" Her voice keeps rising. "I'm going to be sitting home in Manhattan while you're out "closing deals" at parties in LA? That's not how I saw things going."

I hate fighting in a car, the confinement is too limiting in thought and space. "Can we please talk about this when we get home?"

"Home? *There you go again*," she says, sounding like she's given up. "This isn't my home, Harrison. And as much as you hate it, this baby goes where I go."

She's getting close to those lines, if crossed it can be hard to undo the damage already done. "Tatum," I warn, getting her attention. "I don't hate that you're having my baby— whether that be in LA, New York, or Nova Scotia—don't turn me into the bad guy for something I never said or even inferred. I'm going to say this again. We'll talk about it when we get home. I'm not doing it in the car."

"Maybe you don't get that choice. I don't have a say? God, I thought you were different. Sure, you have an arrogant side, but it wasn't jerk macho."

I grip the steering wheel, my anger starting to boil.

"That's a lot of fucking accusations in a four-block radius. Keep going, Tatum, and we'll fucking do this and get it out of the way."

"I don't want to get it out of the way. I want it resolved. You have me living in a purgatory not knowing if I'm going to heaven or hell."

"Hell, being LA? Wow," I say, shaking my head.

"To me, it is. Watching you at that party wasn't what I expected to see. You know I get jealous and although I'm working on that, I don't like women shoved in my face."

"You're confusing what you think happened and reality."

She scoffs so loud and then laughs deliriously that I glance over at her. "Me confusing reality. That's rich. And while we're at this, why are you driving your pregnant girlfriend when you've been drinking?"

She backs her bark with her bite, cutting her teeth deep. I need to take a breath, take a walk, put some space between us. I pull into my garage and cut the engine, ready to face her head on with this since that's the road she's choosing to travel tonight.

She gets out so fast that I don't even have time to help her. I follow her inside the house. She takes off her heels and then storms down the hall. "This was supposed to be my birthday present, not Decker's back in party mode weekend."

I expect the sound of a door slamming. I don't get that, though. Walking slowly toward the bedroom, my frame fills the doorway. I don't breach the entrance, giving her all the space she fucking needs to cool down. When she comes out of the closet with her suitcase in hand and dumps it on the bed, I ask, "What are you doing?"

"I'm leaving."

"It's eleven o'clock at night. Where are you going?"

"I'm sure there's a redeye I can catch," she replies with her back to me.

My eyes practically bulge out of my head. "You're flying home?"

Whipping back, she says, "Yes. *Exactly*. Home."

Now I'm pissed. "That's it. That's fucking it." I walk into the bedroom and shut the damn suitcase to the sound of her gasp. "You're not running away from this, away from me. This isn't what you do anymore. You have to break the pattern, Tatum."

"Every time I stay, I'm the one who gets screwed." The anger has left her shoulders sagging. Defeat rings through her tone, but I'm not sure what she thinks she's lost. An argument? Me? What she thought her life would be?

I'm lost in her hurricane as it destroys everything in her path. *Am I next?* No. I refuse to be. More than I did before, I get why she's defensive. Her parents suck. But I'm not like them. I desperately want her in my life. I love her, for fuck's sake. Now calls for being honest with that love though. "The second we touch on something too close for comfort, you barricade yourself behind walls too thick to break through."

Her arms cross over her chest in indignation. I've seen it too many times to play naïve. Her chin is raised as she mentally gathers her weapons together. I try to end this deadlock we find ourselves in, not wanting to fight with her about things that keep resurfacing. "You only get mad when you feel attacked. We may not know every little fucking thing about each other, but I've seen you for who you are, and you've seen me. I'm not a fucking stranger, Tatum—"

Her gaze hits me in the chest, slicing me up the center until she reaches my eyes. Fires shine so bright that she could light up the universe with her anger. It takes her a few seconds to come to me, the woman I know so well inside the walls of her apartment. Vulnerability douses the flames, and she says, "I'm lost in your world, Harrison, an outsider that feels misplaced."

"We're together, so why would you feel that way?"

"Because I'm standing in the middle of a party of strangers being hit on while you schmoozed. Why bother taking me at all?" *She does have a point. I hated that too.*

"I'm sorry for leaving you. I guess I always saw you as more of a party girl or socialite and would like to be there."

A humorless laugh rattles her chest as she looks down at the suitcase on the bed. "I used to revel in those titles, feeling I had earned them after endless partying for years." She looks up at me, and says, "I've never felt ashamed of being either. Until now." She moves toward the bathroom and with her back to me, she adds, "You're right. It's too late for me to figure out how to fly home right now. I'm tired, so I'm going to bed."

"It's probably best if we both get some rest, so we can figure this out tomorrow." I walk to the door to give her privacy. I didn't have a drink earlier, but I'm damn well having one now.

Before I leave, I say, "For the record, I didn't have anything except Perrier to drink because the things that I thought mattered when I was living in LA full-time don't anymore. Only you and that baby do."

She sucks in a staggered breath, and then I hear her start crying. I go to her, rubbing her shoulders, and kiss the back of her head. "It's going to be okay, Tate."

Turning in my hold, she hugs me so tight that I can't see her face. "Promise me. Promise me that you'll always be there for the baby, even if you can't be there for me."

"I'm going to be there for both of you. I love you, Tate."

Tilting her head, the tears glisten making her eyes look like precious gemstones. "Promise me, Harrison."

It's an easy promise for me to keep, so I reply, "I promise."

I come to bed just over an hour later. An hour of staring at the glittering city of LA had me wanting to make this right with her. She wants security. A place to call home for a family. She wants New York.

Although I want LA, I don't want to lose her. We have a lot to work through, the details of how our relationship will move forward. But it will be best discussed in the daylight and on full stomachs.

I climb into bed next to her sleeping body. She didn't tell me she was going to sleep but I understand we were standing our grounds in separate parts of the house. The pregnancy is taking a toll on her already and I know she needs more sleep.

Though her back is to me, I slide around her, wanting our bodies to mold together like they do at her apartment. Maybe then she'll feel what she can't see—that it doesn't matter where we live as long as we're together.

My mind is too busy for sleep and one of the memories that flashes is when I went to go pick up my clothes from the drycleaners after returning from Catalina . . .

I HANG the hanger on the hook in my car. It's weeks overdue, but with my sister being in the accident and niece still in the hospital, my laundry from Catalina wasn't a priority. My mom dropped it off though and I was down to my last day before they donated them. I don't mind the donation, but I was partial to the shirt I was wearing with Tatum.

She liked it.

That meant I would keep it in hopes of wearing it for her again. I made a promise to her, made her my mission, and unlike her pact, I intended to keep it.

Once I get home, I carry the plastic-wrapped clothes into my closet and rip off the packaging. A Ziploc dangles from the neck of the hanger. I open it to pull out a white piece of paper.

Probably one of the women working at the cleaners slipping me her number. It happens at businesses quite a bit.

I unfold it and read:

Tatum
   Her number written just below.

STANDING THERE SMILING LIKE A GOOFBALL, *I add the number to my phone.* "She broke her own pact. For me."

Once Madison and my niece are home, settled, I'll plan my quest to win Tatum over.

When the dust settles.

THE SUN HASN'T RISEN, but I need to hit the water to clear my head before tackling the day. I slip out of bed and find my trunks. I pull them on hopping on one foot and then the other down the hall. I shove a banana in my mouth and grab a bottle of water as I head for the back door.

It takes me a minute to scroll the surf report to figure out the conditions before I decide which board I want to ride. With my board in the back of my old pickup truck, I text a good friend who's in town for a few days from Hawaii: *Sorry I missed yesterday. You out in the water this morning? I'm heading over.*

When I see the three dots on the screen, I laugh. He's always up early for a surf. The message reads: Evan Ashford - *Down at the usual. Just arrived.*

He generally surfs in the same place, so I drive my truck down to meet him.

Easy to spot, he's built for the sport, has that Hawaiian tan, and a million-dollar grin. He comes toward me. "Good to see you, brother."

"You too, man." I reach in and dig my board from the back. "How goes it?"

"You know, busy. Wife, family. Business."

"You're still managing to squeeze some surfing in?"

"Trust me, Mallory would make me. I'm a bear of irritability if I don't kneel to the ocean altar at least two times a week. I miss the days when I could surf all day. But I won't complain. Life is good. What's going on in yours?"

We head over to the sand and rub wax all over the boards. I've known Evan a few years, not before he settled down, but I've heard some stories.

I say, "I'm out in New York with my license to get some business. Your old stomping grounds, right?"

He looks out at the water as the sun rises. "High school days. It's been a long time since I called that place home."

"I'm with a girl out there."

"Yeah? You thinking about growing some roots in the city?"

"She's the first one who ever made me consider it and now I want that."

We bump fists and then stand, tossing the wax with some of his stuff. Just before we drop our boards in the water, Evan says, "I talk a lot of shit about missing the surf, but I'd miss my girl more. Seems like a good trade off and you coming out ahead if she's worth the sacrifice."

"She is."

"Glad to hear it. I get first wave."

"Naturally." We both start paddling out.

Evan's words stay with me—*"I'd miss my girl more"*—as I burn out my muscles on wave after wave. Now that I have Tatum in my life, I'd miss her more than anything else as well. When it's good, it's fan-fucking-tastic.

Now we have to work on those bad times.

Before I back out the truck, Evan calls, "Come see me in Hawaii sometime and bring your girl. It's paradise out there."

With my arm hanging out the window, I laugh. "I just might take you up on that offer."

"Hope you do."

When I get back to the house, it's just gone nine. I'm later than I wanted to be, but glad that it appears she's still in bed. I walk lightly down the hall, not wanting to wake her. I'll take a quick shower and then make her breakfast. We can sit on the deck and I know she'll start coming around to maybe splitting our time if that's even possible.

We just need to get the conversation going so we can plan our lives because her walls don't scare me.

And I intend to comfort her from fears. I'm not leaving this home permanently. We will be able to afford both places. The party life of LA can go, but this place . . . this place I chose for a family. Even if we're only here part-time, it will be worth it. *Hoping Tatum can see that too. Eventually.*

When I enter my room, the covers are rumpled, and the bed is empty. "Tatum?" I look to the bathroom, but the door is wide open and she's not in there. "Tatum?"

I know.

Deep down, my heart already knows.

But I do it because I need to prove it to my brain. I open the closet door to verify her suitcase is missing.

Just like she is.

Fuck.

Tatum is gone.

30

Tatum

WHAT HAVE I DONE?

My shell is so hard it's become a detriment. Harrison Decker loves me. And I love him. "I love him so much that it hurts, Natalie. Like physical pain. So much that he makes me feel out of control."

"That's not him . . ." Her head wobbles in debate. "It might be him as well, but it's definitely your hormones. You're pregnant. All kinds of changes are happening in there. Do you know how many fights I've picked with Nick in the past few months over the stupidest stuff?"

"A lot," Nick says from the couch. His eyes are fixed on the TV, but clearly, his ears are eavesdropping.

She rolls her eyes, but then says, "You guys moved so fast, and now you're having a baby. So many emotions are involved in this that I don't want you to act rash. Granted, you left, and that's rash."

Nick nods. "Rash."

I'm tempted to flip both of them off out of aggravation, but again, that would be rash, thus proving their point.

It's Saturday, so they're both home, but I could probably do without the peanut gallery in the living room, especially since we're talking about his best friend. But him being here isn't all for naught. He gets up during a commercial break and stands in front of the open fridge staring in. "Harrison is broken-hearted."

"Did he say that?" I ask, moving to the edge of the barstool.

He looks back at me. "No, guys don't talk like that, but I can tell. Kind of obvious anyway since he came back to an empty bed."

"He came back?" I sound so stupid. Of course, he came back, but it begs the question: *Why'd he leave me?*

"He lives there, Tate."

Natalie is staring at me. She can read my mind too well, so I avoid looking at her altogether. And then start whistling since I'm already in the hot seat.

That's not going to stop her. "Tatum Eloise Devreux."

She's full-name calling me out? Crap. I'm in trouble now.

I look at her. "Yes," I gulp through the response.

"He went surfing to clear his head. Nick and Andrew do that too."

"She's speaking facts," Nick slips in and then pops a grape in his mouth.

Natalie comes around the island and stands right beside me. Swiveling me on the stool to face her, she levels her eyes to mine and lowers her voice. "Did you actually think Harrison wasn't coming back?"

"He lives there. I knew he was coming back at some point. I just . . . he knows my triggers, and leaving is the biggie for me. Why would he leave when the night before he said we'll talk in the morning? What kind of message does that send for me to wake up alone?"

"I don't know," she says, her body out of energy. She pulls the stool next to me out to sit down. "I don't know, but you guys can't seem to catch a break. Maybe—"

"Don't say it, Nat," Nick says, this time wholeheartedly involved in the conversation as he returns to the couch.

"Say what?" I ask.

Natalie hits Nick with a glare before turning back to me. "Destiny. It will find a way if you're meant to be."

"And if we're not?"

"Then it will lead you to who you're supposed to be with."

"Destiny sounds like a drunk girl you have to buy cab fare for to get her to go home at the end of the night."

"That's very . . . specific, but I can see it," she replies, and then hops off the stool again. "I'll be back. Time to pee for the three hundredth time today."

"I've not gotten to that stage. Thank goodness."

Nick looks toward the front of the house where his wife just disappeared. Then, seemingly pleased the coast is clear, he turns around on the couch. "We should talk, Tatum."

"I'm right here."

"Look, I say this because I care about you."

I almost feel as if I've disappointed him. "That's not a good start."

"I'm going to be very direct because Natalie likes to make every short story long. I love that woman and everything about her, but we don't have that kind of time."

Now he has me on the lookout for her. "Okay, shoot."

"You and Nat are a team, a force to be reckoned with, a dynamic duo, the great Nat and Tat. Like it literally is a thing.

But she worries about you. She feels guilty, like she's letting you down by moving on with her life. Not that she ever forgets you. She doesn't at all, but she cares enough to want the best for you, to want you to find the happiness that I know she's found."

I could be defensive or keep my guard up with him, but nothing Nick is saying is new. Natalie and I are a dynamic duo, but Batman and Robin had other love interests, even if Catwoman was a poor choice. But that's a whole other issue I wrote a paper about in college. I got an A+. *Anywho*, I say, "She has. She's so lucky to have you."

"Is it luck? Maybe. Though you know Cookie doesn't believe in luck."

"She believes in destiny."

"That's what Natalie is to me. She's not only my wife. She's my eternity. I love her that much."

She scored with Nick Christiansen.

Is it wrong to be this stinkin' happy for your best friend? I could tear up . . . *and I do.* I'm blaming those hormones Natalie was just talking about. I was a boohooing mess on the flight home because *Home Alone* was on. *What is this craziness?*

Yep, rash.

I realize now that I acted rashly.

I can hear the water running in the bathroom. Peeking down the hall, I know we're running out of time. He says, "My point being . . ." Thank God, he's getting to his point. I'm even stressed she'll overhear. "I realized early on that it's not choosing you or me for Natalie. We all have the capacity to love and love big. What Natalie and I have is different than what you two share. Harrison, or whoever you fall in love with, will love you enough to understand we're not competing. We're family."

"That's why you've always welcomed me into your home without a single question. You just opened your heart."

"Natalie loves you. That means I do too. So you're not alone. Not ever. But we hope you find the same kind of love that Natalie and I share. I vote for Harrison, but that's a given. You go where your heart leads you."

"I think Cookie's rubbing off on you."

"I'm okay with that."

The door opens down the hall, and Natalie's shoes echo as she returns. "Ugh. My bladder is the size of a peanut. So annoying." She stops at the entrance to the living room and puts her hands on her hips. "Wow, Nick," she says to the back of his head. "You couldn't entertain our guest for two minutes while I was gone?"

With his eyes glued to the TV, he replies, "It's not a guest. It's Tatum."

My heart swells with the feels. I'm not a guest. *I'm family.* He didn't have to say it for me to know what he meant.

She sits down next to me again, spinning to face me. "I thought I heard you guys talking."

Nick says, "Must have been the announcers." If she only knew what a softie he is. What am I saying? She knows. She married that sweetheart of a man.

Natalie goes over to the back of him and kisses him on the head. To me, she says, "He's a big lug when sports are on, but he's my big lug. Before I forget, the cooking class starts next week. Are you still in?"

I don't have those same interests, but maybe it's time I learned a new skill. "I'm in."

"Good. That will be fun."

Slipping off the stool, I reach down and grab my bag. "I think I'm going home to rest. It's been a long day already, and you really have me rethinking things."

Natalie walks with me to the door.

"Good talking to you, Nick." I have no intention of spoiling his cover, but I will take his advice to heart. After all, they only want the best for me.

He waves over his head, but he never looks back. "Yeah, you, too."

Grabbing the handle of my suitcase, I roll it to the front door. Before she has a chance to call him for help, Nick's already coming to carry it down to the sidewalk for me. "Got it."

I hug Natalie because I realize she's carried the burden of my happiness since we were kids. She's the one who stepped in when my parents upset me or, worse, ignored me altogether. It's time I let her live free from the weight of her worry for me.

"Love you."

"Love you, too," she says.

When we step back, I say, "I'm going to be okay."

"Yes, you are. You've always been the strongest person I know."

"I say that about you."

We smile at each other, and then I say, "See you soon."

"See you soon."

Riding in the back of a car heading home, I pull out my phone. I'll give Harrison full credit for texting and calling right away. I didn't expect to see twenty missed calls and more than a handful of texts by the time I landed, but I'm not upset by it.

I'm about to text, but I decide I want to hear his voice and for him to hear mine. There's no misinterpretation that way. That also means I have to wait to get home. No way am I having this conversation in the back of a rideshare.

I hurry to my apartment as soon as I arrive. My heart is

racing, and I'm not sure of the words I should use other than I'm sorry. But I roll my suitcase inside and kick the door closed. With the phone in my hand, I drop my bag on the counter and head for the windows. I need light.

It makes no sense, but the sun pouring in makes this feel less heavy. The phone rings, and I stand there with my heart trying to beat out of my chest. "Tatum," he says as if he's breathing again.

"Hi."

"Hi."

An uncomfortable silence invades, and an apology suddenly doesn't seem like a viable option of getting us back together. A long-winded explanation maybe? "I'm sorry I left." Okay, well, direct is always good. Let's just hope he can appreciate that angle.

The silence lingers though I know he's still there because I can hear his breathing. In the past, he's mentioned the first one who speaks loses. It's a sales technique of his. But the quiet between us is painful and stretching, so I say, "Harrison, are you still there?"

"I'm here."

"I . . . I'm not sure how to make this right."

"Can I be honest with you, Tatum?"

"Of course. I hope you're always honest with me."

"I'm not mad at you. I'm disappointed. I was only gone a few hours. I don't know why you would leave. Why would you leave at a time like that?"

"If you want my honesty, I thought you had already left me. I know that doesn't make sense, but I wasn't thinking rationally. I was thinking through the pain, and all I wanted was for it to go away."

"Did it go away?

"No, it got worse."

"I appreciate you apologizing. I know that's not easy to do, especially when your reason for doing it makes sense to you. But you gave me enough time to think about what was happening, and it's a lot. I know you're going through a lot, and maybe this isn't the right time for us."

"Wait, no. That's—"

"Time is what you need, Tatum. Your life is changing dramatically. I'm not saying I want you out there dating because fuck no, that's not happening."

"Then what are you saying, Harrison?" *Please don't say you've given up on me too. That I'm not enough for you to want to stay for.*

"I want you to want me how I want you."

It's a tongue twister, but, "I love you."

"I love you, too. But I want us together because we want to be together. Not because you're pregnant. Am I the man you'd choose if you weren't having my baby? Don't answer right now. When you know and you're certain, call me."

"Harris—" The line goes dead, along with my heart.

I had it all, and I realized too late.

31

Tatum

"I MISSED WHAT BRAISING IS," I WHISPER TO NATALIE.

A spatula slaps the cutting board in front of me. "Zip it, Ms?" Chef Marcelles yells in an intense French accent from right behind me.

I turn around and say, "Devreux."

"Ah. Oui. Oui. French. Tres magnifique." He comes closer. "No talking in my class. Oui?"

"Oui?"

When I turn back to Natalie with wide eyes, she gets my drift without using words: *he's an asshole.*

"That class was intense," I say, "like Marcelle, and that was only the first one."

"It was incredible, right?" Natalie cheerfully raves, hands in the air and all. "And who knew that brown butter was a secret weapon for the perfect short ribs? Not me."

"I thought brown butter was just butter that's cooked until brown?"

She laughs. "It is." Staring down at the rest of her shopping list, she says, "I have a lot of shopping tomorrow for short ribs. I want to practice before Cookie and Corbin fly in next month for Juni and Andrew's delivery. The guys have a bet going, and Nick's going with the Fourth of July."

"That's too early. I'm feeling July eighteenth."

"Really?" she asks as if I just told her she won a million dollars a week for life sweepstakes. "I told Nick the same date."

"Great minds and all. Hey, before you take off, can I ask your advice?"

She adjusts her bag to the crook of her arm. "I'd be offended if you didn't."

"You know how Harrison and I are taking a little break?"

"Yes." *Of course, she does.*

Harrison has flown back and forth a few times. I only know that because I'm told I can come over because the coast is clear.

Beyond that, I have no idea if he's had to show anyone else properties in New York. I have no clue what he's done in New York at all. I've felt blind about anything to do with him, and that just feels wrong.

My offer was accepted on the property next to Nat and Nick, but I've only spoken to Robert about that. He's organized the various building inspections, and I'm about to sign a contract. That's still a surprise to Natalie and Nick, though. Unless Harrison's spilled the beans to Nick already. *Wouldn't Nat tell me if she knew, though?* Once again, I have no idea, and I hate that it feels like they're living a whole other life that I'm not privy to. I wonder if Harrison feels the same. *I wonder if he asks about me when he's here.*

"I want to call him. It's already been eleven days." I look down at my watch. "Seventeen hours and some odd minutes, but the apartment's not the same without him cooking or hogging the shower, taking up the side of the bed that I don't use, and I'm always cold. He was a really great heater at night."

"So what you're saying is that you miss him?"

Sometimes it's just best to cut to the chase. "I miss him, Nat. Does that make me sad that me missing him is the biggest revelation I've had since he's been gone?"

"I think it's a good thing, and quite honestly, exactly what he wants you to realize." She touches my belly. I never mind when she does. I even get to touch her belly that's just recently popped out a little. She basically looks like she ate a hoagie for lunch.

We move off to the side of the restaurant doors where they hold the cooking class. She goes on, "The question seemed simple, but it's really complex. If you weren't pregnant, would you want to be with him?" *Yes. One hundred times, yes.*

"I was doing that already. I was living that life and want it back. I want him back."

"Then you have your answer."

"I guess I do." We hug goodbye and head in separate directions. It's tempting to want the perfect setting to make confessions of the heart, but I don't want to waste any time. So I call him.

The trill of a female laughing fills the line, and I hold the phone away from my face to double-check that I didn't misdial. Nope. Harrison Decker is at the top of the screen. The voice says, "Hello?"

"Sorry, I got the wrong number."

I end the call and look around. Leaning against the jagged rock of the refined restaurant, I go numb.

Well, I guess that answers the other part of my question—*does he want me to call him as Nat suggested? To ask him to come back to me . . .* Or was that his get-out-of-jail-free card?

He said he'd always be there for me. For us. He said he loved me. He said I was his future.

But just like my parents, other things are far more tempting. Far more . . . worth staying elsewhere for. And I got a good idea what sort of women he's gravitated to in the past. Women who literally threw themselves at him. *How could I trust him to be alone out there when I saw how he was hounded?*

Eventually, most men would give in. Even a man like Harrison, who I thought was one of the good ones. Turns out, he was quick to hang up on me, and it seems, quick to replace me.

I place a hand on my middle. I've been such a fool for thinking he wanted me to figure out the meaning of life and come running. It worked too, but no more. "It's okay, baby. We have each other now. We don't need anyone."

I push off the building and get in a cab.

There will be no calls or texts, spending all day pining and the nights crying from his absence. Harrison Decker can go to hell for all I care.

If I mean that little to him . . . tears overflow the barriers of my lower lids, but I'm quick to wipe them away. I can't believe I'm crying over a man.

Never again.

~ Harrison ~

"It's so good to see you," Cookie says, welcoming me in. She leads me to the kitchen where the smell of blueberry muffins causes my stomach to growl. "Help yourself."

She pours a glass of milk, and it reminds me of stopping

by after school to do homework and play video games with Nick.

"I wanted to get your advice."

"On Tatum?"

"How'd you know?"

She shrugs and gazes out the window. When she turns back, she says, "I remember both of my sons being in a similar state over Juni and Natalie. "What do you want to know, Harrison? I'll help you the best I can."

"I'm not sure what happened. She lets her fear of getting hurt protect her from ever receiving love."

Nodding, she then takes a sip of iced tea. She doesn't rush her response, taking her time to mull it over. "That is a tough one. She's hard on herself, and to protect her heart, she builds walls around it. How close am I?"

"Very."

She grins.

"How do I get through to her that I won't hurt her?" I ask.

"You don't, silly. No one makes that promise to everyone and can keep it. The problem lies in the woman herself. Tatum made that promise to herself. The key is to get her to unlock a door and let you in."

"You're probably right." I eat a muffin because how do I not when they look and smell amazing.

"I'm always right. Did you confirm her birthday? It's in June, correct?"

"How'd you know that?"

"Because you're an Aries and the most complementary sign is Gemini. Leave it to destiny to cause a ruckus between you two. We're also in retrograde, but I don't like to tempt fate by focusing on that too much."

I wash the muffin down. She asks, "What are you doing

wasting time here anyway? I have a feeling you both need to lower your walls and enjoy what's inside."

She's right. It's not great revelation stuff. "Boiling it down, we need to stop being asses to each other."

"That sounds like a good start."

I go around the island to embrace her. "Thank you."

"You're welcome."

Walking back to my car, I start to mumble because she makes a whole lot of sense without saying much.

There are two things that are true:

1. There's no winning Tatum's heart until she takes the walls down. It's a losing battle otherwise.
2. She's doing the best she can. So am I. I hope we can meet in the middle from here on out.

WILL SHE COME AROUND? I want her in my life. She's my future. *They* are my future.

She rang when I was with Madison, but then hung up. And hasn't called since. *She still isn't ready.*

What if waiting isn't enough?

~ Tatum - July ~

My office door opens, and Natalie twirls in. "I need a favor."

I set my pen down on the pink pad and say, "Go on . . ."

"I have a client who wants a whirlwind weekend with his girlfriend, soon-to-be fiancée if all things go as planned."

"My favorite."

"You know why that is? Because you're a romantic."

"No, Natalie. I'm a professional event architect. Instead of going down memory lane, talk to me. Give me the W's."

"The sweetest couple ever. Surprise proposal. This Saturday. Catalina. Because they love each other."

Dropping my head to the side, I ask, "Catalina?"

"Come on. Don't poo-poo the idea. It's a very romantic location."

I give her that. But that doesn't make it easier. Memories of my time with Harrison are always swimming around in my head. This only makes it worse. "Anyway, I have it all set up. I just have to fly out there and make sure it goes off without a hitch."

"So, what's the favor?"

She only has to look at me before I'm shaking my head. "No. No. No. No. No. Natalie. Not this one. Not this time."

"Please? Nick and I have to go to Juni's candle lighting ceremony on Saturday."

"What the hell is that?"

"It apparently shows the baby the way out."

I cover my mouth. It was that or gasp, so I let that confusion we're all feeling go. "What? Nooo."

"Yes. And since we said we'll be at the birthing center with her, we had to say yes to the candle ceremony. Juni wanted me to give you your invitation."

She holds it out for me. "When do I fly out?"

It's been a month since I've spoken to Harrison, and every landmark we pass reminds me of a certain someone. When I arrive at the hotel on Catalina, my heart's racing, a little sweat's gathering under the collar, and I'm feeling sick at the scene of my crime of passion. I'd forgotten how gorgeous this place is.

I'm told to settle in, so I grab my case and head across the lobby to find a chair.

Sitting there minding my own business, a woman next to me says, "Is it illegal to pick poppies since it's the state flower?"

"I don't think so. I actually got them as a gift once." My heart clenches around the absence that's felt. "It was actually really sweet. He traveled all the way from California with them. They were raggedy with missing petals. Bent and broken. Still so romantic."

"That does sound sweet. I'm trying to help my brother, actually. He wants to surprise his girlfriend."

"That's what I'm here for too. Well, not your brother. That would be weird, but a surprise proposal."

"If you knew him, it wouldn't be weird. He's an amazing man and even better brother."

I sit back, realizing she's going to talk about him whether I'm a part of the conversation or she's sitting alone. It's endearing to hear how close they are, though.

"You sound very close. That's sweet."

"We are. He was the first one I called when I was in a car accident a few years back. He didn't leave my hotel room unless we forced him out shopping."

I close the small pad on my lap and drop it and the pen in my bag so I can give her my full attention.

"My daughter spent her first birthday in the hospital. All due to my psycho ex," she says.

"What happened?"

"He threatened to hurt me if I didn't get in the car. He was saying he just wanted to talk, but I shouldn't have trusted him. I was just trying to do the right thing since Harlow's his daughter."

My tummy clenches. "You got in the car?"

"My brothers had warned me, but I didn't listen." Her eyes go to the screensaver on her phone—the cutest little dark-haired beauty. She glances at me, the emotion raw on her face as if this is a fresh memory.

"How is she doing now?"

"She's amazing. Doesn't remember anything, but it's better that way. He crashed us right into a tree. He died instantly. I only survived because of my family."

I glance back at the photo again. She has the prettiest blue eyes, and I'm reminded of . . . *don't go there*. "Sounds like you got one of the good ones."

A hotel attendant comes up to her and hands her a card key. "Ms. Decker, your room is ready."

"Decker?" I say unable to keep my mouth shut. "I know a Harrison Decker." I'm mastering the art of sounding like a crazy person.

Jumping to her feet, she says, "That's my brother. Well, one of them. I have three. Wow, crazy small world." The smile falters, and she says, "You're Tatum."

I stand and nod. Now I'm not sure what to say or do. My gut tells me to run, but my heart tells me to stay.

"He told me all about you," she says, and then laughs lightly as if recalling a fond memory. "I remember him saying your soul was golden the first time he met you. That was when we were in the hospital."

"What do you mean?"

"Talk about timing. Harry came off the best weekend of his life, and the minute the ferry docked, I called him. He spent the next three months nursing me back to health while sleeping night after night in Harlow's hospital room.

You were all he talked about. The days became weeks, and those became months." She reaches to touch my hand wrapped around my suitcase handle. "I feel like I owe you an apology."

"You don't."

"I took away his soul mate, so yeah, a lot of guilt is carried with that."

"But we found our way back to each other," I say without a second thought. That just rolled off my tongue so naturally.

She smiles. "He feels the same—two souls that are forever connected." Turning to look around, she returns her gaze to mine, and she says, "It's not too late." I have no idea why his sister thinks that. Harrison has made it pretty clear. *He wants to surprise his girlfriend.* And now, he's here to start a new life with someone else. *Why does his sister think it's not too late?* It's almost so cruel being here now. Knowing that *he* has moved on. *Has fallen in love with someone else.*

We've bonded on some level, two strangers who were there for each other, so I feel a hug is in order. We embrace each other, and I whisper, "I would have done anything for your brother."

"Then let him be a part of your life." *That ship has sailed.* Or has it? What did she mean suggesting that he still cares about me . . . *two souls that are forever connected?* Have I got my wires crossed? Is she here for another brother? If so, maybe what I should have said was, "I would do anything for your brother." Present tense. Because I still love him. Want him.

When she leaves, I decide right then and there that we've had too many signs. That man is my soul mate, and I can't let him get away.

But first, I need to handle this surprise proposal.

32

Harrison

"Harry?"

"In here." I straighten my shirt, trying to flatten a wrinkle across the front. I'm keeping it casual but classy. As instructed.

My sister's heels click across the Saltillo tiles of the suite as she rushes into the room where I'm staying. Fortunately, I'm dressed. "What's up?" I ask.

Out of breath, she leans one hand on the doorframe as if that will help her catch it. "I just met Tatum." The name alone gets my heart pumping to an erratic rhythm.

Pressing my palm to my chest, I ask, "What do you mean you just met Tatum?"

"She's here. In the lobby right now." The words don't make sense, and my expression must match that confusion because she goes on to say, "We just got to talking and—"

"Does she know I'm here?" What the hell is going on? Why didn't Natalie come? She knew I'd be here, so it makes it awkward that she sent Tatum instead. Or did Tatum volunteer? That doesn't seem logical since the woman won't talk to me on the phone or in text, so why would she want to see me in person? *What is she up to?*

I'd hired STJ because I like to give my friends business, but was that a mistake? I don't want today to turn into a spectacle. It's important that it goes off without a hitch.

Maddie's arm comes down, and she moves closer, picking up a bottle of my cologne and plucking the cap off. "Of course not, but we quickly realized who the other person was."

"How?"

"The front desk clerk called me Ms. Decker. That got Tatum's attention."

"I bet it did," I mumble, walking to the open patio door that leads to a private balcony, the same balcony where I made love to her under the stars and . . . *made love, created love, fell in love.* That's what we did that night. God, I miss her. I miss her smile, her laughter, her voice, her touch . . . I just miss her. And I hate that I have no idea when that will end. If she'll ever trust me enough to love her with everything I have.

"She doesn't seem upset, Harry."

"*She's not upset?* Are you sure you met the right Tatum? *My* Tatum? My Tatum is always upset. It's a part of her charm."

"Sounds like it." My sister's expression softens. "And can you call her *your* Tatum a few more times. I don't think the people in the back heard you."

"Funny."

"Most call me delightful. As for *your* Tatum, from what you've told me over the years and from just meeting her, I can unequivocally give you my endorsement. She's a perfect match for you."

After my eyebrows shoot up, I have to get better about controlling my reactions, especially if Tatum is here to tell me this break is better than our relationship. "Geez, thanks, sis. But tell me, you got that from just meeting her for thirty seconds in the lobby of the hotel?"

"No, we were there a few minutes, shared stories, and became fast friends before we figured out who the other person was." *Fast friends.* This would have been great news if I were still with her, but now my sister gets time with the woman I would give anything to have. She smells the cologne and then replaces the cap. "That smells good. Definitely wear that for her."

"I'm not wearing anything for her. We're not together. *Currently.*"

"Currently leaves room for hope and love." Giddy, she comes closer and starts fidgeting with my shirt. My sister has experienced the worst in life when it comes to love, but she still remains a romantic. I hope she gets the fairy tale ending she deserves. She says, "Don't be so stubborn, Harrison. That's what got you into this mess."

Removing her hands, I hold them between mine. I love my sister, but this isn't something she can fix. No matter how good her intentions. "No, what got me into this is . . ." I slow my words and hold my tongue. Releasing her hands, I think about what I really want to say, what I want to shout from the rooftops. Tatum's having my baby, and I still haven't told a soul. Well, other than the surprise party crowd. But my family doesn't know anything. Nick and Andrew know, and they're not telling anyone.

I need to respect Tatum and her wishes, so until she's ready to tell the world, I need to remain silent on the matter.

Not the matter, the baby. Our baby.

A pinch in my chest has me wondering if I'm having a stroke or a heart attack or just can't seem to find my rhythm these days. I rub my hand over to ease the pain. It doesn't work. Never does. It showed up the day Tatum left and stayed. To say I have suspicions that the two events are related is an understatement.

I turn my back to the balcony and the memories we made out there. Not that I can escape them in this room, which is the same one where we spent the night together. It was hers, but being back here, I can't help but feel the ghosts of us together.

Madison has me wanting to leap from the room to rush down and find Tatum to tell her how I feel—the good and bad—laying it all out on the table. I'm not sure if we're a good match, as my sister said, or we mold easily and over-stayed our welcome. What I do know is that I've missed her so fucking much this past month that it's not natural to feel this kind of constant ache in my soul.

But this must be handled very carefully. I can't miss any steps when it comes to Tatum. We did that the first time, and look how that ended.

"It doesn't matter, Maddie. Sounds like you got fairly deep into conversation about our relationship, though. Why would she tell you all of this? Not only are you a stranger but you're my sister," I say.

"Maybe because I *am* your sister. Maybe she knows I'll tell you everything. *Maybe*, Harrison, you use that heart of yours and let it guide you for a while instead of trying to find a reason for everything. Love is an emotion. It doesn't always make sense." Checking her watch, she adds, "We need to leave. Are you ready?"

"I've invested too much time and energy into this to turn

back now. This is about doing what's right for the family. It's time I do my duty."

She comes to me and straightens the collar of my white shirt. "You look very handsome."

"It's not about me. Let's go."

33

Tatum

"You tricked me."

"It's not a trick when you love him," Natalie starts, completely unashamed by her actions.

Shifting the phone to my other ear, I taste a cucumber lobster bite before the caterer finishes loading the tray. I'm starved, having to work a proposal event for the father of my child to another woman, and my best friend is denying all culpability in the matter. I say, "That's why the contact information was missing. I asked for it how many times? Until I got here, I had no idea who our client was. It's not totally foreign to work with event representatives for the location like we're doing here, but you knew, didn't you?" Pointing at the appetizer cucumber bites, I whisper, "Add a hint of sea salt. Thanks."

"Just give him this one chance, Tate."

"I've given him two. But apparently, I get no credit for that. It's all about innocent Harrison. He's a big boy. He helped create this mess, and he can dig himself out of it. Next, you'll harp on about a third time."

"Third time's a charm. I know firsthand with Nick."

I grab a piece of bruschetta and walk out to the proposal site. "Natalie, do you hear what you're saying?" She's got to be off her rocker. "You want me to ruin a beautiful marriage proposal that you designed and organized for my own selfish gains."

"Yes. I do. Call me a horrible person, but if it makes everyone involved happy, why wouldn't you do this?"

Everyone? I can't imagine the woman he's about to propose to is going to be too happy about this. My friend's hormones are definitely clouding her better judgment. "Natalie, our business could be destroyed if I purposely ruin the event."

"Love is powerful. Everyone will understand. I bet most will even support it."

"You're talking crazy. You need to get to the candle ceremony, and I need to check on the flower arrangements for the dinner."

"Tatum?"

My patience has worn thin, but I know it's not with her. It's coming, the breakdown I've been dreading for a month, the one I raise my chin above and put off. "Natalie, I need to go do my job."

"Tate—"

I hang up. I've never hung up on her, but this is taking things too far. Heading for the door, I tell the caterer, "It looks great. Thank you." I rush outside, wishing it was winter to help cool my heated face. I'm met with the heat of the day instead.

With my suppressed emotions bubbling to the surface, I struggle to hide behind a stiff upper lip. I can't do this. Why would my best friend put me in this position? I'm strong on the outside, but this is just too much. I walk the length of the dinner table, checking to make sure everything's in place.

He may break my heart and me while he's at it, but I won't let him ruin my reputation. It doesn't matter that I was so easily replaced. He'll be in LA, and I'll be back in the city. We'll live our own lives separately. The baby is the only reason we need to have any contact, and as much as I never imagined I'd be raising a child alone, I can do it. That way, we don't ever have to come face-to-face again.

I grab a bottle of water from the bar and leave to go back to my room. There has to be a way to avoid having Harrison's family bear witness to my heartbreak. Who can I call to step in for me?

My phone buzzes in my pocket. I pull it out, knowing I'm not answering any calls, but texts are a necessary evil. Cookie Christiansen: *I heard you were in LA. I'd love to see you if you have time in your busy schedule.*

That's it. *I need Cookie.*

She arrives as if she had nothing better to do today than assist me. After hugs and greetings, she waits while I get dressed for the event, and says, "This doesn't sound like Harrison at all. Meeting a girl and moving quickly is not so shocking because he was a spontaneous kid. But proposing? That doesn't sound like him. Should I call Nick? Wouldn't Nick be a part of it?" She peeks into the bathroom, and our eyes meet in the reflection. "He'd invite me, and I knew nothing about it."

"It's clearly very last minute, which is why they hired our company to plan it for them." I don't miss the effects of alcohol while pregnant. I miss giving fewer cares while I'm drinking, especially tonight. Cookie thinks I need to face my demons head-on. Why does mine have to be so handsome, though? I can only imagine how gorgeous his soon-to-be fiancée will be. He lands very pretty women.

I step back and brush down the front of my pale-yellow dress. I always let the brides, wives, girlfriends, and in this case, fiancée own the spotlight.

Cookie's admiring smile makes me feel I've done something right. I wiggle the belt to make sure it stays in place and then hold my arms wide. "All good?"

"Beautiful."

"Hope not too beautiful. It's not my day." Despite the fact that it's the love of my life, it's their day.

"Oh honey, come here." She brings me into her mother fold and rubs my back. "I'm at a loss of what to say. That Harrison would do this to you . . . I'm so sorry. I don't understand what's going on in his head."

Before the tears that are gathering can fall, I tilt my head back and take a quick and deep breath. "I'm ready. Let's go."

The hillside pavilion is stunning, with the sunset in the background. The table is set, the crystal sparkling, and the arch of the proposal area with orange and yellow flowers wrapped around it are perfection. I direct the photographer to capture the magic for our portfolio just as guests start to arrive.

From the file, the dinner bringing two families together for the first time is the cover. The proposal is the surprise. As soon as the question is popped, a yes is secured, dinner will be served and then my duties are done. I won't be staying another minute on this island or even in the state. I want to be as far away from this place as possible.

The woman of the night arrives wearing a white satin dress straight from the runway. By her height and physical attributes, she could be a model. She circulates through the small crowd, kissing everybody on two cheeks.

But there's no sign of Harrison yet.

Cookie comes up behind me, and whispers, "Not that you would do this . . . I mean, you're not me, but it's a proposal, not an exchange of wedding vows. So there's not a justice of the peace to ask if there are any objections. But if the love of my life were getting engaged, I might have a few things to say about it."

I look at her over my shoulder as she sips her champagne so innocently. "And here I thought I was trouble with a capital T."

"Sometimes we have to stop worrying about others and go after what we want. Incoming at ten o'clock."

My gaze darts straight for him. He hasn't seen me as I hide in the shadows, but there's no mistaking that even among family, he stands out.

"Tatum?"

Turning around, I find Nora. "Hello, it's so good to see you again."

"You, too. You look lovely in that color."

"Thank you. Congratulations for tonight."

She shifts, and then says, "Thank you."

Before any awkwardness can sneak in, I say, "I need to check—"

"He misses you."

My feet stop. My breathing stops. My heart. All of me because he misses me. I'm not ready to turn around and confess everything, but I can admit, "I miss him, too."

"You should tell him."

What kind of alternate universe am I living in that everyone is rooting for the crazy ex-girlfriend? And pregnant, but they don't know about that big detail. Yet.

But Nora's right. So are Cookie and Natalie. And it seems anyone else I speak to. I bet even Madison. So with my heart thumping loud enough for everyone in the Big Apple to hear, I start thinking maybe this isn't so crazy. Maybe this is my moment to tell Harrison that I still love him.

A knife is tapped against a glass, and a man I don't recognize starts speaking. "We're so glad you could be here to celebrate this special occasion for us and our families. . ."

I frantically search for the one man who already changed my destiny but still holds my fate in his hands. When I find him in the crowd, his eyes are already locked on me. Pain. Happiness. And everything in between is working through his features. The woman in the white dress leans over and whispers something in his ear, but his eyes are still mine. I'm willing to bet his heart is as well.

She starts walking toward the man with the microphone. Her name is Natasha. *Figures.* He then calls, "Harrison?"

But Harrison doesn't move a muscle.

"Harrison?" is called louder over the speakers, snapping him out of the connection we have.

I won't give it up. I won't give him up.

Cookie whispers, "Now's your chance."

"I object!" I shout over the small crowd. "I object to this sham!"

I hear Cookie giggling and turn back to see Madison laughing along with her. Madison gives me a thumbs-up and says, "You got this."

"I do. I got this."

Natasha asks, "Why is she saying my proposal is a sham?"

Mic man puts his arm around her and starts soothing her. "It'll be okay, tookie wookie."

I thought I had this until I see Harrison still working his way up to her. "Harrison?" I yell over everyone as he pulls the ring box from his pocket. "I love you. And you love me. I always based a lot of my worth on my looks. But you're not drawn to that. You love my soul, who I am on the inside, and that's more important."

"Your beauty is . . . to see, Tate. Your . . . like a rose just for me."

Cupping my ear, I yell, "What? I can't hear you."

He grabs the microphone, and says, "Your beauty is for the world to see. Your soul blooms like a rose for me. Come here, Tate."

I seek Nora's approval, not sure why, but it would be nice to have, considering the death glares I'm getting from Natasha's side.

To Nora, I say, "I love him."

She nods, and relief washes through her. "Go get him then."

As silence falls over the group, I hurry through to get to Harrison. I don't know how this will turn out—my biggest triumph or greatest defeat. But I believe love is on my side. Stopping with a few feet remaining between us, I realize everything has to be aired. No secrets and no hidden fears. "You left me like everyone else, and when I called, and I heard a woman's laughter."

Madison calls from the back. "That was me. He was with me when you called." I turn back to Harrison, and he's nodding. "You didn't even give me a chance to explain. I think that's when you blocked me."

"It was. I thought you moved on without me."

"I couldn't. I can't. Never. When I was at my lowest, when my niece was in ICU, you were the person I called."

"When?"

"Almost five years, but that doesn't matter now. I just need you to know that I called, but you didn't answer. And I'm okay with that now because I got the second chance I needed." Bringing my hand to his mouth, he kisses it like when we lie together naked. I love that he's not afraid to show the intimacy that exists between us. "I can't get you out from under my skin. But now it's worse. You've invaded my heart, you own my soul, and now you're carrying my baby." An audible gasp is heard from behind me. "Oh shit."

"It's okay," I say, laughing. "I don't think you still need the microphone, though."

He gives it to the first mic guy and then takes my hands. "We've fucked up. Both of us have."

"You were right. I leave first to avoid being left behind."

"I won't leave you, Tatum." Touching my stomach, he says, "I won't leave this baby or any of the other four kids we have."

"Four?"

His smile is so smug and adorable that he might be able to talk me into this. When I smile, he says, "I've missed seeing your face and your naked body, but most of all, I miss you. Just everything from not knowing where your own dishes are stored to the bed you hog without apology to how you cling to me when you're sleeping. Your laugh and love of being silly, like falling on your ass in a candy shop, and how animated you are when you talk about your work. I missed you, Tatum. All of you."

He kisses me. Grabbing my face, he steps into my space, and we kiss, taking advantage of this opportunity. "I love you," he whispers against my lips.

"I need to say something, Harrison. You seem to think I'm only with you because of the baby." I hold onto him not wanting to ever let go as we talk with only a breath separating us. "The baby didn't bring us together. Catalina did. Life did. Destiny."

"I realized the same thing. Whatever brought us together is doing it again."

We kiss again, ready for our happily ever after to begin.

Natasha whines, "This was supposed be about me."

Harrison turns to mic guy and says, "Don't do it, Dawson."

I say, "I'm confused."

"Oh, yeah, this is my brother Dawson." Harrison looks at me with a huge grin practically splitting his face in half. "And this is my Tatum." I shake his hand, and we do the greeting, noticeably leaving Natasha out of it.

He says, "I've heard a lot about you." Distracted, Dawson moves around Harrison and speaks under his breath to Natasha, "I think we need to talk."

When they start weaving their way toward the exit, Harrison says, "My other brother couldn't make it. He just doesn't like Natasha."

"*Ah.* And your dad?"

"Thinking about an office in Dallas, so he traveled there."

Poking him in the chest, I warn, "Not for you. Just setting that straight right now."

He chuckles. "Don't worry. I don't want to be anywhere else than with you."

A phone rings in the background just as our lips press together in a kiss.

Along with everyone else, we look out to see Cookie with the phone to her ear. Holding it up, she says, "Juni's having her baby."

That's when it dawns on me. She's supposed to be at the candle ceremony, so why is she here? I laugh because I knew that couldn't be a real thing. I turn to Harrison, and my knees weaken just from being in his arms again. "I think we've been set up."

"I think the universe did it long before our friends."

Despite his hold on me tightening, I tap his chin. "A-ha! Natalie knew it was Dawson's day, didn't she?"

"Yes, she's the one I hired to pull it off."

"She pulled off more than a . . . actually, since the proposal didn't happen, we could stay and enjoy the meal, and then catch a flight home in the morning?"

"I have a suite. You're very familiar with it."

I lean against him, ready to claw his clothes off right here. "Oh yeah? Is it *our* suite?"

"I requested it."

"Maybe we should retire early."

"After dinner," he replies, tucking hair behind my ear. "You're eating for two."

"You're going to spoil me, aren't you?" *Please say yes.*

"Every chance I get, baby."

EPILOGUE 1

Harrison

Poppy Eloise Decker

I'm smitten.

One week early, our baby came roaring into this world, demanding all the attention. I'll give it. I'll give her whatever she wants.

Nothing went to plan.

Everything happened exactly how it was supposed to, though, and I'm good with that. How can I complain when I'm holding my daughter in my arms? My baby girl is going to be so loved that she'll expect nothing less.

Tatum chose the first name, giving me a little shout-out. She told me we'll always have a little California in New York State since she stole me from the West Coast. I came willingly, but we vacation out there a couple of times a year. I kept the house and added her name on it. Life is good as long as we're together.

But seeing Tatum truly content within her life makes my life even better.

We live next door to our best friends. We're godparents to their little guy, James Nicholas, Poppy's best friend. And one house down from them is Andrew and Juni. Reed is the oldest of the baby crew and already showing great leadership qualities like his dad, making Andrew very proud.

The only ones missing in this little girl's life are her maternal grandparents. They'll eventually be back in the city, but I can't say they're missed. As for the blank check . . . it cleared for the full eighteen million. Not one word was ever said.

Tatum yawns, opening her eyes. "I thought you put Poppy in her crib?"

"I wanted to hold her a little longer."

Maintaining our hushed tones, she adds, "You're spoiling her."

"There are worse things I could spoil her with than daddy hugs."

She reaches over with a smile on her face and rubs the top of Poppy's bald-ish head. "I remember the first time you called me baby. I thought that was the best thing ever. But seeing you hold your actual baby, that wins hands down."

"One day, she's not going to fit in my arms, and that will break my heart."

"Wait until she starts dating." *Not funny.*

"Slow your roll, little mama. It's too soon to talk about that."

Tatum sits up and rests against my arm, her head on my shoulder so we can both stare at this little wonderment. "I always thought it was pride, or you forgot about me, that kept you from texting. It was hurt feelings on my part for the longest time. Now I realize it was timing. We weren't supposed to be together yet. Look what patience brought us."

I kiss the top of her head, and then say, "Happiness."

EPILOGUE 2

Tatum

ONE YEAR LATER . . .

I DON'T REMEMBER why I thought single-momming this kid would be my only option. Then I realized that double-parenting with Harrison is the dream I never thought I could have. But I do. *I have him.*

I've never loved anyone as much as I love him and Poppy. I finally understand what Nick was talking about. I'll always love my best friend. Through thick and thin, we were a team. That still stands, but now we've expanded our family.

Natalie stands at the front of the conference room, and says, "It's with great joy that today STJ becomes Devreux St. James." We narrowly avoided the STD acronym. "Here's to a long partnership built on success and friendship. Here's to Tatum Devreux."

The round of applause is appreciated, but these days, it's

simpler things, like promotions that are the only limelight I see these days, so I'm out of habit. Heat floods my cheeks, but I know I earned this partnership. Natalie came to me after my plan had been in place for less than a year. The company thrived. All while we bounced our sweet babies on our knees.

We employ one nanny, and so far, Mrs. Westrich, a seventy-four-year-old retired preschool teacher, is working out great. She also cooks. *Bonus.* Since I gave up on the cooking class, it's nice to have a home-cooked meal instead of eating out of throwaway containers every night.

After putting Poppy to bed, I jog downstairs, ready to cover a few miles on the treadmill. When I enter the basement gym, Harrison is already on it.

Shirtless.

Sweat dripping slowly down his back.

Defined abs that were made for licking.

Deep tan from his last visit out west.

The man is trying to kill me with that sexy body.

Or more precisely, knock me up again. He can't get off that four. I like to give him a hard time. That means, I strut around the place in barely-there workout gear when we're home alone. "Hi, sexy," I say, leaning against the door.

He spots me in the mirror, a smirk already in play.

"I was wondering if I could have my turn riding that large, oh-so big piece of equipment?" I bite my lip and watch him drool.

"You talking about this treadmill . . .?" He grabs his crotch, cuz yeah, he's a guy. "Or this big piece of equipment, little lady?"

Tossing my towel onto the weight bench, I stride toward him. "I'm not talking about the treadmill."

The treadmill comes to a stop, and he hops off. He

doesn't bother wiping the sweat off because he knows that turns me on. Kissing me, I can taste the salt and feel his hardness against me.

"I was thinking maybe we could make another baby."

This time, the smile is genuine. "I was hoping you'd say that." He takes my hand and leads me upstairs. When we reach our bedroom, he clicks on a lamp and stands beside the bed. "But first, I want to ask you something."

A bag of candy is on my pillow, so I reach for it, unsure how it got there. "You bought me Twizzlers? How'd you remember they're my favorite?"

"Because I remember everything about you, baby." He drops down on one knee and holds out a ring box.

"And here I was excited about the candy. Are you proposing to me?"

"I am. You're a woman who buys anything you want, but money doesn't buy what we have. Love and dedication do."

I didn't expect to get emotional. I assumed it would come, and I was actually fine with waiting, but now that I see my gorgeous man and his golden soul kneeling before me, I feel the weight of importance and acceptance at this moment. He gave me that. He gave me the life and love, the confidence, and a hard time when needed. He loved me just the way I am. "I will," I say, bending down to kiss him.

Weaving his fingers into my hair, he kisses me and then pulls back. "Do you still want me to ask you?"

"Oh, yes. Sorry. I got excited. Carry on."

"At times, I thought we were crazy. But then I realized we're crazy in love. I love you with all of my being, Tate. Will you marry me?"

Sitting on his bent knee, I wrap my arms around him, and say, "I will. I do. With you forever and ever."

And we did, kissing happily ever after.

The End.

Never Got Over You and The One I Want are set in this world. *Read both FREE in Kindle Unlimited!*

Never Got Over You is Natalie & Nick.

The One I Want is Juni & Andrew.

If you enjoyed Crazy in Love, make sure to read/listen to Never Got Over You where you meet Nick and Natalie. This is a sweep you off your feet, feel-so-good epic romance.

Turn the page for a sneak peek.

NEVER GOT OVER YOU

CHAPTER 1

Natalie St. James

I'm the first to admit I have no business taking another shot.

Especially after the past two.

But what's a girl to do when a room full of strangers is chanting my name and a particularly wild best friend places the shot hat on my head along with a small glass of liquor in my hand?

I drink.

In a little hole-in-the-wall hidden from the main street in Avalon on Catalina Island, I down the liquid like a champ, then promptly proceed to fall from grace, also known as the barstool.

My eyes close, bracing for impact, except . . . someone catches me just before landing. With my breath caught in my throat, I hang in the balance of arms made of steel and open my eyes.

Laughter fades away with any drunken shame that threatened as I stare into the soulful eyes of a stranger.

"Hi," whispers the future hero of my dirty dreams . . . *oh, wait.*

Maybe I'm unconscious? Maybe I was knocked out cold, and I'm dreaming. I blink. Why are my eyes open? Letting my lids fall, I keep them closed long enough to pray, "Please let him be real. If he's not, I'm begging you to leave me in this dream a little longer." My lids drift back open to find him still staring at me.

"Are you okay?"

"Perfect," I reply. *I think.* I'm not sure if I actually voice the response or not. I feel pretty damn perfect in his arms, though, the response still fitting in any circumstance that involves me, him, and those arms wrapped around my body.

Naked would be nice, but I'll save that for our second date.

His brow furrows, but a smile curls the corners of his lips.

The fog of alcohol clouds my mind, creating a heavy blanket on my brain. Regardless, I try to calculate the odds of a ridiculously sexy stranger—the exact man I'd craft if Create-a-Hottie was an actual thing—being in the right place at the right time to catch me if I fell.

It's impossible, so the only logical answer to this conundrum is that either he is the best college graduation gift ever or I'm dreaming. "How are you so hot?" I ask, worried he'll disappear in a puff of smoke and mirrors. Clamping my eyes closed again, I whisper, "Dear Lord, please don't let him be a mirage."

"I'm real." *Yes!*

Does that mean my friend set up this encounter for me? She's always been a great gift giver. It is our job, after all. I squint one eye open, biting my bottom lip. "*Mm*, so real," I purr. *Too perfect to be real, though. I must be dreaming.*

His grin creates dimples that could compete with the Grand Canyon. *How did I know I liked dimples enough to add them into this delirium?* I don't know, but score one for me.

"I think you're going to be okay," my dream man says, his voice as delectable as his face.

Wait, what? No. "As for me being okay, not so fast, buddy. No need to rush toward the waking hours. Anyway . . ." I drape my hand across my forehead. "Dream or real, I'm going to need mouth-to-mouth resuscitation."

His dimples dig deeper. "Is that so?"

"*So* right," I pant.

"Do you think I should call a paramedic?"

"That's a little kinky for me, but if you're into it . . ." I press my lips into a pretty little pout to seriously consider this twist. "Nah. Changed my mind. I only want you. Just the two of us resuscitating each other."

"You want me?" he asks, surprise tingeing his tone as he cocks an eyebrow. He readjusts me in his strong, manly arms. "Circling back to the real part, you do realize you're not dreaming, right?"

I reach up and wrap my arms around his neck, wanting to melt in his arms again. Totally obsessed with how I fit so perfectly, I pull him closer and hold tight. "You do realize you're stupidly attractive, right?"

He chuckles, his grin lifting higher on one side.

That smirk would totally get me into bed, given what it's doing to me while dreaming. I close my eyes again. "I'm ready."

"For what?" His deep, dulcet tones vibrate through my body.

"Resuscitation. I'm ready. Resuscitate away."

When nothing happens, I peek one eye open. He's still

staring at me with the smirk I'm ready to kiss off his sexy face, and whispers, "I don't think you need me—"

"Trust me." Opening both eyes, I also run my fingers through his shiny, chestnut-hued hair, taking in the feel of the soft strands. "I really, *really* need you."

When he leans down, I prepare my lips with a quick lick before meeting his . . . or at least, that's the direction I hope this dream is going.

"I was thinking—"

"Yes?" My gaze floats from his mouth to his eyes again.

"We've been at this a while. Maybe we should get you off the floor?" His head tilts to the side, and the industrial lights above him shine bright in my eyes, almost like a place of business, a restaurant, or a bar would hang. My senses begin to return, starting with the stench of old beer scenting the air.

"Yuck." Next comes a wave of cedar-y cologne and salty air. That's a scent I approve of, but that's when something else hits me. *What if I'm not dreaming?*

"Up you go," he says, shadowing me again as he tries to lift me to my feet.

I don't budge. "Dream or not, I quite enjoy being horizontal with you."

"Are you always this, *should we say*, flirtatious?" he asks, laughter punctuating his question.

"Not when I'm awake, no."

As if he couldn't be more gorgeous, little lines whisker from the outer corners of his eyes, enticing me to drag my fingertip along each one. I don't, but I want to. "Are your eyes hazel or brown? It's hard to tell in this light."

"Brown."

"Brown does them a disservice. A kaleidoscope of colors

is trapped inside them. I'm going to need a closer look in the sunshine."

"The sun will be setting soon."

"Then we should hurry."

A restrained chuckle wriggles his lips. "You can stare into my eyes, but I have to warn you, once you do, you'll fall madly in love with me. And I'm leaving tomorrow, so if we're falling in love, you better get to the loving part since you've already fallen."

"Good point."

"Get up, Natalie," my best friend says, rudely barging into my fantasy and peering at me from beside his shoulder. "The floor is filthy! Now you're going to have to wash your hair."

My eyes shift her way. "Please go away and let me have this one little dream, Tatum."

Snapping her fingers twice in front of my face has me jerking my head back. "You're wide awake and making a fool of yourself."

Noise from the crowded bar filters into my consciousness. Instead of looking around to confirm, I stare into Dreamy's eyes a moment longer and then exhale as embarrassment becomes reality, returning me to the present. "You're real, aren't you?"

A slow nod accompanies a smug expression.

The heat of my cheeks has me pressing my hands to them in hopes of cooling my skin down. "Do you mind helping me up?"

"I need to know something first."

"What?" I ask, knowing I should leave before I'm sober enough to realize how absurd I've been behaving.

Still holding me in his arms as if I'm light as a feather, he leans closer with his eyes on my mouth. When his gaze rises to meet mine, he asks, "Did you fall in love?"

My heart rate spikes, and the sound of it beating whooshes in my ears. Maybe I did hit my head because I swear at that moment, the one with my dream man so close I can kiss him or even lick him if I want, I can answer honestly.

Despite all the physical signs of me feeling otherwise, I reply, "You know. I think it's time for me to go." *Before the last few minutes really sink in.*

My feet are set on solid flooring while his hands remain on the underside of my forearms to steady me. Like the perfect gentleman. "I wish—"

"Nat," Tatum says under her breath. She moves in and grabs my hand.

"What?"

Her hair catches the light when she flips it over her shoulder, an exhausted sigh following right after. Every blonde needs a brunette bestie, and Tatum Devreux was destined to be mine since our mothers exchanged silver spoons from Tiffany's as baby shower gifts. I'm not exactly the calm to her wild ways, but she can out party me any day.

"A party on a yacht down in the harbor. We have to go now, though."

Panic rises in my chest. I know I should want to hightail it out of here to save myself from further mortification, but I don't want to go. I'm perfectly content right here.

I'm not shy about it. I look straight at him, but I'm smacked with a dose of candor I wasn't ready for, my ego crushed under his expression that mirrors pity. Now I regret not making a quick getaway when I had the chance.

My stomach plummets to the floor I was just hovering

above. "Yeah, it's time to go," I tell Tatum, my hand pressing to my belly in an attempt to keep myself together. My hand is grabbed, and I'm tugged after her as she calls, "Ciao, darlings."

I turn back to catch Mr . . . *Dreamy, Smug, Sexy, Pity-er of Drunk Girls* watching me. I'm left with two options to make an escape without further incident. I *could* blame the craziness on a head injury, or I *could* just leave. "So . . . thanks," I say awkwardly as I back toward the door. *Yes. Choosing the latter.*

"Are you sure you're okay?" His voice carries over the lively crowd.

I dust the dirt off my ass. "I'm fine. Guess I'm not a tequila girl."

"You drank rum," he replies with a lopsided smile that could sweep me off my feet again if I'm not careful.

"Rum. Tequila. Same difference." I wave off the idea because it doesn't really matter. "I'm not good with liquor." That should settle it, but I make the mistake of daring to look into his eyes again. The five feet between us virtually disappears, and mentally, I'm back in his arms again, reading the prose that makes up his features. It would take me days to interpret, capturing not only his thoughts but a history that's worn in the light lines. He makes it hard to look away.

Stepping forward, he raises his hand and then lowers it to his side again as conflict invades his expression. "You sure you're okay? You might have a concussion."

I can't say I'm not touched by his concern. Grinning, I ask, "Does a concussion involve my heart?"

"What's happening with your heart?"

"It's beating like crazy."

Smiles are exchanged. "I think you're experiencing something else, but if you'd like me to call an ambulance—"

"Nope," Tatum cuts in, yanking me toward the door again, and laughs. "He's cute, but we don't want to miss the yacht." She whips the straw hat off me and tosses it to him.

I twist to look back. "Thanks for the lift. *Literally*."

"Anytime," he says with his eyes set on mine. When he shoves his hands in his pockets, he looks like he's posing for a Ralph Lauren ad. Tan. Rugged good looks. Tall. Those dreamy eyes and a grin that call me back to him. But life isn't a dream. It's time to return to reality.

Goodbye, dream man. It was nice hanging with . . . onto you.

DOWNLOAD your copy from Amazon or read FREE in Kindle Unlimited today!

To keep up to date with her writing and more, visit S.L. Scott's website: **www.slscottauthor.com**

To receive the newsletter about all of her publishing adventures, free books, giveaways, steals and more:

https://geni.us/intheknow

Follow me on TikTok: https://geni.us/SLTikTok
Follow on IG: https://geni.us/IGSLS
Follow on Bookbub: https://geni.us/SLScottBB

THANK YOU

Thank you so much for reading my book. Writing is a dream and wouldn't have come true without you.

Your support means the world to me. Please leave a review where you purchased your book.

My family has been incredible during this chaotic year. They are my biggest cheerleaders and I'm the most fortunate wife and mom in the world to have them.

What an awesome team I have. They are literally the best. Thank you Andrea, Jenny, Kristen, and Marion. You made this book so special and on a crazy deadline. I'm sorry about that. I love you!

To my audiobook production team at One Night Stand Studios and the incredible narrators - Jacob Morgan and CJ Bloom: Thank you for bringing my books to life. I adore listening to you and working with you so much!

And finally, but not least, thank you to the Wildfire Marketing team and my Rockin' Readers. My heart is full because of you!